SAND & STORM

MOONFIRE TRILOGY BOOK 1

PATTY JANSEN

GET FREE EBOOKS

CHAPTER 1

THE WEATHER STATION stood by the side of the road, a tiny hut, once painted white but now a dust-stained yellow, surrounded by a rolling stubble field that disappeared into the hazy horizon.

"There you are," Pashtan said. He let the reins rest and the two donkeys came to a halt. The cart stopped with its usual creaking and groaning.

Javes gathered his equipment and jumped off the front bench. His boots, when they hit the ground, threw up a little cloud of dust. Over the past few weeks, they had gone from dark brown polished leather to smudged grey. Mother would kill him when he came home, and as the end of his field assignment neared, that thought occurred to him more often. *Home*, where he could go back to being a *tryhard* and sitting in the back of the class, being laughed at by the fellow students.

Yes, he dreaded that time. There was the prick Rolan who had been boasting about going to Solmeni. Yoshi who was going to Twin Bridges, and Branto and Siana, who had both scored assignments on the coast. Even Lana, who was going to work for the library in Tiverius, and had clearly been disappointed with her placement, had a more interesting job than his.

Yet, in one way, he didn't mind it. For one, no one here knew who he was.

He trudged across the dry gravel road to the weather station, checked for scorpions as Pashtan had told him he should always do, undid the latch and opened the door.

The station wasn't big enough to step inside, with each side barely as wide as a man. The door was long and tall and needed to be secured against the wind, lest it blow shut on him and injure his hands or damage the equipment.

There were no scorpions inside the shady den, but a legion of spiders had woven together all the equipment inside. The barygraph was barely visible under the silk. Wow. He used the corner of his notebook to push aside the white filaments. The owner of the web scurried behind the power board that held the connection plugs to the telegraph line that he'd been assured was going to be built in the future.

Ew, he hated spiders.

Javes folded out the shelf that formed a little worktable and secured it with the piece of metal that was neatly stowed on the inside of the door for that purpose. He lifted the barygraph machine from the bottom shelf onto the table, took out the roll, unscrewed the rings that held the recording paper onto it and let the paper fall to the bottom of the cabinet, all curled up.

He wiped sweat from his forehead. Now that the breeze of movement from sitting on the cart had stopped, the air was more searing than ever.

He took a clean, flat sheet from his folder, threaded it between the roll and the rings and tightened the screws again. He set the machine back and moved the bellows, with the arm holding the pencil, back into position.

He wiped his forehead again. Sweat threatened to run into his eyes. His forearms glistened with it.

He picked up the curl of paper with the barygraph scribbles for the past two weeks and slotted it in his folder, using a fold of his shirt to open the covers. Whoever at the Scriptorium had thought that issuing students with *black* folders was a good idea?

All right, done.

He folded away the table. Then he shut the door and climbed back onto the cart, where Pashtan waited, slowly chewing his tobacco. Pashtan leaned against the backrest of the seat, with his hands folded in his lap. He wore the loose grey-white robe that locals called a *temuz*. His face was infuriatingly free of sweat.

Javes sat down next to him, and tried to mimic his tutor's stoic demeanour, but the sweat had crept into his right eye and it stung.

"And?" Pashtan said, pushing the wad of tobacco like a lump into his cheek.

Javes gave his tutor a quizzing look. And what? "I got the readouts."

"What did it say?"

Oh. Well. "I . . ."

"You haven't looked."

"No." Javes admitted. And damn it, he had to wipe his face again.

He opened the folder while wiping the sweat off with his elbow, and started riffling through the papers. He also should have marked the paper with the place and date where he had collected it, he realised. But it was just so hot here that he could barely think.

"Do you want to be a meteorologist, boy?"

"Yes. Why?" Javes looked into his tutor's eyes. For the past two weeks, Pashtan had asked him these uncomfortable questions. He had also stubbornly refused to call Javes by his name.

"I ask because you need to have a hunger to learn."

"I do want to learn," Javes scoffed. He was tempted to add, *It's just so hot*, but he'd made that mistake before and reaped the reward of Pashtan's scolding him for being a soft city boy for the next few days.

"I see very little evidence of that. Come on, have a look at the readout. Tell me what you see."

His ears burning, Javes located the paper in the folder. First, he wrote the number of the station and the date in the corner. Pashtan was looking at him. His silence was worse than his scorn would have been.

He slowly unrolled the paper. Over the past two weeks, the expanding and contracting bellows in the barygraph had made a squiggly line over the paper—with a sharp spike a few days ago, and another yesterday.

Javes stared at it, trying to decide what that meant. He'd never seen a sonorics spike like that. "I think a spider got into the equipment."

"Why do you think so?"

Javes showed him the readout.

Pashtan's brown eyes widened.

"What is it?" Javes asked.

"Dust devils in the area. We don't normally see them as far south as this."

Pashtan didn't explain what dust devils were, and Javes was scared to ask in case it was something else he should have known but didn't. By the expression on Pashtan's face, he could guess it was not a good thing.

But not to worry. He had only two days left in this forsaken dust-bowl of a place, and he could go back home. Back to where the students in his year would hide his books, or, like last year, replace the text of a speech he was going to make with a lewd picture, all because they discovered that his father owned the Singing Lark Hotel, where guests paid by the hour, not the night, and where few people went up to a room alone.

And yes, his father owned it, and no, Javes wasn't terribly proud of it, but his father said that was business. You sometimes had to put aside things you didn't like if other people wanted to pay for it. He said he had plans for the place and was waiting for the right time.

But these stupid boys in his year had discovered that his father owned it, and they called his father a pimp, and Javes had tried to explain about the waiting for a good time, but that just made the lewd jokes worse. Asking those boys what *their* fathers had done to provide people with work and salaries hadn't helped either.

And the worst thing about the lewd pictures was that all these stupid boys had girls that they talked about having kissed, and Javes had only ever looked at girls from behind, in class.

That was waiting for him at home.

When they had made the round trip past all the stations, Pashtan steered the cart back towards the town. It was getting towards the end of the afternoon, the time when the weather was at its hottest. The air shimmered above the stubble fields. A few scraggly trees hung onto a handful of measly leaves, but most appeared to consist primarily of dead branches.

A tiny village, a loosely strewn collection of blocky white houses, lay in a valley to the right. Last week, Javes had accompanied Pashtan into the village at midday, where they had stopped at a drinking place. Over a jug of blissfully iced beer, irate farmers had told them of the drought, how it was all the fault of people in the capital, and especially the meteorologist. Javes happened to study under Vikius han Maronian and knew that he was the least likely person to wish anyone ill. And besides, meteorologists didn't control the weather, they measured it and tried to predict it.

"Farming has always been dicey in this region," Pashtan had told him after they left.

"But they can't blame anyone for the weather!"

"That's all they have left to blame."

"They don't have to blame anyone. Weather just *is*. No one has the blame for it."

"You can't possibly understand their mindset."

"What I don't understand is that if it's so terrible, why don't they just leave? They don't have to spend their lives in this place. There are plenty of other farming towns that would be happy to have them."

"If they've lived in this area and farmed the land for hundreds of years? Seriously, boy, at times I wonder what they teach you there in that city. Do they teach you that nothing of tradition has value and everything must be measured in the currency of money? Is that why no one in Tiverius cares about our region, and why the railway they promised us is still unbuilt, and senators of the doga come to all regions except ours?"

His ears still burned from that conversation when he remembered it, which was every time they passed this miserable village on the way home.

Because Pashtan was right about those things. The promise of a railway to the northern district was a great standing joke in Tiverius, and the saying "promising railways to the north" was a saying that stood for promising castles in the air and having no intention to honour those promises.

Pashtan had studied in Tiverius; he had said so when Javes had just arrived after a long and dusty journey by train to Watya and by bus from there.

Javes stole glances at his tutor's dark, weather-beaten face, with its deep crevices and dark eyes, hidden by deep folds of skin, that squinted ahead at the road. Imagine having the misfortune of having been born here, and having to fight this sort of ridicule all your life.

Imagine coming to Tiverius as a student and finding that there were virtually no students from your region there. Imagine hearing for the first time of all the tasteless jokes that were being made at dinner parties, in eating houses, even in the doga, about your region and your people.

That would be pretty bad.

But really, he wasn't here to solve the problems of the suppressed people of the north. What could he do about it anyway? People already laughed when he opened his mouth and that was just when he talked about normal things.

The hot wind whipped up drifts of dust that stuck to Javes' sweaty skin. The donkeys plodded along. The cart bumped and creaked. The little village disappeared behind the hill, and then the next one and the next one. Javes wished he was home in his cool room.

All of a sudden Pashtan sat up straight. "Whoa!" He pulled the reins. The donkeys stopped, snorting.

Pashtan stood up on the driver's seat, peering ahead.

Javes started, "What's going on—"

"Boy. Quick, get the cover."

Javes didn't want to say *I have a name*. He stared ahead, trying to make out what Pashtan was seeing. Just dust and more dust. On the ground, in the air. It was hard to see any kind of distance, in fact.

"Come on, do as I say and be quick."

"What is it?"

"Dust devil." Pashtan jumped off the driver's seat. He started unharnessing the donkeys.

Javes went to the back of the cart. He found the cloth that they would put over the cart when it stood in front of the house at night and unfolded it, still glancing at the horizon. What did a dust devil even look like?

But Pashtan was far too busy for him to ask. He'd probably be annoyed at yet another stupid question from the city boy with no name.

He threw the cloth over the bed of the wagon, tied down the straps on one side, pulled the rest of the cloth over and started on the other side.

By that time, he became aware of a low keening sound.

"What's that?" he asked.

And boy, had it gone dusty all of a sudden. He could barely see past the front of the cart, where Pashtan had turned the donkeys around in the harness so that they faced the cart.

"The cloth!" he yelled at Javes. "Give it to me!"

"I thought you said to put it over the cart. So I did."

"Over the *animals!* By the thousand flaming stars. Why does Tiverius keep sending me these numbwits." He stomped off to the back of the cart and started undoing all the straps that Javes had just tied up.

The keening sound increased. Javes' hair whipped around his face. Sand stung the exposed skin on his face and hands. He pulled the hood of his robe over his head.

"Come on, useless lump, help me."

Javes tried to grab the other end of the flapping cover and was lashed in the face by the rope that whipped about in the wind. Then the fabric was torn from his hands.

Pashtan dragged the cloth over the donkeys. "TIE . . . IT . . . DOWN . . . ON . . . YOUR . . . SIDE!" His voice was blown in shards over the roaring of the wind.

Javes managed to grab hold of the flapping cloth. Sand blew in his eyes, in his mouth. He couldn't see anything anymore. With fingers that were numb from the biting sand, he tied the cloth onto the harness.

"Pashtan, I've done it. What now?"

There was no answer. Javes called again, "Pashtan!"

There was a muffled sound of a voice.

The wind had increased so much that Javes could barely still stand up, even if he was on the protected side of the cart. He ducked under the shelter they had just made out of the cloth and the donkeys, and met the heaving flank of one of the donkeys. He crouched there, threading his fingers through the fur. Sand whirled around his and the donkey's feet, and he had to keep pulling his feet out.

The donkey started fidgeting.

"Calm down, be still. It's only a dust storm. It will soon be over."

Through the roaring of the wind came the keening sound again, like a dog whining. What *was* that? A crash sounded nearby. The donkey shied. A corner of the cloth lifted briefly. Some of the cloth must have come loose, because it flapped like crazy, and the sand was coming in. The cloth didn't cover him properly anymore. He reached for the corner that was being tossed about by the wind.

It was *dark* out there. He couldn't see the cart, or Pashtan.

Something out there made a loud, *Wheeeeeuuuuuuuuuuu* keening noise, like a howling wolf.

Javes grew very, very scared.

What if they were buried in sand? What if he died here? What would people at home say about him? Would his parents even care in their pretty house with their dinner parties and two older sons who ran successful businesses? Would students in his year care?

WHEEEEEUUUUUUUUUU

The keening became so loud that his ears hurt, and his head hurt. And then a huge shape loomed out of the raging dust. It looked vaguely human, but was at least three times taller. The outlines were fuzzy and they crackled with lightning. The thing appeared to have arms and long claws for hands. The eyes burned with an evil red glow like hot coals.

But that was . . . the mud monster out of his childhood nightmares that would wake him up and send him screaming and running to his parents. His brothers used to tease him about it.

He hadn't thought about it for a long time, had never believed it was real, but here it was, and there would be no escape into wakefulness this time.

It roared and stretched two claw-like hands towards the cart.

Javes might have screamed, he wasn't sure. But he let himself drop under the cloth and pressed himself against the donkey's heaving flank.

"It's nothing, it's only my imagination. It's nothing, it's nothing."

Something went *crunch* and jolted the harness.

He said to himself, "It's nothing, it's nothing. It can't see me." Just like he used to do as a little boy, hidden under the blankets of his bed.

Crunch.

Wheeeeeuuuuuuuuuuu

The cloth jerked. The other donkey's legs disappeared, as it bolted, or blew away, or . . . was eaten. Javes held his breath. Surely he was next?

He closed his eyes. He held his breath.

Wheeeeeuuuuuuuuuuu

He waited, and waited.

Did he imagine it or did the sound become weaker?

He waited. He counted to ten, keeping his eyes closed.

Yes, he had not imagined it, the fury of the wind lessened. The cloth slackened. Sand stopped lashing against his trouser legs and stopped whirling around his feet.

And there was utter, deadly silence.

Javes pushed the cloth aside, upsetting an avalanche of dust that cascaded to the ground, where the road was barely visible.

"Pashtan?"

The only reply was a donkey snort. The animal closest to him was jerking its head up as if to get out from underneath the cloth.

Javes undid the ties and pulled the cloth off. It had ripped in half. Everything that should have been there—the second donkey, Pashtan —was missing.

He searched the dusty ground, but saw only rills of sand with every now and then bits of stubble poking through.

The air was still very dusty, and he couldn't see much more than during a misty winter day in Tiverius.

Ah, there was the second donkey, lying on its side.

Javes ploughed through the sand, but when he got there, it was clear the animal wouldn't go anywhere anymore. Its entire side had been shaven away by the scouring sand, exposing ribs. The animal was not quite dead, and it made him sick to look at it.

He would have to kill it.

Pashtan would know what to do.

Then again Pashtan had taken shelter on the same side as the unfortunate donkey.

"Pashtan?" he called again.

There was no answer.

Javes walked around, looking for a stick to kill the poor donkey, but of course there were no sticks to be found. He knew that, too. To see an animal suffer like that made him sick, but the thought of having to kill it made him sick, too, and where *was* Pashtan anyway?

Then he noticed a lump under the sand.

Mercy, his grandfather would say.

Javes ploughed through the sand and pushed the top of the mound off.

A piece of cloth stuck out of the sand. It was Pashtan's *temuz*, dusty, ripped, stained with orange from the dirt.

Pashtan lay on his stomach, his hands by his side as if he were sleeping. But his eyes were open and there was sand in them. There was also sand in his mouth, open because his tongue was swollen and black. The skin was peeling off his face.

Javes reeled back, looking around him. The cart was broken, one donkey dead, his tutor dead.

That terrible thing that looked like the mud monster was still out there. It might come back, and he was all alone with little water and less food.

He didn't think the town was too far away. He could walk that far, couldn't he?

Because the cart was on its side and one of the wheels was broken, and the axle, too, and most of the stuff that was in there he didn't need for survival, except the water, so he took that. He had no bag to carry it, so he ripped a piece off the cloth.

He was going to tie the water bottle and the cloth to the donkey, but he wasn't sure that the animal would be able to walk. It tottered around looking none too healthy. Instead, he tied the bottle to his back. The donkey's reins had snapped, so he replaced one by the rope from the cover.

All this he did with trembling hands and while constantly looking at the horizon all around him.

But the dust devil did not come back.

He shouldered a corner of the cloth—in case the devil came back and they needed to hide again—and led the donkey away from the destruction.

CHAPTER 2

THE BIER WAS the size of a dinner platter.

Two Eagle Knights carried it across the shoreline to the water, walking slowly so that they didn't slip on the algae-covered boulders. Both men were splendid in their formal outfits, with their red tunics, shorthair cloaks and the ornate hilts on their daggers. Their solemn faces belied the splendour and colour of the display.

The tiny body that lay on the foam cushion on the bier was too grey, too fragile, dressed in the smallest clothes to be found, which still resembled giant sacks on the tiny figure. The eyes were barely formed, the fingers ended in nailless stumps and the skin was shiny, almost transparent.

Isandor waited on the ocean's edge for the two Knights to carry their load his way. He could easily pick up the entire floating platform with the foam cushion and the body in his arms. He lifted it from the bier and, making sure that his wooden leg was secure in a crevice before continuing, carefully turned around on the slippery rocks until he faced the ocean.

A breeze blew hair across his face, and he shook the long locks aside.

He lowered the platform to the water.

The waves washed over the oyster-encrusted rocks, driving foam into crevices, tugging at the floating platform.

Isandor stopped the lapping waves from claiming their prize with one hand. With the other, he gently stroked the little head, not even the size of his palm. The skin was already as cold as the water.

Behind him, Jevaithi sniffed. She was seated in a chair that the Knights had put higher on the shoreline, where the ground was more even. She looked fragile, a pale face protruding from her white furs. A tear ran down her cheek. She wiped it away with the back of her hand, but a new tear came.

The next wave came in, and Isandor let go of the cushion. The waves carried the platform and its load back and forth a few times before pulling it out to sea.

Isandor clambered back up the rocks. He stood next to Jevaithi, with his hand on her shoulder, watching how the waves pulled the tiny body on its final journey, away from the shore. It floated past the rocks overgrown with seaweed, past the little island before the coast whose rocks were stained with seagull droppings. Then it went out the bay, where the Legless Lions frolicked in the water, until it vanished from sight.

They watched, flanked by silent, motionless Knights.

"Let's go home," Jevaithi said after a long silence.

She rose from the chair, wiping tears from her cheeks with her one hand. Isandor steadied her and a Knight rushed over to take her other arm, where, these days, she wore a white-painted wooden pole with a hook, now that neither of them needed to hide that they were Imperfect.

"It never gets easier." Her voice was hoarse.

Isandor shook his head. It only got harder. Every time they hoped that this was the time that the palace would see a healthy child, and every time the cramps started early, or Jevaithi suddenly lost blood and the child would come. Sometimes already lifeless, sometimes, like this morning, it would fight for a bit before slowly sliding into death.

"Better next time," Jevaithi said. She held her chin up, challenging him.

Isandor wanted to say, *There won't be a next time*, but they'd had so many arguments about this already, and having another during the funeral procession in front of the guards and courtiers was hardly appropriate.

He was tired of seeing his sister suffer. The midwife had told him that each time another child was torn prematurely from her womb, there was a greater chance that she would bleed to death. Using different men, eating strict diets and restricting her movement to within the palace made no difference.

Two courtiers had come from the coach that waited on the road and lifted the chair that Jevaithi had vacated, putting it back into the cabin. Isandor lifted Jevaithi up the stairs and climbed in next to her, holding her hand. She felt so frail and weak. Her hands were so cold, even though the weather was mild. He was losing her already, in more ways than one.

The two Eagle Knights who had accompanied them mounted their birds, magnificent animals with white heads, tan feathers and fierce orange eyes. One of them, Isandor's friend Supreme Rider Barton, met Isandor's eyes in an understanding look. He understood about the royal heir, a girl borne by the queen, he understood about stubborn family members, having dealt with a frail mother too stubborn to accept the help she so clearly needed.

Isandor gestured to his advisor to join him for a drink later.

Rider Barton nodded to him and both birds took off, carrying their riders back towards the eyrie in the City of Glass on the other side of the bay. The courtiers got on their horses, tall white- and brown-spotted steeds.

Right now, Isandor wished that he was still an Eagle Knight and could take off and forget about all this difficult stuff while flying over the countryside, with the wind in his hair.

The coach driver climbed into the front seat, flicked the reins and set the white bears into motion. The coach jolted, the bells on the harness tinkled, but the sound brought no joy today.

The sad procession made its way back over the bumpy farming track along the shoreline. The grass was green underfoot and the hills displayed a patchwork of farm fields dotted with the last flowers of the year. Here and there dirty patches of snow had survived the summer, soon to be covered again with fresh snow.

The road was quiet.

Sometimes a farmer with a cart, or a herder with sheep, would come the other way. That person would stop, take the animals or the cart off the road and wait for the royal procession to pass. Sometimes they passed farmhouses; children and their grandparents and aunties who were not working in the fields would come out to the doorstep to look. Workers in the cabbage fields would down their tools and stand still, solemnly looking at the ground.

Isandor acknowledged the people with a wave of his hand. They were good people, who had helped build the southern land of Peria into what it was today: happy, prosperous and thriving. He should be happy about all the things they had achieved, but the question of the royal heir hung over him like a bucket about to spill over. They needed to do something. Jevaithi was, like himself, thirty-six, and somehow needed to be made to agree to a different solution. There were a few options, but getting her to agree to any of them seemed impossible.

She was the queen and the heir needed to be her daughter. She flatly refused to discuss any other option.

He could remind her that so many women in the City of Glass could not bear children. He could remind her that it was especially bad in the Thilleian house.

But she would just say that he couldn't possibly understand, having grown up in the Outer City instead of in the palace, without being constantly reminded that it was her task to serve the people.

Isandor felt like pulling out his hair, like banging his head against the wall.

The procession joined the busier main road that led into the outer reaches of the city. From the road he could see the new Harbour District, opened seven years ago, when the ice floes receded far enough for ships from eastern Chevakia and even from Arania to come in with their goods. Today, in the golden sunlight, it was a riot of colour, abundance and many different people.

The City of Glass had transformed into a vibrant community since the Heart that radiated icefire and that kept the land in eternal winter had been destroyed twenty years ago.

The palace lay in its oasis-like garden sanctuary, sheltered from the city noise by the surrounding wall. The coach turned into the gates and up the driveway, lined with little trees clipped to look like green balls on sticks.

The building itself was almost entirely made of glass: clear glass, coloured glass, black glass, cloudy glass, mirrored glass, thick sheets cut into squares, rectangles or triangles and welded together. It looked as if they had been randomly thrown in a heap, but the position of each piece was calculated so that it caught the light and reflected it into the building as much as possible.

A servant held open the main door for the porters who came into the coach and carried Jevaithi in her chair inside the atrium, a huge hall where the walls leaned inwards to join each other at the very top. The many planes and angles of the glass played with the low light, scattering dots of reflected light throughout the space.

Jevaithi held up her hand. "Stop. Let me out. I can walk."

The servant protested. "But Your Highness, the midwife said—"

"She said not to overdo it, but didn't say not to do anything at all. I feel like walking. It's not far."

The porters set the chair down.

Jevaithi got out. Isandor came to take her arm, but he had to do his best not to snap at her—because snapping at the queen in public would never do. He had heard the midwife give the same warning that the servant had heard. Why did Jevaithi always twist things to reflect the things she wanted to hear?

The lift doors opened.

Isandor led Jevaithi in. A servant got in with them and operated the control panel. They rode to the top floor in tense silence.

Upstairs, Isandor took Jevaithi to the luxurious bedroom that overlooked the shore. The maids had been in to change the bed and clean the room after the morning's disaster, but the floor was still wet where Jevaithi had stood, crying and clutching her belly, with blood running down her legs.

Jevaithi took a few steps into the room, and turned to him. "We should try Rider Carro again. Or maybe there is a man of standing we haven't yet tried—"

"Jevaithi, please."

"He must be in the Knighthood, because I don't want any of those lazy nobles who are just pushing to get their blood on the throne—"

"Jevaithi, stop."

"We should also go back to trying it in the natural way. All this business with putting men's seed in bottles is strange to me—"

"Jevaithi, are you going to listen to me?"

She gave him her best I-am-the-queen-why-should-I-listen-to-anyone face, but said nothing, because he was her twin brother and she was sure to know he wouldn't take that treatment.

Isandor took a deep breath and continued in a low voice, "I've had enough." And oh, by the skylights, he'd had enough, more than enough. He could not deal with this anymore on top of all the other frustrations of late, and especially the glacial pace of the last phase of rebuilding the country: to produce robust laws. He was no lawyer; it was BORING in capital letters.

Jevaithi stared at him, outrage on her face. "*You've* had enough? What about me? Don't you think *I* haven't had enough? You think that I do all of this for fun?"

"No, but I've still had enough."

"There *is* no enough. I either have a child and stay queen or give control of the throne to others. Do you think we have any other options?"

"Yes, we do, and—"

"We need an heir. There needs to be a little princess on the throne. She needs to be my daughter."

"That's not going to happen."

"How can you say that? There is so much we haven't yet tried. So many different men we can still try."

"What difference do you think it will make?"

"Why are you saying there is something wrong with me?"

"I'm not saying that."

"Yes, you are." Her eyes blazed.

"Jevaithi, please stop it." He hated it when she went like this. He took a deep breath and continued in a lower, more controlled, voice, "Maybe we should give it a rest. Maybe we should look for another option."

"No. I'll do it. We'll try again. I'll do it. I won't fail my country."

"You're not failing your country. The people will understand." Many women had the same problem.

"No, they won't. And I won't fail them. Just give me . . . a bit of time to recover. Two weeks will do."

"Don't be silly. The midwife said you might die."

"Stop telling me what to do!"

"You might die! Just for once listen to me. There are other solutions. Let's use them."

"No! No, no, no." She clamped her hands over her ears.

"Listen to me. I love you and I don't want you to die. And I'm sick of seeing you suffer like this. I will—"

"No. No!" She burst into tears.

Isandor closed her in his arms. She cried in great wracking sobs.

A feeling of great helplessness came over him. Arguing with her always led to this. He understood how she had grown up amongst a group of leering Eagle Knights in the days when the Knights ruled the land in her name and she lived as a prisoner in a gilded cage while the Knights bickered over which of them was going to father her children.

He did understand all of that, and he understood how that life had made her frightened, damaged, but she didn't aid her cause by acting like a spoilt child.

He helped her change into a comfortable gown and installed her in the bed. He asked a maid to bring the queen some tea, and went down to the atrium, feeling empty and dejected.

Short of yelling at her, what could he do to make her see sense?

Had he really signed up to be a puppet king just so that he could watch her grow increasingly mad?

"Isandor."

Isandor's friend Rider Carro of the Eagle Knights came out of the entrance from the atrium to the downstairs hallway. He'd been on patrol and was still wearing his shorthair cloak. His cheeks were red from the cold air. "I heard what happened. Is it true?"

"Sadly, yes."

"Accept my condolences."

"Thank you."

A brief moment of silence passed between them. Carro pressed his lips together. He was the same age as Isandor, and at one point, years ago, the child Jevaithi had lost had been his, back when they still had hope that changing the blood of the father would make a difference.

In silence, he led his friend into his private study at the far end of the downstairs corridor, a room that jutted into the garden, and had a view of the bay with its dark blue water and large rocks where legless lions would lie in the sun.

"Drink?" he asked Carro.

Carro didn't refuse as he normally did when he was still on duty or planned to be flying later in the day, so he had probably come off duty. Isandor went to the cupboard against the back wall and found a bottle of yellowish, syrupy fluid. He was in the mood for Chevakian honey liquor.

Carro brought the glasses, Isandor poured and they both sat down on the couch in companionable silence.

Isandor sipped from his glass, letting the mellow taste of the liquor roll over his tongue.

There was a time they used to drink bloodwine, but it had become expensive lately. Young people these days thought that to drink the blood of an animal was barbaric. Back then, he'd never seen it that way. Meat was all they ate because the land was frozen and there was nothing else, and the blood was a by-product of the meat. It was all they had. But bloodwine—blood mixed with distillate—was not a great, durable or refined product, and, like so many in the City of Glass today, Isandor had lost the taste for it.

He sighed. "I don't know what to do about Jevaithi." *What to do about my entire life.*

"What do you mean—what to do about her?"

"She can't go on like this. It's been—like—the twentieth child she's lost. The midwife says that every child is bigger risk, and yet she won't listen to any arguments."

"She's the queen."

"She's my sister, and I can't see her suffer any longer. She wants to try again, but there's no point. It's not going to make any difference."

Carro sipped from his drink. "You should try a breeder."

"Yeah." Isandor blew out a breath. "But that means going through the whole selection and approval process again."

Isandor *had* tried a breeder five years ago, but after he had selected the girl, Jevaithi insisted on getting involved in the choice and hovered around while he visited the girl, and even asked about the bedroom particulars.

Then he had told her to lay off, and she had refused to speak to him for two months.

He shuddered at the thought.

Why did his sister smake both their lives so difficult?

The thought of having to go through the selection process again, including the gossip spreading all over town, and the lewd jokes in the bars, the weaselly attitude of the girl's parents, the sickly visit to her house to perform the deed, which he'd never felt less like doing. How had noble men been able to pay fertile women to have their children for so long? How were they still doing it?

Carro said, "Adoption?"

He turned to Carro. "We can't adopt a child, because if we adopt a child from the Thillei clan, the Pirosians will be angry and if we adopt a Pirosian girl, then the Thillei will be put out." And a flare-up of the clan conflicts had the potential to shatter the fragile prosperity they'd been able to build.

Carro nodded. "A breeder, then."

Isandor cringed. "Who can we consider? We did a lot of work choosing a breeder last time."

Back then, they had chosen a woman who had given birth to many children already, one of the professional breeders. And that hadn't worked either, at least for the only time he had been able to bring himself to visit her.

She reminded Isandor too much of his foster mother and the men who visited her. He remembered sitting in the snow outside the limpet in the Outer City, waiting until his mother had finished with her customer. When carrying a child for a noble, that man would be able to buy her services until the child was born. The whole idea of it made him feel sick.

Carro continued, "I could find you a strong breeder with Thilleian blood, so that the princess will resemble you and Jevaithi." That was another problem: if finally a child was born and it was a boy, they would have to start all over again. The City of Glass must have a *Queen*.

Carro sipped from his drink, in deep thought. "I'll make some investigations."

"Please be discreet," Isandor said. "Offer a good fee, but don't make a big fuss. Contact some regular breeders. Talk to them, but don't say who it's for. Ask them if they are booked."

Carro said he would do it, finished his drink and made for the door, leaving Isandor alone in the silence of his office. He finished his drink, too, set the glass on the table and went to his desk, but he couldn't concentrate, and leaned his head in his hands.

He thought of Jevaithi, who was possibly writing letters to men she wanted to try, stubborn as ever. Queen Maraithe, the mother he had never known and who had never held him, had wasted away as a skeleton under the imprisonment of Rider Cornatan and his Knights of the old guard, who had ruled the land with an iron fist after her death.

By all accounts, she had been quite deranged, calling out for help at every whim, asking the servants to attend her most ridiculous needs. He'd heard that in her last year, she had a servant devoted solely to washing her backside in the outroom. He had also heard rumours, more reliable because they came from Rider Barton who had seen it, that she would eat strange things and that apparently those outroom visits grew increasingly frequent and nasty.

He could see Jevaithi set on the same course.

She desperately wanted a child, and she would do everything possible, and impossible, for it. She would ruin her relationship with him and with all her advisors for that one goal.

There was a knock on the door.

"Come in." Isandor lifted his head from his hands.

A member of the palace guard came in with the words, "The mail is here, Your Majesty."

Isandor accepted a small pile of letters. Most of the mail that came to the palace would go to the correspondence service, but these were considered too personal or important for the secretaries to deal with.

He spread the letters on the table.

One was the monthly report from the treasury detailing public expenditure. Most of it had gone into the Harbour District, which was still far from finished, and now the citizens were complaining that too many foreigners lived and had businesses there.

A letter from the town administrator of Bordertown was about the progression on the duplication of the railway tracks and the joint project between Peria and Chevakia to build a faster cable train down the steep escarpment that allowed for easier movement of goods between the two countries. And he was reminded that he'd promised to investigate the opening of the land route through the mountains. Yet more work to do.

The last letter was a dust-stained envelope bearing the seal of the

Chevakian doga, which was their government assembly. Across the front, his name was written in loopy handwriting.

Sadorius han Chevonian, or Sady.

Long-time proctor of Chevakia, husband to Isandor's foster mother—who had once been a breeder in the City of Glass—and father of the last child she would ever have.

To see his familiar handwriting brought memories of Sady's large house with its many courtyards; the straight, tree-lined streets of Tiverius, the Chevakian capital; warm sunny weather; and dinners around the table in the large kitchen.

He lifted the envelope to his nose as if he could smell the essence of Tiverius on the paper. Oh, the memories of enjoyable times.

He inserted his finger under the flap and ripped it open, looking forward to reading about everyday life in the house. His foster mother Loriane was very ill, but if anything bad had happened, Sady would have sent a telegraph message.

He unfolded the paper inside, and then breathed out disappointment. Sady was writing to him in his capacity as King of Peria. The letter was addressed to the Knight Council and contained no personal in formation.

I have in the past year or so observed a number of meteorological changes that I find troubling. I think I mentioned during our last visit to the City of Glass that the northern half of Chevakia is gripped by a severe drought. The drought has still not broken. Villagers have walked away from their fields and are coming into town. They speak of dust devils, whirlwinds that destroy their crops and sometimes their towns. The entire northern region is slowly turning into a desert. Even in Tiverius, we are feeling the effects of the drought. The water stores are low, and this year farmers were forced to plant their crops early for the fear of missing out on rain. For the first time in known history, the Solmeni River has stopped flowing and the legendary falls are dry.

I'm facing an influx of people from the north, and we're having enough trouble coping with our regular citizens. The situation is achingly familiar to the one we faced after the sonorics explosion in the City of Glass: we have refugees, but nowhere to house them and no resources to give them. This is only from our own country so far, but according to my meteorologist, Arania faces worse problems. There are people on the move in Arania in the direc-

tion of the border. When the refugees come across the border, we will have to deal with them.

Most worryingly, my chief meteorologist and his students have observed some anomalous increases in sonorics. We have seen these spikes occurring over the past years, but they had been on a strong diminishing trend. We are now seeing a reversal of that trend.

Isandor's heart thudded in his throat. What the Chevakians called sonorics was the same as icefire, and yes, he had sometimes seen flickers of the golden light dancing over the shoreline when he looked out of his bedroom window at night.

The Heart was really destroyed, wasn't it?

CHAPTER 3

THE WAY TO TOWN seemed longer than any distance Javes had ever walked in his life.

Once he moved away from the scene of destruction, the layer of dust deposited on the ground grew thinner, and he was able to follow the road. But the sand radiated heat through the soles of his shoes and the donkey was so fidgety that he gave it most of the water, which it drank from his hand, licking his arm and his shirt and the bottle. Then he didn't want to drink from a bottle covered in donkey slobber and grew very thirsty himself. Surely the town couldn't be that far away? Or had he walked in the wrong direction?

With every breeze, he looked over his shoulder, checking that visibility wasn't getting worse, and the dust devil wasn't coming back. With every step, he felt more hesitant about having left the bodies and the cart behind, and he argued with himself about the reasons. The cart was broken, he couldn't fix it and he couldn't carry the bodies anyway, so it was all right, wasn't it?

It was almost dark when Javes plodded to the top of a hill and looked down on the blocky houses of the town of Ysherra. The sky was deep blue and purple at the horizon, the glow of lights in windows and courtyards warm and orange, and the dust cast a thin haze over the landscape, where the surrounding hills were just visible.

Had Javes any tears left, he would have cried with relief, but his eyes stung with dryness, his lips were cracked and bleeding and the skin on his face felt like sandpaper.

He could drink an entire bottle of water, and he had no tears left.

The town housed no more than five hundred people but was still one of the larger towns in the region.

Pashtan's house was on the other side, and Javes dreaded walking through town. Pashtan might not have any relatives here—in fact he'd been coy about the subject of relatives—but everyone knew him.

It looked like the devil had come through the town as well. One house had been reduced to rubble, and lot of townsfolk were helping to remove fallen debris. An old woman sat in the dirt, crying.

"There is the student!" someone yelled.

Within moments, Javes was surrounded by dusty, dark people. They were all yelling at the same time.

"Where has the dust devil gone?" a man screamed. "Where are all my horses?"

"Is it coming back?" another man wanted to know.

"The devils are meant to stay in the desert," a woman said, her voice indignant. "They don't come as far south as this. Pashtan said so."

"Pashtan said nothing like this could happen."

"I don't know why you ever believed him. He's not even from here and knows nothing about our land."

"Pashtan is dead!" Javes called out over the din.

A good number of people fell quiet. They stared at him.

"Dead?" a woman said.

"Yes, dead. You know, not alive. Same as the other cart donkey. Had the flesh ripped from its bones. The cart was turned over and everything covered in dust." He wiped his face. He didn't think he'd ever felt more exhausted in his life.

More people fell quiet.

"And you survived?" a man said, his voice incredulous. "The city kid? What sort of magic is that?"

"It's not magic. It's only because—"

"You survived! That's a sign. You should have Pashtan's position."

"You could not possibly do any worse than call dust devils into town!"

"He did that because you cheated him out of two bottles

of cider—"

"Quiet!" Javes called.

People stopped yelling.

"I will contact the meteorology department for a replacement meteorologist—"

"What are you talking about? There has been a sign. He died while you were here. You survived and he died. That's a sign. We have a new meteorologist."

Several people nodded their agreement. "It's a sign."

No, no. Javes was overcome with a feeling of total horror. "I can't stay because I'm not finished with my education yet." That was the only thing he could think of saying, and it came out really lame. But his mouth was dry and his mind blank. He shuddered at the thought of spending his entire life in Pashtan's simple square house with its two rooms, of trudging past all the weather stations in a donkey cart every day, day in day out, and sitting at the plain wooden desk every night to work out the curves and trends and traipse to the telegraph office every few days to send the results to Tiverius.

The life of a regional meteorologist.

That was not what he had signed up for, was it?

He made some sort of excuse, left the scene and led the donkey through the town. The collapsed house was not the only sign of damage. In some places, roofing had been ripped off.

In other places, dust had heaped in corners and on ledges. The poor olive trees that grew by the side of the road looked even dustier and more forlorn than they usually did. They had lost branches, mostly dead ones eaten through with termites.

Whispers accompanied him down the road: that Pashtan was dead, that dust devils were coming into town, the he was going to protect them because Pashtan could not.

He wanted to scream at them that a meteorologist does not control the weather, but that would be a lost cause. It was what they believed: that the meteorologist could make it rain. And Pashtan, clearly, had failed to deliver and had been served his sentence.

He shuddered.

Javes pushed open the squeaky gate to the house and led the donkey into the shed at the back. The poor animal was covered in dust. As soon as he came into the yard, the goats bounded up to the gate, and crowded around him and the donkey. There were twelve, white with brown spots. They had ten kids between them and they were all bleating and pushing in a throng of hairy bodies.

"Out of the way, out of the way!" Javes yelled.

Not that they listened.

He wrestled himself out of the goat-crowd and pulled a bale of hay down from the loft of the shed. They attacked it as soon as it hit the ground.

Next, he led the poor dazed donkey into its pen. Javes took the brush and combed out its fur while it drank from the bucket. He filled the trough with fresh hay.

Then when all the animals had been tended to, he dragged his sore and tired body inside.

It was too dark to see inside, so he fumbled for the light, taking several tries to work the spark lighter. Finally the oil light lit the simple room with a warm glow that belied the circumstances. Javes realised that not only had the cart been destroyed, he had left all the measurements with it. He would have to go back so that he could report the measurements to Tiverius as Pashtan did.

He would also have to return to get Pashtan and the donkey's bodies and deal with them in an appropriate manner, even if no one in this forsaken town seemed to care much about funerals and such things.

He found half a loaf of bread in the cooler box and a jar of jam in the cupboard. He poured goat's milk from the big jug, realising that he would have to milk the goats tomorrow morning, a job that he was none too proficient in.

While eating, he pulled a slate from the shelf. With a stylus, he wrote on it:

Plan to get out of here

1. Retrieve cart and bodies. Funeral.

2. Appoint someone to take care of goats.

3. Write to Tiverius for a replacement meteorologist.

No, scratch that. He knew what they would say. They'd say they already had a meteorologist there—him—and would just stick him in the position, unqualified as he was. Because meteorologists were thin on the ground and much in demand, and of course only the people from the right families got positions in the city.

So, rephrase that last point:

3. Train someone to take measurements.

Because, much as he wanted to, he could not just leave the town without a meteorologist. If nothing else, it would be recorded against his reputation and he would be forever stuck with doing the jobs no one wanted.

There. He held the slate up and then put it on the shelf so he could see it.

His only issue was money. Yes. That was definitely an issue. No one in this town had any money. He had some savings and money that his grandfather had given him, but it was in Tiverius and of no use to him here.

Well, damn it. That was a plan, but it wasn't going to get him out of here any time soon.

He'd forgotten to check the oil level on the lamp before lighting it, and you could not refill the reservoir when it was hot, so when the light sputtered out, that was the end of it.

He should go to sleep, but it was still quite early, people were talking outside, the walls of the house still radiated heat, and his mind churned.

He went to sit on the back step of the house, which looked out over the back yard where the donkey slept in its shed and the goats lay like hairy lumps under the olive tree in the corner.

The air still carried a tang of dust, and from elsewhere in the town came sounds of hammering as people repaired the damage done by the dust devil.

The sky above was finally turning its usual black, and stars were coming out. Then, above the far northern horizon, he saw something he had never seen before: a faint shimmering of green light. It flickered like flames across the sky.

What was that?

JAVES GOT UP BEFORE DAWN. It was just too hot to sleep and he wanted to get started with his tasks. It took him much longer than it had taken Pashtan to milk the goats, and he was already tired by the time it was light and he went to the neighbour's house.

The man, a middle-aged peddler of tools and metalware by the name of Arukat, came to the door. He had a dark, wizened face that looked much older than Javes suspected he was, because his daughter was at that age where her limbs started lengthening and she looked awkward in advance of the pending arrival of femininity, which was yet to touch her youthful features.

In a town the size of Ysherra, Javes did not have to explain what had happened.

"So, you'll be in town a bit longer, then?" Arukat said.

"I won't leave Ysherra without meteorologist." It wasn't exactly the same thing, and Javes felt terrible about skirting the issue, so he launched into the reason why he had come. "Could you lend me your sand cart so I can bring back what's left of Pashtan's cart and deal with the bodies?"

"Bodies?"

"They need a decent funeral."

"Even the donkey?" Arukat laughed.

But people in this town helped each other, so he took Javes out the back to this jumble of sheds that contained a collection of metal parts that, in Tiverius, would be called a *dump*. The sand cart, so named because of its broad wheels that allowed it to roll over dunes of loose sand, stood in the corner. He'd be needing two donkeys, Arukat informed him, and yes, he was happy to lend Javes a donkey as well.

"Really, what you need is a camel, but they're stroppy beasts and take some getting used to. My donkey will do the job."

"Do I owe you anything?"

"Just bring us some rain."

Javes left the yard with the cart and the donkey, feeling the darkness creep up on him. If he wasn't careful, he'd be stuck in this place for the rest of his life, and that life would likely not be long if he couldn't deliver the rain everyone wanted.

When he brought the cart into the back yard, Pashtan's donkey gave him the evil eye.

"I'm sorry," he said, patting the side of the donkey's neck. "We're both stuck in this dump. Today's job is going to be awful, but I have to do something."

In his short time in Ysherra, Javes had found that the harsh life in this district did not favour elaborate ceremonies. When villagers died in town, family took the body to the field of bones, where large vultures waited in surrounding trees. Javes had gone past it on his trips with Pashtan, and and its stench reached to the next hilltop. When people died while they were out of town, other people just . . . left them there. Going back to look for people who were certainly dead was considered asking for bad luck.

But he wasn't brought up that way, and he didn't think it was right.

He decided that he should take Pashtan's body to the field of bones, much as the thought revolted him. Then he should see what he could salvage of the cart to see if he could repair it. Then maybe he could sell some of the goats to buy another donkey. Or sell some of the goats and the donkey to buy a camel.

But he should also do the round of his weather stations today and send the data to Tiverius, because above all, he needed to make a good impression doing the job he'd come here to do. He wanted to go home so badly, but he must never fail doing that.

Not much later, he left town on his own, sitting atop the driver's seat of Arukat's sand cart, feeling very empty and insecure. He hoped he'd rigged the donkey correctly and taken everything he needed. He'd watched Pashtan do all the things that needed to be prepared for a day in the field every day, and even when Pashtan had told him to do them, he'd still watched over him, making sure that they were done correctly.

The trail was hard to follow at times, where dust had blown over the road. The wind had since erased many of the tracks that he and the donkey had made last night. He was glad he had the sand cart with its big wheels.

First he went around the field stations. He collected the measurements; he replaced the paper in the barygraphs. At some point he would need to find out where to get more paper and where to get pens. And he needed to find a young boy who would want to be taught to do this job while he went to finish his education—and then never came back?

That didn't feel right either.

The day grew hot. The air shimmered above the dry fields. Groves of olive trees stood waiting for rains that had stayed away for months. Occasionally a small breeze would ruffle the branches, showing the silver undersides of the leaves. Many trees, too, had dead branches. Even the olives were dying, people said.

It was after midday that Javes had finished the round and turned back to the spot where the sand devil had overwhelmed them.

He could see the spot from the top of the next hill. It was where giant vultures flapped around, fighting each other. Sometimes, he could see them carry chunks of meat in their claws back to their young.

Coming over the final crest of the hill, he had not expected the level of destruction he found. At night, wild dogs had ripped at the carcass of the donkey, tearing it to shreds. It was this that the vultures had been fighting over.

He shooed away the vultures, which took to the air with big flapping wings and indignant squawks.

Pashtan's body was mostly still buried under the sand. An animal had taken a bite out of the exposed shoulder, but mostly the scavengers had gone for the easy meal. Javes covered the body up some more. The donkey would have to stay here, but he'd deal with Pashtan's body the very last.

First he went to have a look at the cart.

It had blown over, and the axle and one of the wheels had broken. When it fell, the tray had become warped and the side had split.

All of the measuring equipment lay in the dust.

Javes brought the sand cart as close as possible. First he collected all the meteorological equipment. The spare barygraphs, the box with paper, the leads and connectors for the telegraph line. He stacked all these things in the far corner of the tray. Then he tried to right the cart. In one way or another, he would have to return it to town so that he could fix it, or get a new axle and wheel fitted. But since materials were scarce, he would have to bring the old wheel so that a carpenter could repair it. He pulled the wheel off the broken axle and heaved it into the cart with the equipment. Then, using ropes and a few planks, he rigged the broken cart to the back of the sand cart so that it stood on only one wheel.

Then he turned the remaining planks that had broken off the side of the cart into a bier which he tied to the back of the construction.

By this time, the vultures had returned to the site. He brought the cart up to where the body lay buried. He swept the sand off and pulled Pashtan by the clothes.

Whoa! He upset a great nest of insects. They swarmed from the body over his hands. He jumped around to wipe them all off.

The smell was *urghh*. He tied a cloth around his mouth.

He was starting to understand the reason for the local attitude.

But eventually, he managed to get the body onto the bier, shooed away the vultures and climbed up on the cart.

It had become so heavy that the donkeys had trouble setting it into motion. He should have borrowed a camel after all. So he had to get back off, also to shoo the vultures away again, and help the donkeys to pull the weight.

Finally the construction creaked into motion.

It was hard to keep the cart moving, because the single wheel of the cart at the back kept getting stuck, and that meant Javes had to push, next to the body that was starting to smell really bad. He felt sick and sweaty and filthy, and knew there would be no relaxing bath at the end of the day.

By the time the shadows were long, he arrived at the field of bones. Here, he untied the bier and dragged it in to the area marked by a low stone wall. The smell here was even worse. A big vulture sat in a dead tree in the middle of the patch. It was a magnificent bird, with golden feathers, a collar of long loose black feathers, a bare and black-skinned head and a blood-red eye.

Walking inside the field was another experience altogether. Bones and skulls crushed under his feet with each step, no matter how much he watched out for them. Some still had scraps of cloth attached. The breeze brought wafts of stench mixed with an earthy smell.

He dragged the bier to a spot where none of the skeletons seemed too recent. He would have liked to leave the whole construction there, but he knew he'd need the wood, so he tipped it over. The body rolled on its side, trailing insects and maggots.

Holding his breath, Javes retreated.

In Tiverius, where people were smart enough to bury the dead, a funeral celebrant would say some words in the memory of the dead person, and the family would gather before the body was covered.

Now, what did the celebrant say again at funerals?

Another thought: did Pashtan have any relatives, and how could they be contacted?

As Javes stood there, trying to think of something to say, the sun sank below the horizon. Three vultures sat in the tree, waiting for him to leave. The donkeys stood, miserable, harnessed in front of the cart.

All of a sudden, one of the vultures squawked and flew up. The other two followed it, and there was the distinctive sound of foot-steps crunching on bones.

Javes turned around.

A man had come into the graveyard, leading a camel by the reins; at least Javes thought it was a man. He was covered from head to toe in cloth, sand-coloured like the desert. The camel wore . . . leather armour, for want of a better word. Leather plates covered the beast's head, back and sides. It also wore kneepads.

"Who are you? What . . . what are you doing here?" Javes stammered.

The man held out his hand. On it lay a strange object: a ball with pieces of wire coming out of it at two opposing ends. Made of polished silver-like metal, it glittered in the last of the daylight.

"What's that?" Javes asked.

The man held the thing out to him, pushing it in his hands.

"I don't have any money for things like this."

The man wagged a finger, the skin dirt-ingrained and wrinkled. The nails were painted blue.

"Here then, if you want it back." Javes held the thing out to the man, who refused to accept it. He backed away, and then crouched at Pashtan's body. He searched the pockets of Pashtan's *temuz* and found some coins and a key. Then his trousers, and found some more coins. Then he inspected the hands, found that Pashtan wore several silver rings, and snapped the fingers clean off the body to retrieve them. He then extracted a knife from his robe and cut clothes from around the neck of the body. As it turned out, Pashtan was wearing a necklace, too. Javes looked away, not wanting to see how the man retrieved it. The wet crunch of bones made him feel sick.

The man stuffed everything in his pockets. He bowed to Javes and left again, without having spoken a single word, leading the camel by the reins.

CHAPTER 4

THE HEART WAS really destroyed, wasn't it?

His mind racing, Isandor sat in his office, watching as the mist rose from the ocean and rolled over the City of Glass, cloaking it in a grey, humid, cold blanket. Here was another thing that didn't happen much as recently as last year. So many signs proved that after the supposed destruction of the Heart, the world hadn't finished changing yet. In fact, change was speeding up.

The weather, the continuing fertility problems, the flashes of icefire that wouldn't die, and now Sady's letter all added to the worry that gnawed in his stomach. Up until now, Peria was the only country that had done well out of the destruction of the Heart, going from an ice-covered wasteland to a cool highland with rolling green meadows.

He'd heard of Chevakia's drought, but had somehow not associated it with the goings-on in the City of Glass, even if Sady had told him that Chevakia's climate hinged on the low-pressure systems that were pushed off the southern plateau by icefire.

The changes affected the whole world and he didn't like the direction in which things were going. What could he do about it?

First of all, he should check that the Heart had not somehow regenerated. At first he went to the scene of destruction a lot, but these days—he probably hadn't been there for at least three years. That might have been exceedingly short-sighted. The machine had been made by an ancient society much more advanced than theirs. Who knew what capabilities it had?

Isandor went into the bedroom.

He half-expected Jevaithi to start talking about her next breeding scheme, but she was asleep. She lay on her side, one naked shoulder protruding from above the blanket. It moved up and down slowly with her breaths. Her hair—honey-coloured and loose—fell over the pillow.

For many years, he had slept next to her, but right now, he felt that he had never understood what drove her to this desperate attitude towards having a child, which was obviously not going to happen.

She was slipping away from him, and he wasn't sure what to do about it. He protected her, but she didn't want protection. She wanted to tell everyone what to do, but she had no clear vision for the land, and she still acted as if the Knights had all the say. Possibly she had never learned to see beyond her room in the glass palace where she grew up, hidden from the people by her mother and later by the Knights, while they fought over which of them was going to father the heir to the throne.

He understood how these experiences had scarred her, but not how in twenty years those scars had never healed.

He quietly collected his fur boots from the wardrobe in the bedroom. In the hallway, he donned his fur cloak. Then he went back to his study and extracted a box from the very top shelf of his bookcase. It was a thing of beauty, made from wood inlaid with mother of pearl. The lid looked grey, and not even running his hand over it removed all of the caked-on dust of the years.

It had been so long that he had used this.

He undid the latch and opened the lid. It creaked. Inside the box, he found the little device with the dial that had been given to him by the Chevakian meteorologists when he and Jevaithi and a band of survivors returned to the City of Glass in the season following its destruction. The Chevakians had developed all kinds of devices to measure icefire, and Isandor had walked through the ruins of the city with this little thing, recording the numbers that the little hand pointed at, and sending them through to Chevakia, where the other refugees waited for news that their city was safe enough for them to return home. In those early days, icefire contaminated everything, but it had gradually vanished until even foreigners who were not normally resistant to it could live in the city.

Isandor stuck the device in his pocket and closed the box.

He left the building through the atrium, rejected the offer of a guard or a coach, and walked through the gate into the city. It was only afternoon, but already it was starting to get dark, especially at the street level where the tall buildings of the city cast their shadows. Soon the sun would disappear under the horizon and would not be seen again for all of winter. The days would be bleak, with only the merest glimmer of light. It had been, in past years, the season that icefire was the strongest. If it was true that the menace was coming back, that the machine had somehow regenerated and was again sending out its rays that killed anyone not born in the City of Glass, he needed to find out before winter.

Ahead, a tall forbidding fence blocked the street. In the part of the city that he had just crossed, people had been able to restore the ages-old structures after the explosion of icefire. Washing down all surfaces and painting over the raw stone walls helped dull the contamination and, gradually, people had moved in. The section ahead, however, had been deemed too contaminated and damaged to rebuild. Maybe it was time for another review of that assessment, but in all honesty the City of Glass didn't *need* any more housing. There was plenty of space to build, the native population had shrunk through infertility and people leaving, and the foreigners disliked the idea of living in the tall towers that housed the ghosts of past civilisations, some of them known, some unknown. Most importantly, they hadn't needed the space, because the foreigners had been happy to build the types of housing they thought the City of Glass lacked.

There was a guard post in front of the fence to make sure that louts didn't endanger themselves by climbing it.

A single Eagle Knight stood guard in the little watch house, looking extremely bored.

He sprang into action when Isandor approached. "Your Majesty, what an honour to see you here. How can I help?"

"I'd like to go in," Isandor said.

"Yes, certainly." The Knight found a bunch of keys on his belt and opened the gate with a creak. Isandor went through.

The area on the other side of the fence had barely been touched since the day of the explosion.

Rubble and glass that had blown off the facades of buildings lay where it had fallen twenty years ago, covered in a layer of dust. The open sides of people's former houses showed the furniture still inside, much of it rotted and covered in seagull shit.

Isandor had already left the city when the explosion happened, but he had heard from his foster mother how giant figures made out of icefire had burst out of the ground and had destroyed everything in their path. Apparently, they had once been children, which the leadership of the Knights had changed into icefire sinks.

He could barely comprehend the cruelty of that act. It would have required embedding a stone in their bodies.

The further he walked into this ghost quarter of the city, the more prominent and twisted the wreckage became. At times it was hard to understand that the mangled mess of metal had once been tall towers that had stood here since before the start of any written history of the City of Glass.

Isandor remembered how, when he was a boy, these streets used to be full of colourful people, mostly nobles with the golden tattoos on their cheeks and their pretty furs and beautiful, impractical clothes, sitting in beautiful sleds pulled by magnificent bears with colourful harnesses with bells that tinkled at each step. He remembered the fashion stores with their extravagant dresses of layers upon layers of thin gauze and outlandish frills, and the stores that sold little miniature trees that were the rage with the rich people. He remembered the grotesque sculptures of molten coloured glass that had dripped down the sides of buildings like candle wax: a reminder of a disaster much older than living memory that seemed to exist as a kind of afterthought to the vapid, showy, self-absorbed life that these nobles led in their palaces of glass and stone.

And he was glad for the change.

From an inward-looking society with a weird, indulgent, detached nobility and a commoner class in dire poverty, the City of Glass had gone to a vibrant port city where the strange customs of old had almost died out, along with the nobility that perpetuated them.

Few of the old nobles remained.

Many of them had gone to Chevakia, where the old queen consort lived and, by all accounts, still plotted crazy schemes against the world. But she was very, very old now.

Others were said to have gone into Arania, but no one knew for sure about those, because contact with Arania was sporadic at best.

Before the explosion, the old palace had been the tallest building in the city, but it had split into pieces at the foundation, ripped apart from the inside while the ground had peeled open like the skin of a fruit.

The building's facade had fallen into the courtyard and flattened the old palace gates. The result was an impenetrable mess of bent metal and broken stone, punctuated with jagged sheets of broken glass, some of which had lost none of their cutting sharpness in the many seasons of wind, rain and snow.

Isandor knew how to get across safely. During a previous visit, he had daubed dots of paint along the path: where to put his hands so that he didn't get cuts, and which sheets were stable enough to support his weight.

It had taken such a long time for the effects of icefire to wear off that not even the animals had moved back into this section of the ruins, one reason why this part of the city was off-limits to the public, because one did not want to risk foreign children playing here and dying of icefire exposure, or falling into any of the holes.

He extracted the little Chevakian device from his pocket and took the cover off the front. He waved it in the air and studied the thin needle on the dial.

The engraved print on the dial was tiny and in Chevakian numbers. The needle sat at between the numbers twenty-five and thirty. That stood for twenty-five in motes per cube, a Chevakian measurement unit for icefire. At this level, exposure was mildly dangerous for Chevakians, especially long term.

He held up his free hand, concentrated on it and flicked his fingers. A few feeble golden sparks flew from his fingers.

Years ago, that needle had sat right up against the left-hand side of the dial and, while sifting through the ruins, looking to recover resources and people, he had to be careful not to burn his tools or even his assistants with great jolts of golden lightning that would fly unbidden from his hands. He belonged to the few who could use icefire, whom some called magicians, but he had never learned to control it properly.

Icefire was disappearing, and when it was gone, there would be no more evil and no more sorcerers. The world would be better that way. It already was better.

He came to the edge of the maw that the explosion had opened up into the ground. The hole was deep and dark and spanned several floors. He checked the needle, but it hadn't shifted from its position.

Someone had lowered a ladder which took Isandor to one floor below ground level. It was dark here, the ground uneven and slippery through fine dust, and you had to be careful not to fall into the opening to the next level down. On his previous visit he had left a light at the bottom of the ladder and it still sat there, because no one had been here since then.

The light was an ancient thing, a glass bulb on a metal stand with a lever at the bottom. The glass bulb itself used icefire to produce its glow, and when Isandor moved up the lever, it flicked on. But oh, it gave off such a feeble, lifeless glow that it barely even showed the ground a few steps ahead.

At least this was an indication that the machine under the ground hadn't come back to life.

But he also remembered the elation of finding these old lights in the bottom of boxes of bric-a-brac at market stalls in the Outer City where he had grown up. He would take the haul to the sleeping shelf in his mother's limpet and would marvel at the bright glow. He would read about all the amazing things that used to exist in the City of Glass and that ran on icefire. The trains for example. Not Chevakian noisy, stinky ones that went chug-chug-chug, but ones that whizzed over rails at great speed with barely a sound.

When icefire was gone, that would never again be possible.

But icefire brought permanent winter to the land. It made it impossible to grow crops. It killed many people in the world.

It was beautiful and dangerous. It tempted those who could wield it into evil deeds. Even while standing here, he could feel its call.

Isandor walked down the corridor, footsteps muffled by years of built-up dust. A trail of footsteps showed the path he had taken the last time he'd come here.

At the end of the hallway, he turned into a door that led to a staircase. Surrounded by stone walls, the stairs had survived, but the giant spiralling walkway that started at the bottom of the stairs was truly dangerous ground.

Sections of ceiling had collapsed and in places part of the walkway had fallen onto the next level down. There were also sections where the stone would look intact but would crumble at the slightest touch.

When he had first come here, there had been a good number of skeletons strewn on the ground, but those had since fallen to dust. He couldn't even see where the one with the Knight's cloak lay anymore.

He slowly picked his way down the spiralling walkway, stopping occasionally to check his measuring device. The icefire levels did not rise much as he progressed. If anything, they fell a bit.

At the bottom of the spiral walkway, the scene of destruction came into view. Where the big, chunky machine that people called the Heart had stood, there was a scar in the rocky ground. Bits of metal lay strewn over the chamber, most of them bent and twisted and heaped up at the bottom of the walls. It was hard to imagine the force of the explosion that had thrown them there. There were pipes ripped from their attachments, metal threads clean snapped off, glass that had melted and re-formed into grotesque shapes, stained and broken and bits of flexible material burnt to a crisp.

Isandor could not even begin to think how it had all fitted together and how much force must have been involved in bending metal so. He understood even less why people had wanted to build this machine that killed. Was it because it emitted icefire and allowed only those people who were immune to it to live in their opulent city?

That ancient, advanced society was the greatest mystery of all.

He checked his meter again. The icefire levels had fallen to nineteen motes per cube. This device was well and truly dead. Yet, Isandor could feel the pricking of icefire at the edges of his awareness. Something, somewhere still produced the deadly magic.

Isandor finished speaking and looked around the Knights' Council, seated around a large round table in the middle of the Council hall in the palace.

This was one of the most delicately built rooms, where builders had taken glass sculptures to another level and where coloured lights reflected from wall to wall in a display of glittering splendour, catching and retaining so much light that this far into autumn, they still weren't using lamps.

Supreme Rider Barton and Carro sat to his right, Jevaithi to his left. The members of the Knights upper command filled the rest of the spots. All the faces around the table were serious.

"So that is the situation," Isandor said, putting both his hands on the table. "I think we can no longer deny that this is happening. The machine may have been destroyed, and I checked it, and it's still very much destroyed, but somewhere another source of icefire exists. One or more sources, maybe. We need to find them and destroy them, too. There is no way that we can allow our land to slide back into eternal winter."

Rider Barton, who was easily the oldest person at the table, said, "I've heard people talk about icefire coming back. It's time that we acknowledge that there is a problem."

"What can we do about it?" Rider Jeito asked, practical as always.

Isandor liked having her on the council, because she was not much inclined to want to listen to endless talk. He said, "This is where I encourage you to think and come up with suggestions. For the immediate future, I have this plan: I will ask Brother Veshi to supply the street patrols with icefire sinks so that they can siphon off any flare-ups."

Brother Veshi, a black-clad and bearded man on the other side of the table, nodded. "We can do that no problem. We've put the sinks in storage, but I know exactly where they are. Give me a few days and I'll have them retrieved and ready for use."

Isandor turned to Carro and Rider Barton. "I want you to identify those in the Knighthood who can spot these flare-ups and task them with making them harmless." Since Knights were mostly from the Pirosian clan, they couldn't see the flare-ups, but Isandor had encouraged the Knights to recruit from all sections of the population. The first Chevakian-born Knights were coming up through the ranks, and a few from the Thillei clan were already on duty.

Rider Barton nodded. "We can do that."

"Recruit extra people if necessary."

There were more nods around the table. More people was always good. It meant more funds and more resources. The Knights were always arguing that they wanted more people.

Isandor continued, "I will write to Chevakia to see what their meteorologists know about this new phenomenon."

There were more nods around the table. Aside from being deadly to Chevakians, icefire had controlled much of the weather in Chevakia.

"I also want you to send out as many patrols as you can fit out with the Chevakian barymeters. I don't know how many devices you have, but send out that many patrols. Send them each to different areas. Just a fly-over inspection will do at this point, unless they spot something very obvious or interesting. Map the results before the next meeting."

Supreme Rider Barton said, "I will see to that."

"It could be that we worry for no reason and that there are simply lingering fields of icefire." Isandor spread his hands. They had gone through periodic flare-ups in the past. At which point did one decide that this was something different? "It could be part of the land shedding icefire that built up in the soil. I don't know. We will work to try to understand it. If there are other sources, we will destroy them."

"Should we warn people?" Carro asked.

A chill went over Isandor's back. That was another loaded question. There were so many foreigners in the City of Glass these days. Should he warn people and risk panic, or not warn people and risk being called dishonest and then have panic anyway?

Isandor sighed. "Maybe just the foreigners."

CHAPTER 5

ZAINA WIPED her hands on the legs of her overalls and sauntered to the workshop's entrance, where the open door provided access to the building from the street and where two of her young mechanics stood talking with the man who owned the carpentry shop next door.

The youngsters looked up at her, and the neighbour, in his early middle age, nodded at her. His brown Chevakian eyes were kind.

"How's business?" she asked him.

"I didn't see you at the *Sailor's Rest* last night. Have you heard the news?"

"About the warning? Yes, I have. I live above the *Silver Gull*. I was there last night." She remembered the rowdy meeting where the palace official was besieged by many questions, mainly asked by foreigners who lived in the Harbour District of the City of Glass. The poor man had tried to answer questions, but most of the time his voice had been drowned out by shouts of protest and more questions. Zaina had never understood why people needed to protest to authorities about things that those authorities didn't control.

The carpenter said, "What do you think? Is it as dangerous as they say?"

"Icefire is dangerous, no doubt about it." She'd listened to the stories of the sorcerers of the past, told by old men at the bar.

"Dangerous enough to leave?"

"I didn't hear leaving town in their suggestions."

He shook his head. "No, but a lot of people in the Sailor's Rest were talking about it."

"Well, I'm not leaving." She had seen the golden glimmers over the water in the harbour, and had seen the sparks that sprang from the bashing together of two pieces of metal. She had figured that this was probably icefire and the fact that she could see it meant that she likely had some resistance to it, unlike the poor Chevakians who had no resistance whatsoever and were all panicking.

"I got my leather jacket, just in case," the man said. *He* was half-Chevakian.

"My overalls will do." You should wear thick clothing, most people said, and never expose more skin to the air than necessary, keep all doors and windows closed and stay indoors as much as possible.

"So," the man said. "What are your plans? It would be hard to shift your entire workshop."

"I'll wait and see. It's too early to worry. It might yet go away."

"Well, they wouldn't warn everyone about it if they thought it was going to go away, right?"

Zaina shrugged. "I really don't know. I'm cynical enough to question their motives."

The man gave her a sharp look. "What? You think they want us out?"

"Well, most commerce in the City of Glass is in the hands of foreigners. They can't be happy about that."

"Yeah, but . . . icefire is something anyone can measure. They can't make it up."

"They can't lie about it, but machines exist that produce it, so . . ." She spread her hands and let them sink. "What's to say that they won't have built a little machine that produces just enough to chase us all away?"

"Hmmm," the neighbour said and then they were silent for a bit. Did anyone in the Harbour District really trust the Knight Council? As far as Zaina was concerned, the Perian nobles who lived in the citadel in the Aranian capital Kadrish had been all too quickly accepted into the inner circles of the king. That alone was a reason to be wary of them.

Zaina said, "Come on, boys, let's go back to work. That truck is not servicing itself."

The three of them went back into the workshop. The boys worked on the truck and Zaina was meant to be doing administration, but she sat in her office staring at the wall.

She wasn't sure what to do about the warning. Nothing, probably. Back when Chevakia was in a panic about icefire leaking over the borders and putting up barriers to stop it and when the massive explosion happened and the barriers shattered, the only thing King Orik in Arania had said was that if a lot of Chevakians died, he would send his army into Tiverius and do to the Chevakian capital what the Chevakians had done to Kadrish during the last war. He had stood on the balcony, and Zaina remembered standing in the crowd below, holding her mother's hand. She remembered cheering with the people, because she had been five or six and didn't understand wars, nor, for that matter, the orchestrated lies told by the citadel and the court astrologers.

But still, she thought that if a lot of people had died of exposure to icefire back then, she would have heard the stories from her mother and her mother's generation. That she would remember an atmosphere of fear.

So did she need to start planning for the inevitable and pack up the workshop? She couldn't see herself moving to Chevakia. Her appearance would ring alarm bells. Her hooked nose and deep-set, light-coloured eyes marked her as Aranian.

And there was no way that she could go back home.

IN THE EVENING, after work, Zaina sat at her usual table in the *Silver Gull* over a mug of cider and a plate of fish and seaweed cakes. Those had taken some getting used to, but she had finally been long enough in the City of Glass to develop a certain tolerance for seaweed cakes. That was one thing she did miss about Arania: the food.

The door to the drinking room opened to let in two of her friends. Eshtar was Chevakian, but had come from the far north of the country, a long way from the capital. She had heard life was harsh there. The other was Marek, like herself an Aranian refugee.

They sat down at the table.

Since most patrons were foreigners, the talk in the drinking room was all of the icefire warning. A couple of men at the table next to them were discussing a plan to go to Tiverius. On the other side, a group of Chevakian women discussed protective clothing, holding up samples and testing them for fabric thickness.

"Yeah," Marek said, looking at the women. He often did that: continued a conversation that hadn't yet started. His expression was as worried as Zaina felt.

They were silent for a bit longer.

"Yeah," Marek said again.

"What are you going to do?" Eshtar asked. His dark-skinned face looked serious.

"What can I do?" Marek said. "I've got nowhere to go."

"You could come with me. I'd go back home."

"And what are Chevakians going to think of me?"

"That could be a problem," Eshtar admitted.

For most of the Aranians here, going home was not an option. Like Zaina, they had fled oppressive circumstances and feared for their lives should they ever return.

The door clanged and a group of three men came in. They wore blue armbands with the eagle symbol of the Knight Council. Proper Knights would wear a uniform, so these had to be helpers, or something.

They strode onto the middle of the floor.

"Listen up, everyone," said one of the men, in a thick Chevakian accent. "We all heard the warnings about icefire, and I trust that you have heard them, too. The council has asked us to make a register of all the foreigners in the City of Glass so that they can easily be warned when there is an emergency."

"I'll put my name on no flaming register," Marek said under his breath.

Zaina had to agree.

"The register will be operated through the Knight Council and the Business Council. If you employ any people or run a business, you will be required to register as a condition to continue to operate your business and you will be responsible for registering your foreign employees."

Someone in the audience said, "Fuck that. It's not a register, it's a ploy to screw more tax out of us."

There were some noises of agreement to that.

Another one of the three men said, "I can assure you, this is a scheme to assure your safety and that of your junior employees." He was a local, but Zaina was looking at the third man in the group, who had stayed behind. He freed one of the tables by evicting the patrons —they took their glasses and retreated to the side of the room. He wiped the table with a cloth and deposited a stack of papers in the middle, presumably for registration. Then he pulled back a chair and sat down, looking into the audience. His hooked nose and light eyes made him distinctly Aranian.

The Chevakian man continued, "All foreigners should come and collect a form from my colleague here, fill it out and hand it back to us. If you have any questions or need translation, we are here to help."

A number of people got up and went to the table. The Aranian gave them forms while studying them with his light grey eyes. Some people asked him questions.

Soon, a queue had formed. The vast majority of the people were Chevakians, but some Aranians had also joined. Those were the brave ones.

"I'm still not registering," Marek said. "I don't care what they say."

Zaina shook her head. "I don't have any foreign employees, so I can't see why I should."

"He said 'For the continuation of business.' "

"Screw that."

Eshtar said, "I can't see the problem. You're both honest people. The Knight Council is an honest organisation. What can they do with the information anyway?"

"When Aranian authorities are concerned, the word 'honest' has no meaning," Zaina said.

"But Arania is not involved."

"What about that guy at the table?"

"They're just sending him to speak to Aranians who need someone to translate. You're so suspicious."

"Trust me, we have good reason to be."

"Well, I'm going." Eshtar rose and joined the queue.

Marek and Zaina remained at the table, both holding their drinks.

"This is bad news," Marek said.

Zaina nodded. And then, because she had been friendly with him for months and because she felt that she could ask this sort of thing, she asked, "Who is after you?"

"The National Conscription Service. I was allocated a place in the Special Patrol."

"Shit." Those were the frontline troops sent as test cases to extremely dangerous places. "What's the record for the number of missions survived by one of those people? Seven, I believe."

Marek folded his hands around his glass and sighed. "And for having fled conscription, I can never return. I am viewed as a coward, because I refused to sign up for certain death."

Zaina looked at his face. Usually the men allocated to the Special Patrol were ones who the king and other men in power thought posed the most danger to their position. Popular minor princes.

He looked up. "What about you? I'm guessing you're fleeing the Mothers Register."

Zaina nodded. "My mother was dirt poor. She put me on there because she said I was growing up pretty and maybe a prince might want me in his harem. You know . . ." She shrugged. A prince would feed and house her, and becoming a mother to his children would lift her status enormously, especially if there were a lot of them. So she didn't *blame* her mother for putting her name on it. For most poor girls, it was the only way out of poverty. "Once I became a mechanic, I applied to have my name removed."

He sucked in a breath.

"Yeah, not my smartest move ever."

Eshtar returned to the table and sat down. "Well, that was simple."

"What did they want to know?" Marek asked.

"Name, where you came from and where you live. That's all. You should do it, too, especially you, Zaina, because of your business. I overheard someone asking if they were going to require all businesses to register, and the man said they were. You don't want to get into trouble."

"Nope," Zaina said. She drained the last of her cider and plonked the glass on the table. "Let's go."

Eshtar's eyes widened. "But . . ."

"Nope. I'm not going to register as long as I can avoid it."

While she weaved her way between the tables towards the door, with Marek and Eshtar, the Aranian official's eyes met hers.

ZAINA LIVED in a room above the drinking room of the meltery, but the only way to get there was around the back of the building through an alley that ran between the building and the eatery next door. The whole area was a seedy place—there were hookers outside the main doors to the meltery at night—but when she arrived here, she had no money, and the place had grown on her. Besides, the kitchen was good.

At this time of the day, the brothel was starting to get busy. Two fresh and perky hookers stood on either side of the meltery's entrance, twirling their butts and bosoms at any passing male. One of the women eyed Zaina while she said her goodbyes to her friends in the street. Eshtar and Marek both lived in different establishments.

Zaina'd had an unfortunate encounter with that particular hooker. A few days after coming here, she had deposited a few coins in the groove between the woman's pushed-up breasts for an evening's worth of table service. She figured that since these hookers in the Harbour District had no morals, they would not mind serving a woman for a change. She hadn't even asked the woman to come upstairs with her, just to bring her drinks and jiggle her tits in Zaina's face, or sit on her lap for a bit, maybe.

That had been a dumb move. These women catered only to men, and since that day, this woman—and she was incredibly voluptuous and desirable—had studiously avoided Zaina.

Because *We don't do that sort of thing here.* Gah. Now she was forever marked and memorable to this woman and her friends. And she had wanted to keep quiet.

The guesthouse patrons had their own entrance through a small hall where everyone left their wet and snowy cloaks and boots. A creaking wooden staircase led to the upper floor.

It wasn't raining or snowing yet, but Zaina took off her boots anyway. She wasn't crazy enough to leave them, though. They were good boots and expensive to replace if some jerk took off with them, and she wouldn't put that past any of the patrons in the upstairs corridor.

A couple of men stood talking in Chevakian. They fell quiet as she passed, and continued again when she was at the end of the corridor.

Zaina unlocked the door to her room—and found it was already open. That was strange. She remembered locking it this morning. She didn't give the cleaners permission to come into the room when she wasn't there.

As she stepped into the room the thought flitted through her mind that maybe it wasn't such a good idea and at the same time she noticed the dark silhouette, knew it was too late, and a man grabbed her around the bottom half of her face, his hand across her mouth, while wrestling her into the room and pushing the door shut with his backside.

Zaina grabbed the arm that held her with both her hands and tried to pull the hand off her mouth. It smelled like tobacco—Aranian tobacco. The man was too strong. He dragged her to the hard-backed chair that stood at the table against the wall and pushed her down.

"Not a word or I'll kill you," he said in Aranian. Damn it, by his accent she suspected that this was someone from the Royal Service.

He let go of her mouth and tied her hands behind the chair.

He lit the little oil light that stood on the bedside stand. When he came around the front of the chair, it backlit his silhouette.

He was tall and broad, a mountain of flesh and muscle. Most of his head was shaven, with the exception of a round patch on the crown of his head, where he wore a ponytail, dark and glistening with oil, the plait fastened with several metal ties.

The skin on his head bore red tattoos.

It was not just someone from the Royal Service. It was Prince Nayek himself.

Zaina sat, petrified. What had she done to deserve this? Her position on the mothers list was low. Many, many women would be called up before it was her turn.

"You may wonder why I'm here," Nayek began.

Well, *wonder* was an understatement. She would have told him so if she hadn't been so scared, and that would have been cocky, even if he hadn't been the prince.

"Usually, when I call a woman from the list, there is only one thing I need from her."

A quick fuck and then a child. The royal family paid the women. It wasn't much, but in the poverty-stricken quarters of Kadrish, it was hard cash and came with the chance that a child of yours might develop into a prince's favourite —or the king's if you were lucky— and you might benefit from it, or maybe have a second child and be paid even better.

Nayek said, "Normally."

He trailed a fingernail over the line of her cheek. Zaina did her best not to flinch away from him. She wasn't terribly fond of men most of the time, but was even less fond of those who got their way by using force. She knew she shouldn't fight him—everyone said that it would end badly if she did—but, hell, if he was going to force himself on her, she was going to bite his balls off.

"Yes, normally." He withdrew his hand. "But I get sick of women who undress themselves before I have even asked them."

There was not going to be any danger of her doing that. In fact, he was going to have to rip the overalls from her if that was what he wanted.

"I thought I could make better use of you."

Zaina didn't like the tone in his voice. She didn't want to be "made use" of.

"Those women are weak and useful only for one thing. They do not think, they do not observe, they do not have any use besides being a chattering fuckhole. But some women, when they are pretty and smart, make good collectors of information. I guess you have many friends in this town."

What was he on about? "Not that many." It was the first thing she'd said, and her voice sounded high even to her ears. So, he was after Marek?

"Enough, probably. I guess you have Chevakian friends, local friends. I guess an engine workshop, in a place where engines are not that common, attracts a fair share of well-off people."

"Compared to King Orik, no one is well-off here." That was a standard Aranian reply, drilled into all young children from the moment they could speak.

He laughed. "I see your mother taught you what to say after all."

Zaina clenched her fists. One did not say anything bad about her mother. She wanted to say that *he* seemed to have forgotten that slurs on mothers was one of the rudest things one could say in Arania, but no doubt he did it on purpose, to see how she reacted. And she was not going to give him the pleasure of being able to punish her.

"Your mother was a seamstress in General Pakori's court. The General took a liking to you until you developed a stubborn, rude attitude."

She had never been rude. Stubborn, maybe, and assertive, but girls in Arania weren't allowed to be assertive. Or smart. Or have an opinion that they didn't want to be traded like a piece of furniture to a man whose favours the General wanted.

"After your mother died, you secretly worked in an engine workshop and left the General's household when they found out that you were living with another woman."

Poor, poor Xalia, stabbed to death by a National Service guard for refusing his advances. Girls in Arania weren't allowed to like other girls better than men. Their only allowable aim was to become a mother.

"Imagine," Nayek said. "Imagine having to go back to Arania with that fact widely known."

Zaina held her chin high. She wasn't going to go to Arania or anywhere else. She had no intention of abandoning her business.

"Imagine being inside my palace, while all the other mothers there know who and what you are: a lady-lover."

Zaina shuddered. She had heard many stories of the highborn men's women hurting or even killing each other inside those houses. Once you went in as a mother, the only way out was in a coffin.

"I have your fate in my hand. I could simply let the guys downstairs know that you have no intention to register your business and you're out of here. Once you're gone, I can hunt you for as long as I want. When you return to Arania, you will be easy prey. But you will probably go to Chevakia. Chevakians don't care about you, or about me for that matter. You can run as fast as you can, and I will always find you. Because you should know: no one ever *withdraws* from the mothers register."

Zaina forced herself to think that he was just doing this to freak her out. Why oh why was he so fixated on her?

"I am no longer interested in meek girls. I want someone who will run when she can, who will fight me when she can no longer run, who will try to scratch and bite me and will scream that she hates me when I fuck her."

Zaina made a note that, when it got to that inevitable event, she would not even give him that satisfaction.

"The idea of doing that excites me." He stopped before her, thrusting the crotch of his leather pants towards her face. His excitement was obvious.

"Get away from me before I bite your balls off."

He laughed, but retreated and continued circling her. "Yes, that's what I want." He pushed against the back of her upper arm. He was rock hard. The male scent of him made her gag.

"Look, why don't you just get it over and done with and leave me alone?"

"You think it will be that easy?"

"Then tell me what you want, and I'll tell you if I have any hope of getting it for you, and get out of here anyway."

"If? There is no *if*, lovely Zaina with the sharp tongue, or at least no if that's up to you. *If* you are as smart as I've heard, *if* you do as I say and deliver me the information I want, and *if* I like it enough, and *if* I'm in a good mood, I may scratch your name off that list and let you go. But I have to warn you, I'm not easily pleased. And I *am* very much looking forward to throwing you on the floor and fucking your brains out."

Zaina had no doubt that he would do that, too, maybe even if she did give him what he wanted. One of the benchmarks the king used to determine which of his many sons was going to be his successor was the number of sons each of his favoured sons had. Nayek was sure to be in the running.

The more she thought about it, the more she wanted to run.

"So, do we have an agreement?"

Zaina raised her chin.

He slapped her in the face. Her eyes watered with the sting. "Answer me. Do we have an agreement?"

"I don't even know what you want me to do."

"I was getting to that part, but your tongue keeps distracting me. You're delicious. The fucking will be good."

Zaina clamped her jaws. He was trying to needle her and she should know better than to react. "Tell me what you want me to do. I've got work to do."

"All right, if you're going to be like that." He sat down on the bed.

"You'll have to untie me if you want me to do anything."

"Not so fast. I'll untie you when I'm done."

He let a silence hang between them, as if he expected her to protest. Zaina resolved not to give him any more reasons to stay longer than necessary.

"It's like this: after the explosion of their mysterious machine, a lot of rich people from the City of Glass fled to Arania. They are becoming a powerful force at the citadel. They're still a powerful force here. I want to know, to really understand, where these people come from and how much advice they take from the current king and his council, how their philosophies differ and if they ever visit their home, and if not, why."

"What's that got to do with me?"

"I want you to get me this information from the rich families here. Their family trees, their sons and daughters, their wealth and where it is, and the land and houses they own. Who their friends are, especially if those friends are abroad. I'm especially interested in the family of the king and queen and a branch of it who call themselves House Mara."

"But I don't know any of those people."

"Don't they have trucks?"

Zaina stared at him. She supposed the nobles did have trucks, but she'd never paid much attention to the standing of her customers.

Nayek continued, "The better the information is that you can supply to me, the more likely I am to be lenient towards your request. If you give me satisfactory information, I will tell the Aranian official to overlook the fact that you haven't registered your business. Do we have an agreement?"

Zaina had no idea how she was going to do as he asked, but she nodded. Blood was running down her upper lip.

"Good." He rose, loosened the rope that tied her hands and went to the door. His hand on the door handle, he said, "Oh, and in case you are thinking of bolting, I'm going to stay in this guest house for a bit."

Then he was gone. Zaina slumped on the bed. What was she going to do?

CHAPTER 6

ISANDOR LOOKED around the table. It was time for the Knight Council meeting and once again everyone had gathered around the table. The news about the icefire flashes had created a stir around town and this time more people were in the public gallery, including a good number of people he had never seen in the audience before. They were noisier than usual, too, feeling the need to comment to each other after every speaker. They had now arrived at the main agenda point for the meeting.

Isandor didn't mind the public's scrutiny, but he felt the tension in every word spoken in the hall. Panic would break out if the patrols couldn't bring good news.

He signalled Supreme Rider Barton to start on his report.

"The patrols I sent to the peninsula, the plateau and the mountains have all come back with their reports. Some of the teams measured increased icefire, notably those who went to the mountains. Brother Veshi has assisted me in mapping all the measurements they took. I will show the maps to the council." He made a gesture.

Rider Jeito, seated next to him, took a roll of parchment from underneath the table and rolled it out. She rose, all sinew and hard muscle, and hung the map up on the easel that stood on one end of the table for this purpose.

Isandor was glad that he had taken Chevakia's example and instated a meteorologist and encouraged him to acquire real knowledge about the winds and the sky. Brother Veshi had even travelled to Tiverius to look at their huge meteorology department, and the City of Glass had become a measuring point in the Tiverian data collection scheme but, like most other departments, they lacked resources and people, and there were huge parts of the southern plateau where no measurements were routinely taken.

The map produced by the measurements taken by the Knights showed the layout of the land. Isandor recognised the lines of the southern coast, the bay where the City of Glass lay, the peninsula and the western coast that switched back north to the Aranian mountains. There were some small communities in that area now, but the terrain was still mostly covered in ice, and inhospitable.

Rider Barton gestured for Brother Veshi to explain.

The Brother rose and bowed to the council. He began, "The data is interesting, if not terribly satisfying. Interesting, I'm afraid, in not a very good way. We can see these barygraphic lines here in the Aranian mountains . . ." He gestured at that area on the map. "And we can also see a small concentration of lines over the peninsula. The peninsula location was easiest to deal with. The brief issued to our Knight patrols included a mandate for them to investigate areas of interest on the ground. When they measured this higher concentration of icefire above the peninsula, they landed and investigated. But once they were on the ground, they found that the icefire levels dropped to normal levels again. They could not find any concentration of it, no rock or wreckage that's seeping icefire, as the peninsula consists of nothing but rocks and grass and ice."

Now he pointed at the Aranian mountains.

"However, when we consider this area, it becomes a lot more difficult. Because of the mountainous terrain, we have upwellings of air which disturb the normal airflow. It becomes hard to determine the source of the flow that we're dealing with. As you can see, the barygraphic lines are irregular; they don't follow a clear pattern with a clear source. Each cell of icefire is small and, by itself, not big enough to generate the low pressure cells that influence the weather. I've studied a lot of the Chevakian data on barygraphic cells, which would sometimes spin off the main concentration that used to sit over the City of Glass. Those cells would rotate with the wind patterns, and the further north they went, the weaker they got. This happened over a period of a couple of days. These cells over the Aranian mountains are behaving in a completely different manner. They form and disperse and re-form within periods of less than a day. And of course, being over Arania, going onto the ground and measuring there carries certain risks."

He didn't need to say more. The Perian and Aranian royal families had a long history of disagreements about the exact location of the border.

"How many people live over the border in those mountains?" Jevaithi asked. She had been adamant that she wanted to come to this meeting, even if Isandor said it wasn't necessary.

"More than we like to deal with," Rider Carro said.

There were quiet nods around the table.

No one in the City of Glass was anywhere near ready to test their strengths against a foreign enemy, so it was best not to make any enemies in the first place.

Brother Veshi continued, "In the end, the data from both locations is inconclusive."

"Did you find anything in other locations?" Jeito asked.

"Nothing worth mentioning."

"Not even the Bordertown area?" Isandor asked. Bordertown was where Chevakia's icefire barrier had burst and where a lot of Chevakians had died.

Brother Veshi shook his head. "Bordertown has returned to normal. This is what is baffling about the new data. We have no clue where this icefire comes from. It behaves differently from the way it behaved before. There appears to be no clear source."

"Could it be that it was always there, but we just haven't measured it?" Carro asked.

"In theory, it could be. We haven't had the time or the people to monitor any area other than the city and its surroundings with any kind of regularity. However, consider this map that I made three years ago."

He hung another map on the easel. It looked completely different: as expected, there was a concentration of icefire around the City of Glass—the later map showed that as having disappeared almost completely. There were no further concentrations over the peninsula and nothing over the mountains.

In fact, Isandor was shocked how much it had changed, and not for the better. He said, "Could it be that this phenomenon has always existed, but we've just never seen it because the lingering power of the explosion of the Heart overshadowed these patterns?"

"No, look at the levels."

Isandor squinted at the map and read the levels. Three years ago the cell surrounding the City of Glass had measured twenty motes per cube. It had gone down to eight. The recent map over the Aranian mountains went up to as high as fifty.

"But how can that be?"

Brother Veshi spread his hands. "When I was last in Chevakia, the academics in the meteorology department were talking about how their latest way of thinking is that icefire is something that gets shaped by changes in environment as much as it shapes the environment."

"What do they mean by that?"

"That pockets of icefire can be driven elsewhere by the winds, and that wherever they appear is not necessarily where they were formed."

"That's quite a turnaround in thinking."

They used to teach that the immediate, harmful, effect of icefire would linger in an area and would take months or years to dissipate.

Brother Veshi continued, "They kept stressing to me that they are very much still learning about this new phenomenon."

"I guess that means that they have measured it, too."

"They have, especially along their eastern borders."

"But no one knows for sure where it's coming from?"

"No, we don't. It could be that there is a second machine."

And then no one said anything for a while. All of the people around the table had lived through the horror of the intense cold, through the destruction of the Heart, through the disaster. They had seen thousands of people die, had seen columns of refugees, had seen the City of Glass almost die.

The horror was too great. The land couldn't cope with another disaster.

"But then, where would this thing, this second Heart, be?" Rider Barton asked.

Brother Veshi spread his hands.

It did not need to be said: if the Chevakians were right, and they often were, especially in the subject of meteorology, a second machine could be anywhere. It could be on one of the offshore islands, it could be in the mountains, or along the eastern coast. It could be at the bottom of the ocean, in the areas made treacherous by currents and icebergs.

The people barely had the energy to survive. They didn't have the people or resources to explore the land while looking for a machine, while also needing to acquire the knowledge or resources to destroy it without triggering another explosion.

And worse, if there was a second machine, who was to say there wasn't a third or a fourth?

Isandor set his spiralling thoughts of worry aside. "We must find this machine."

There were nods around the table.

"Find it and destroy it, too." He turned to Brother Veshi. "Do the Chevakians have any data that shows better patterns than we have? Do they have clues where to start looking?"

"They have not mentioned it to me. In fact, they haven't mentioned the possibility of a second Heart. They are trying to cope with people fleeing drought and hunger."

"I guess they consider a second machine not their business," Jeito said. "If there is such a machine, they can't come anywhere near it, so it's not going to be on their land. They have enough problems of their own. They just happen to have a lot of good measurements that may help us."

"What about Arania?" Isandor said.

People frowned at him.

"What do you mean—Arania?" Carro asked.

"Do we get data out of Arania? Do they know about this?"

Several Knights laughed, not in a good way.

"Arania is a lost cause," Rider Jeito said. She would know, because one of her flying partners was half-Aranian. Isandor knew the man: Rider Farey with the eerie pale eyes. "They're backward, still licking their wounds from being defeated by Chevakia in the last war—"

"That was forty years ago," a young Knight said, who would not have been born then.

"That's how backward they are," Jeito said. "As far as I know, Arania has not produced anything important during that time—"

"Apart from princes," someone said in a low voice, and everyone laughed. King Orik of Arania was said to have more than a hundred sons, who were all said to be competing for the throne.

"But the borders to Arania have been sealed," Rider Barton said, serious once more. "We've had no news from Arania, we can't travel to Arania and Aranians don't come here or to Chevakia in large numbers."

Council members nodded. It was true.

Brother Veshi said, "Yet, I agree with the king. This icefire problem does not stop at our borders. If there is a second Heart in the mountains, it *will* affect them. It would be good to know if this is the case, because we will not waste any time looking for something in places where it can't be."

"Are Aranians resistant to icefire?" Isandor looked at Jeito.

"Most of House Mara went to Kadrish, so I guess some of them would be." And House Mara, or course, was an old family within the Thilleian clan in the City of Glass. "They have plenty of money, and I guess what with the Aranian traditions of harems and men acquiring power through sowing their seed as widely as possible—" Her face formed a mask of distaste. "—Their resistance to icefire has been spread as far as the reach of their dicks."

All right, he got the picture. "But it probably has been watered down."

"Or met with some other oddity like the pure Thilleian-Pirosian interbreed thing."

By the skylights, yes. Dacon shapeshifters were half-human, half-beast creatures that listened only to their Thilleian parent, that could not be tamed and that wielded the power of icefire simply by breathing.

Who said that crossings with other clan types could not produce a similar monster?

Isandor shuddered. He still found it hard to believe that the dacon that had helped destroy the expanding wall of icefire twenty years ago had been his daughter, but she had listened on to him. He remembered seeing the wild woman, he remembered sitting on the leather-skinned back while she flew into the inferno. He remembered her dying, old and spent, on the ground in a Chevakian field. That time must never be allowed to return.

Isandor said, "We need to get into contact with King Orik to find out if anything is going on in Arania with regards to icefire."

Jeito snorted. "Do you think they'll tell us?"

"If we don't ask, we won't know."

"True. If you write a letter, I can send a royal patrol," Rider Jeito said. "I've always wanted an excuse to send someone into Arania." She grinned.

She commanded a division of the best, fastest and most highly trained Knights.

"How long would that take?"

"They would be in and out of there within a few days."

"Yes, do that. I'll write a letter. I'll need a good translator."

"I can take care of that," Brother Veshi said.

"Do tell them to take utmost care," Rider Barton commented. As the oldest person at the table, he was probably the only one who had been alive during the Aranian wars. "Arania is a strange place, with strange people who can act in dangerous and unpredictable ways."

Jeito snorted. "Has there ever been a time that a patrol of mine has not taken care?"

Isandor invited Carro to his private quarters after the meeting. Jevaithi said she had work to do, leaving the two men with a platter of tea and cakes brought by a servant.

"Do you really think this is worth making such a big fuss about?" Carro asked. "I know I'm not qualified to speak about icefire, but we've got so many other things to do. We've had flare-ups in the past. Do you think this is any different?"

"Yes, I think so, and people have noticed it. If nothing else, a quick investigation will put us and the citizens at ease. With the destruction of the Heart, icefire was meant to be gone. The people can see that it isn't, and they worry. I'm not the only one who can tell that we've had a flare-up recently, and we need to address it, or the people will get restless. They want answers. They deserve answers. It's our task to give them answers."

"All right." Carro shrugged. He drank from his tea.

For a while, the men sat in silence.

Then Isandor said, "Have you managed to look at breeders?"

"I meant to talk to you about that." Carro slid a folder out of his stack of documents. "I can see a few options, but you won't find all of them acceptable."

Isandor nodded and repressed a shudder. Jevaithi could just have the healer insert the man's seed, but if he was going to use a breeder, tradition had it that he would have to go to the woman's house and do the deed. He did not look forward to that, and the gossip such a visit would entail.

Still, Jevaithi had suffered enough and he loved her. "Show me what you have so far."

"Well . . ." Carro opened the folder on the table next to the cream cakes and tea tray. He rummaged in the stack of letters inside.

"Wait, I just had another confirmation this morning—ah, there it is." He pulled out three sheets of paper.

"I looked at the entire list of breeders and their heritage. In order to avoid disasters that cross-clan crossbreeds can present, the breeder needs to be of Thilleian blood. The fact that the breeder needs to be Thilleian presents an immediate problem, because most breeders are Pirosian. They just happen to have greater fertility."

Isandor nodded. That was the curse of the Thilleian house.

"The other issue being, of course, that many Thilleians were of the nobility, and many of those fled the country and have not come back. With that in mind, these are the Thilleians I could find. This is Dania, who is highly-regarded. Her father is well-off, a member of the Brotherhood. She has lent her services to a number of Knights on the council."

Isandor nodded. He knew Dania. She was his age, far too preoccupied with looking younger, and a terrible gossip to boot. One of his private conditions, that he hadn't yet mentioned to Carro, was that he wanted the fact that the king was using a breeder to be secret until the child was born. There was no way she would keep her mouth shut for that length of time.

Carro waited, and Isandor said nothing. He guessed Carro preferred Dania, but he got the message and turned to the next letter.

"This is Jamato, who's a lot younger. She is well regarded, came to prominence by bearing a child to Rider Barton's son, and had two sets of twins after that."

Isandor knew about the case involving Rider Barton's son. The boy had been barely fifteen, and he'd been out at the Newlight festival without his parents' permission. Jamato had been a predator stalking him. By having children to high-class men, they kept themselves in the money, and the idea of Jamato thrusting her not inconsiderable breasts in a fifteen-year-old boy's face for the purpose of screwing money out of the boy's parents made him ill.

He had seen Jamato strutting about at festivities, wearing skimpy clothes, always hanging onto some rich man's arm, regardless of her state of pregnancy. Isandor liked breeders who just got on with the job without having a side income as whores as well, because that whole selling sexual services thing reminded him far too much of his foster mother, and the times he sat outside his house in the snow-covered alley in the Outer City, because his mother was seeing a client. He liked to have the illusion that for the time of her pregnancy, the breeder was dedicated only to him, and that no one would touch her for that period of time, not even him.

He shook his head. "No. I couldn't do that. She's just an in-your-face money-grubbing whore. Sorry if that offends you."

"It doesn't." Carro turned to the last letter. "And the third possibility is Tamerane, who has only had one child, but she has the highest content of Thilleian blood of all of them. She is twenty-nine, and she doesn't officially hire herself out as breeder; but several people mentioned to me that she is looking to move out of her father's house, and I think she could be persuaded to do it."

"Why is she not a breeder?"

"Apparently she worries that she's not very pretty. Also, she pursues her studies as an academic."

And both things would diminish a woman's desirability in the old-fashioned sense. Yes, at times he wondered why anyone still used this breeder system, and then he remembered that people had no choice and would prefer not to use breeders if they could.

"I like the sound of that one."

"She would be good except for one thing: she is the daughter of Ledor of House Mara."

"That could be a good thing, right?" Still, Isandor felt a bit uneasy.

The high-born, stuffy ancient nobility of House Mara was as far removed from his youth in the Outer City as possible. He didn't know Ledor personally, but he seemed to remember that the man owned a business. He couldn't be *that* old-fashioned, right?

"I don't know . . ." Carro said. "We have to question their motives."

"They will be the same as everyone else's: to get their blood on the throne."

"Yes," Carro said, but he stared out the window.

"Is there anything I should know about?"

"I worry about the family's links to other countries, especially Arania."

"We'd be using her as a *breeder*, nothing else."

"Yes," Carro said again and repeated, "yes. You want me to approach her?"

"I don't like either of the other ones at all, so unless you can find other women with Thilleian blood, yes, I do."

Carro sighed. "These women were hard enough to find. All right, I'll contact her."

CHAPTER 7

$\mathcal{I}$N THE STREETS in the Harbour District, people tended to be friendly. They said "Good Morning" and asked how you were, and sometimes they would try to chat. Except, Zaina discovered, when you were female and had bruises on your face.

She had woken up in the morning with a headache, and checked her face in the little hand mirror, which was one of the few possessions she had that used to belong to her mother. Her eye had gone black and blue, with a blotch of red underneath her eye that looked like she was crying blood.

So yes, she was quite a sight, and people looked away when she passed, even those who normally greeted her, afraid of attracting the attention of the violent lover who considered her his property. Maybe they thought she'd cheated. Maybe they thought she didn't do enough for him.

It was always the woman's fault.

When Zaina entered her workshop, she found her two young male mechanics already at work.

She said, "Good morning."

They replied, but said nothing else, even though one of the boys stared at her face. They didn't dare ask, because she was Aranian, and one didn't ask Aranians about their private problems because you might become involved with the Aranian secret service.

Zaina went into her little office at the back to see what needed to be done today. Let's just pretend nothing had happened, that her face didn't hurt or that she didn't have this huge giant threat hanging over her head.

She tried to force herself to think of work, but could not mask her anger. She had thought that she'd escaped the motherhood register and the vile harems of the princes. Why had Nayek picked her out of the thousands on that list? It couldn't *just* be because she applied to have her name removed.

Prince Nayek would be competing to become his father's official heir. He was well-positioned and had a huge harem. Did he have a rival who was related to her?

She was the oldest child of General Pakori, but because she was a girl, that didn't lend her any status. As far as she knew, Prince Nayek and the General got on well. The General was not in line to the throne, so not a rival. She didn't understand. Why her?

"Are you all right?" asked Jadan, her workshop manager. She came into the office, shut the door and sat on the little bench next to Zaina's desk where customers would sometimes wait for small repairs to their engines. It was quite dark in here with the door shut and the only light coming in through the little window in the door. It lit Jadan's boyish face side-on, showing the planes and angles that Zaina had heard women could acquire through eating the male parts of Legless Lions. Jadan was thin, all arms and legs. When she took her shirt off and walked around the workshop in a singlet, you could see the lines of her muscles under the skin of her upper arms.

"Yeah, I'm all right," Zaina said, without looking up from the ordering book.

"What happened to your face?"

"I had a bit of a disagreement with someone in the bar last night."

"Anyone dangerous? I heard that the Knights have been through the district trying to get all foreigners to register and some weren't happy about that."

"Something to do with that, yeah."

"But you know we are all locals and don't need to register so you shouldn't either."

"Some people think that I should."

"We'll testify that you have no foreign workers and that you can register as an individual."

"Just leave it."

Zaina didn't want to register at all, not as a business, not as an individual.

"Did someone seriously hurt you for that?"

"There are some twisted people in the world. Just take the folder with the repairs jobs for the morning. I'm going to do admin for a bit. I'm . . . fine."

"All right." Jadan unwound her long legs and picked up the workshop schedule book with a hand that would not look out of place on an adolescent boy. "Let me know if I can do anything else."

She left the office and shut the door again.

A moment later, the sound of her voice drifted through the door.

Zaina leant her head in her hands—ouch. Jadan was a good kid. An honest hard worker, if a bit naive about the world and how it would view her as woman who dressed and acted a like a man.

In a way, Zaina was jealous. She was cursed with broad, soft hips, big, heavy boobs and full, feminine lips. Maybe that was it. Maybe Prince Nayek needed to be in town for some other thing, and he thought he'd screw around a bit to add some more children to his name, and maybe he'd heard that men found her attractive.

Maybe Zaina should just . . . leave for a bit until Nayek had left town, and forgotten about her. No, he never forgot. But maybe she could give him some small bits of information that would keep him happy.

How could she even give him what he wanted without compromising her business relationships?

Was there anything she could give him on rich families who were her customers that was going to satisfy him for a bit while she worked out how to get herself to safety?

She rose and went through her customer files. She had a customer who was quite high up in the Eagle Knights. He lived in the eyrie and, like most Knights, did not have a family. He had a lot of money and spent it on the latest fashionable things of quality, including trucks. Zaina liked the man. He was hard-working, honest and she loved talking engines with him. She didn't think this customer had any information that Nayek was happy with.

She had another big customer who ran a stone-masonry business.

He used engines to saw and grind his stone. He had several engines in his workshop, where it was hot, noisy and dusty.

The man himself was neither terribly rich nor influential, but he knew a lot of people. Mostly locals, though, and mostly merchants, not old nobles. She didn't think Nayek would be interested in local gossip.

The trouble was, the old noble families mostly stayed in their old houses in the city centre, where they engaged in discussions about music and art. She had no idea how they survived, but they seemed to do so without working or, heaven forbid, without doing anything that could be interpreted as commerce.

There was one business on her books that she thought was owned by a rich noble family. They had warehouses and shops and owned a couple of ship engines. It was one of the contacts she had inherited when she bought the workshop from its inadequate Chevakian owner, and figured that this particular business would have had a big hand in the workshop's atrocious results. They never paid on time, if they paid at all. She guessed those were the type of people Nayek wanted to know about—they did trade with Arania a lot—but she wasn't going anywhere near those cheats ever again.

And it would just look suspicious if she contacted them after having had a massive argument over delayed payment.

Anyone else?

Most of the sporadic traffic between the City of Glass and Arania went over the sea these days.

She had serviced ship engines and probably did so once a month, but most ships still had sails. They were easier and a lot cheaper. The men who ran and owned both the sailing and steamboats were not nobles, but nobles sometimes invested in ships. Would there be something about ships that she could tell Nayek to keep him happy?

Zaina needed to go out to pick up some engine parts and other supplies she had ordered from Chevakia. The courier's office was close to the harbour and on the way back, she walked along the quay, looking at the ships moored there and the men loading and unloading them. The mist had mostly cleared, and a number of ships were headed out of the bay, cream-coloured sails flapping. All the ships looked unfamiliar to her, but were they local, Chevakian or

Aranian? She knew nothing about ships, and how did one tell an Aranian ship anyway?

If she went around and started asking, people would get suspicious. Heck, any Aranians would even get suspicious if she walked around and didn't ask questions. Aranians were always suspicious.

She was about to leave, when she saw a familiar group of men coming out of the door of one of the dockside meltery: the three men with the Knight Council arm bands. The Aranian was carrying a thick folder with papers, probably filled-out forms. They went along the street into the next building, which was a storage warehouse. Making sure all businesses registered. Damn it.

Right now, she was glad that she had not been able to get business premises in the most popular strip of shops in the district, but it was inevitable that they would come to her warehouse.

Zaina continued along the quay and passed the warehouse where the three men had gone inside. The front-loading door was open and the party stood a few paces inside the door, talking to a man who had to be the warehouse's owner or manager.

As Zaina passed, the Aranian looked at her again, meeting her eyes with an intense look. He knew. He was probably in contact with Nayek.

"Prince Nayek?" Marek said, his voice low.

Zaina was sitting with him at a table in the corner of the meltery room of the *Silver Gull*. The room was busy, with people talking and shouting. A waiter had just brought two glasses of cold cider with drops of sweating condensation on the outside.

Zaina nodded. She had her back to the room, not wanting to draw the attention of anyone else.

Marek's gaze went over her face, resting on her black eye. "Oh, that's crap. Did he do that to you?"

"Yeah. I guess I should be happy he didn't do any worse."

He shuddered visibly. "Was this about you trying to take your name off the register?"

"That, and other things."

"Why pick on you? Why come all the way here just to get back at you?"

Zaina spread her hands. "I wish I knew."

"Oh man." Marek sighed. "What are you going to do?"

"What *can* I do? He said he's going to be staying in a room upstairs—"

"No way. He'd stay in one of the fancier places."

"He's involved with the army. I don't think he needs or likes fancy places. No, I believe him. He's staying upstairs, possibly installing his spies everywhere. He says he'll talk to that Aranian guy who works for the Knight Council about my business registration. I think that guy now knows me. Nayek wants me to spy on high-class families. I don't know any of those, at least not the type of family that he wants information on."

"Not to mention they'd get a bit snippy if they found you spying on them. I hear that some of them still use icefire as weapon. What do you know about spying anyway? Why didn't he ask a soldier?"

"He's given me an impossible task because he wants me to fail. I don't even want to spy on these families. I want to find a way to escape." And be hunted again, and cornered in a different place in the world, where she might not have as many friends to help her.

No, there was only one way she was going to get rid of Nayek: by giving him what he wanted.

"I think you should go to Chevakia," Marek said. "Why don't you go with Eshtar when he goes home?"

Zaina laughed. "And let his wife wonder who I am? I'd attract more attention there than I do here, for all sorts of reasons."

Marek nodded. "Point taken. You can hide in Tiverius."

"He will still come after me."

"I don't know. We low-class Aranians are better off in Chevakia than the high-class ones. We can hide, but they can't if they take guards and all that. They're really visible like that. Not many Chevakians have guards. There are not many Aranians in Chevakia anyway."

"He'll find me." And she didn't think Marek was *that* low-class either if he'd been allocated to the Special Patrol. "I don't want to leave, because no one in Chevakia will help me, if there is trouble. I need a safe place to hide, in the City of Glass." She wanted to turn around and look for spies amongst the patrons, but the act of searching for people would draw attention to her.

"And he won't find you here? You'd be imprisoned inside someone's house. He'd just wait until you came out. You can't stay inside forever."

"Maybe. I'll try to find something. Even Nayek has better things to do than wait for me to show myself." There was this organisation called the Brotherhood of the Light that used to hide orphans who were Imperfect, back in the days when being Imperfect—and being able to use icefire—was considered a bad thing. Maybe they could still hide her.

But what about the workshop?

She could ask Jadan to take care of it.

Marek said that he needed to get some sleep, but that he'd accompany her to her room. Zaina went with him out the door into the misty night, past the hookers, around the side of the building and up the stairs to the floor above the meltery room. The murmur of voices came up through the floor.

The upstairs hallway was empty. Zaina's door was still locked and the room was empty.

Marek looked around while Zaina lit a lamp.

"You really didn't bring anything from home did you?" he asked.

"My home is here. My mother is dead. She was the only person I cared about."

He nodded.

When Marek was gone, Zaina locked the door with the room key. She kept her clothes on when she got into bed.

She was restless and worried. Each time someone came up the stairs, she held her breath, waiting for the doorknob to turn and then for someone to kick in the door.

Then a couple of men had a disagreement with one of the hookers outside, underneath her window. They were quite explicit about their wishes. They wanted her to—what? Bah, men were disgusting.

She must have fallen asleep because all of a sudden, wan grey light filtered into the room.

Zaina jumped out of bed.

Mist cloaked the city, limiting her view to a couple of buildings down the street on each side. It was already quite busy. Damn, she had slept in.

She quickly washed herself. Her face was even more colourful today, with yellow patches added to the colour palette under her eye. Awesome.

There was no one in the corridor except the old Chevakian fellow who had lived in the room at the top of the stairs for years, who was just coming back from a trip to the markets, judging by the shopping bag.

The hookers downstairs were gone. A bread vendor wheeled a cart through the street, and the meltery's owner was cleaning the windows.

He greeted Zaina with a cheerful, "Good morning."

Zaina replied, but she didn't think it was such a good morning at all. For one, she didn't like the look of that guy who sat at the bench in front of the bakery. He pretended to read something, but looked up when Zaina stepped onto the street, and went back to reading too quickly. He was a local with dark hair, pale skin and blue eyes. He wore a brown jacket and khaki trousers in the style that many merchants in the district wore. In fact, there was nothing suspicious about his appearance, other than that merchants at this time of the day had better things to do than sit in front of the bakery and read.

Zaina set out for the workshop. It was only two blocks away, but when she had gone past a couple of buildings, she noticed from the corner of her eye that sure enough, the guy had risen from the bench and was walking behind her.

He kept walking when she entered the workshop and continued along the street until he vanished around the corner of the street—to walk around the block and come back from the other side? Did this guy work for Nayek? Why did Nayek spend so much money and effort on her?

Because she was late, the two boys had already started work. Because she had been nervous, she had forgotten to buy breakfast. The boys looked, but did not ask any questions. They were too young and inexperienced to be of any help or comfort to her in this case. Jadan's shift would not start until later.

Normally, Zaina would work on the workshop floor before Jadan came in, but she didn't want to be in view of the street, where passersby could see her working and spy on her. So she went into her office, even if she didn't normally do the office work until later in the day, and wasn't fond of it.

A letter lay on her desk. The outside of the envelope was blank, and there was no sender.

Damn it.

She put it back on the desk and went into the workshop. "Did anyone come in here?" she asked the young mechanics.

"I didn't see anyone," said Coran, one of the boys.

"Someone brought a letter for you," said Meno, straightening from the work he was doing on a broken axle.

"Who was it?"

He shrugged. "Probably a servant. He said it was payment."

"A foreigner?"

"Nope."

"Did he dress in a brown jacket and khaki pants?"

"No. He wore overalls."

Zaina breathed out. Probably just a payment, as he suggested. She was starting to see ghosts everywhere.

Back in her office, she inserted her finger under the envelope's seal and ripped it open.

Inside, she found not payment, but a folded-up note with Aranian text.

It said,

I am watching. Don't think I will forget our agreement. I will expect the first instalment of information tonight.

Shit.

Zaina folded the paper back up, her heart thudding. What was she going to give him that would keep him happy? She had already scoured her customers' files and found nothing that would be of interest to him. She didn't *know* any of the rich people that he wanted to know about. She could advertise herself to them, but that would only work if the people had engines, and most didn't. Or if they did, she would be dealing only with the servants.

What was she going to do?

Zaina worried about this all day. She did do some work in the workshop, and saw the man in the brown jacket walk past a few times. The last time, she ran after him and asked if he was looking for something.

"A job, maybe," he said.

From close up, she could see how dirty he was. He was missing some of his teeth and dirt had engrained in the skin in the palms of his hands.

"Do you have a job for me? I worked as a message boy."

"I don't send that many messages." He was too old to be a message boy. "Try the mail office, or try in the main street. The shops might need people."

"Yeah, all right." He stuck his hands in his pockets and slouched off.

Whether or not his story was true, or whether he worked for Nayek—both, she thought—he left and she didn't see him again.

But his excuse for hanging around her business gave her an idea. Under the guise of doing administration, she went into the office and wrote out several copies of the same letter: that she was a mechanic, that she knew about steam engines, that she had a workshop, and that she was looking for a caretaker job that involved the care of engines, a job that, hopefully, would include housing on the family's estate.

When that was done, she left one of the letters on her desk, and put the others in the pocket of her jacket and left, giving the boys the excuse of going to pick up a delivery.

"I can do that," Jadan said.

"No, it's all right. I need to talk to someone on the way."

Zaina didn't meet Jadan's eyes. Zaina had always been perfectly open about how she ran her business and who potential customers were and where she went.

She hated deceiving Jadan. No doubt Jadan knew she was being lied to. That was the worst of feelings. Betraying their loyalty and deceiving her friends. She hoped that when Nayek moved on to his next victim, she'd have friends left. She hoped she'd have anything left.

At this time of the year, daylight was getting scarcer and scarcer. The thick cloak of mist that rose from the harbour rendered the world in muted greys. The air was cold, and her breath left puffs of mist in the light of the lanterns.

She kept looking over her shoulder for people following her. She saw spies in every man, pursuers in every doorway, snipers on every rooftop.

Nayek's men were watching her, she was sure of that.

From the Harbour District, she walked up the hill to the main city proper. The buildings here were ancient, tall and built from glass and stone. Floor upon floor of apartments housed mostly local people. Sometimes there would be a smaller building in between, often with a little courtyard containing a display of carved rock and glass sculptures. Sometimes the front yard contained a stable where one or two white bears lounged. Sometimes the stable would even contain a sled, its runners rusted now that it would not go anywhere for most of the year.

The rich people lived in these houses with their extended families and servants.

Zaina didn't know who any of them were, and noticed the distinct lack of *trucks* in the front yards, but she went into each gate, up each doorstep, to each door. She knocked and, when some servant opened, she politely explained who she was and gave her letter for the head of the household.

Most servants were blandly polite and took her letter with an expression of disinterest. One of the servants asked if she had worked for any of her masters' competitors, and Zaina mumbled through some excuses, because she had no idea who her master was, but apparently everyone knew this.

Right.

Well, that was one place where she *wouldn't* get a job.

When she had delivered her letters to every house in this part of the main street, she had one letter left. And there was one house left that was an estate owned by a rich family: the palace. But she couldn't possibly send her letter there. Even if they would give her a job—and they would most certainly not—she respected King Isandor and his twin sister Jevaithi. She'd seen them a few times, from a distance. They were good people, right now mourning the loss of yet another unborn child.

She stood before the gate, looking into the front garden with its clipped bushes. A courtier was leading a horse across the entrance into the stable. He spoke to another man in uniform. They didn't see her, or maybe they were used to ignoring people gawking through the fence.

But she still had the one letter.

Well . . . that was a bummer.

Maybe she'd missed some side streets? But she knew she hadn't. She knew where the mansions were and she had visited them all.

She guessed that rich families were a lot scarcer than she had estimated.

That was because they'd all gone to Arania, a little voice inside her said. Which was why Nayek wanted to know about them. Because no one wanted to repeat the horrors of the last war. Zaina had not been born then, but she had been told by people who were there that the Chevakians ruthlessly slaughtered Aranians, soldiers and civilians alike. So yes, she understood that. Peria was becoming a powerful force in the world. Keeping an eye on these people was not really bad, was it?

But she knew it was bad, simply because Nayek was involved, and he would leave the nice and gentle King Isandor for dead if it came to a fight. But what could she do? Nayek would see her tonight and she needed to give him something. And failing that—and she was failing so hard—she would need to show him that she was doing something.

She walked through the gate up to the guard post. She gave one of the men her letter. He nodded politely at her explanation

And later that night, she met Nayek in the bar, and she told him about the letters. He seemed to be amused that she'd been bold enough to do this, although the quiet threat remained with every word he said. With every move he made, she was afraid that he'd grab her under the table and drag her upstairs, and when their meeting was over, she walked out as fast as she dared, went to her room and bolted the door from the inside.

She had not told him that the palace was one of the places where she had delivered the letters.

CHAPTER 8

ORGANISING A MEETING with Tamerane turned out to be a lot more difficult than Isandor had envisaged. Her family was one of the very old established noble families, as he could have guessed by her name. Those women usually didn't need to be breeders, unless they felt compelled to do so out of duty for their country.

But historically, the royal family had always been more involved with the Knights than with the nobility, and Isandor's youth spent in the Outer City did not help at all. He knew these nobles only as haughty, arrogant and self-absorbed. They considered themselves immune from the decisions made by the Knight Council, they disliked the massive law reform process that they were going through, they didn't sit on the council because they thought themselves too good for that, and of course they didn't think he should be in the palace.

His letter was aimed to please the family, full of empty statements of wanting to bridge the gap between tradition and the forward-looking aspects of the new Knight Council while trying to appeal to matters that nobles liked.

They thought it was crass to talk about money, but a traditional application to a breeder involved mentioning money. He mentioned it, but was sure that they'd hate it.

He grew so doubtful of his plea that he asked Carro how he had heard that this noble daughter, who didn't need to suffer inconvenience and pain through pregnancy and childbirth by renting out her body, was willing to do so.

"I heard it from the librarian," Carro said. He would have gone to the library to check the Thilleian clan's family trees. He might have asked the librarian for advice. Like Isandor, Carro loved books.

Carro continued, "I heard that the girl's father had mentioned it a few times."

Isandor didn't know what to think about it, but he sent his letter, and the next day received a reply from Tamerane's father, that yes, his daughter was available and he would be delighted to negotiate.

It was a bit odd, Isandor thought, because he remembered that the other breeder he had used briefly had answered her own correspondence and that his foster mother used to do the same. Tamerane was twenty-nine, and needed no approval from her parents. And he *had* addressed the letter to her, hadn't he?

Tamerane's father wrote in a very formal tone as if discussing a deal to buy a business or property. It sounded a little condescending, both to his daughter and to Isandor; and, yes, Isandor knew that there were sections in the old nobility who thought that he should leave the palace and let Jevaithi rule alone.

And, yes, there was no law that dealt specifically with the status of the Queen's brother, and the law still said that non-Knights could only sit on the council as observers, a legacy everyone had ignored, but that could be invoked whenever a noble family saw fit. And he had the feeling that Tamerane's father was one of these people who would, unlike other people, not be swayed by the sense that Isandor deserved a spot on the council because he had worked hard to rebuild the country.

Isandor had second thoughts about getting involved with this family, also remembering Carro's warning, but he felt even less like inviting the other two women, and didn't like to make Carro go back to this trivial activity of looking for breeders while he needed to look after the patrols and whatever information they could find on the source of icefire.

The agreement only covered a child. There was no obligation for further involvement with the woman, and he shouldn't try to dig in places where potential problems were nicely tucked away underground. Once the child went to the intended family, breeders never kept in contact.

Normally, the man would invite prospective breeders to his house to discuss business and make agreements, but over the next few days, whenever he tried to broach the subject with Jevaithi, she said or did something that made him hesitate. She would cry about being a failure, or would be studying books and tables of the heritage of eligible men. Or she would talk about making appointments with the midwife.

When Isandor suggested it was too early after the last failed pregnancy, she snapped at him that "I'm not getting any younger." And when he suggested that it might affect her health, she flew up and accused him of writing her off. "I'm not old!" she yelled while getting up from the dinner table, leaving the room and slamming the door behind her.

Isandor met a servant's eyes. The old man had been at the palace since it had been rebuilt. He shook his head. "Women. I feel for you, Your Majesty."

Isandor decided to skirt the entire issue by letting Tamerane come to one of the small meeting rooms at the Eagle Knight's eyrie next door to the palace. The thought of meeting her made him nervous, and not just because Jevaithi didn't approve.

He waited upstairs by pretending to inspect the eagles. Most of them were asleep with their heads tucked under their wings, giant bundles of feathers on yellow feet. It was quiet in the eyrie, with not even a stable boy in sight. A cold and humid wind blew in through the open side of the stable. It didn't bother the birds, but Isandor pulled his cloak closer around him.

Then Rider Carro came to tell him that Tamerane was waiting for him.

Isandor went down to the administrative part of the building, where it was much warmer.

He entered the meeting room and—

Wait, why were there so many people here? He'd expected only one. Instead three people sat on the couches: an older couple and a younger woman.

The other two people on the couches were *her parents*, Ledor and his wife of House Mara. They both nodded to him, but for now, Isandor focused his attention on their daughter.

Carro had been right: Tamerane was an ordinary-looking woman. Very ordinary. She was of stocky build, and carried her weight in all the wrong places. Her breasts were small, her hips flat, but her arms dimply and fleshy and he if hadn't known any better, he might have judged her pregnant already, but that was probably belly fat.

Her face was pale, her nose a bit bigger than was pretty and her brow was heavy. The best part of her was her full head of curly black hair that reminded him of his foster mother and her clear eyes, dark blue, a mark of Thilleian blood.

She rose and dropped into a curtsy, very awkwardly. The expression on her face was, quite frankly, terrified.

Isandor sat down. He accepted a cup of tea from a maid, but couldn't have felt less like drinking it.

An awkward silence passed.

"Thank you for coming," he said.

"No trouble at all, Your Majesty," Tamerane's mother said. She must have been the source of her daughter's dumpy looks. She was round-faced, and red-cheeked like a butcher's wife, but she wore a dress of rich brocade and her hands were cultured, with polished nails and rings. She was of House Roban, another influential noble family, which went to show that money and beauty didn't necessarily go together.

Tamerane's father gave a formal nod. He had a hawk-like face with the big nose and high forehead of the aristocracy, and must be one of the last noble sons to have received the golden tattoos on his cheeks. He wore so many rings on his hands that it was a wonder his fingers didn't fall off. The blue velvet cloak, the colour of House Mara, hung over his shoulders, fastened with a golden clasp emblazoned with the house crest, a seagull.

Isandor had prepared formal questions. They were mostly about the family history. Things that men wanted to know about their breeders usually included any illnesses and criminals in the family. The answers were routinely cross-checked with available resources to determine the family's honesty.

There was nothing in the replies—given by Tamerane's father in a formal tone—that gave cause for worry or suspicion. House Mara owned business concerns. Ledor managed a decent empire of shops and warehouses. Isandor knew a lot of them. They were prestigious businesses and he was proud of them, even if he didn't physically work in any of them.

Tamerane was their true daughter, which was quite rare.

Through all of this, Tamerane herself sat demurely on the couch, looking down with her hands jammed between her knees. She had yet to speak.

Isandor addressed her. "Tamerane, what was the reason that you decided not to officially advertise yourself as a breeder, and that you decided to come here anyway?"

Her father straightened his back. "My daughter thinks there is great honour in being a breeder and serving her country and the distinguished families in this city. We are most honoured by your request."

His wife gave him a sharp glance that Isandor didn't think he was supposed to see. She said in a soft voice, "My daughter told us that she wanted to go abroad for study. We told her that she needed to have her own income or savings to sustain her while she was there."

Isandor understood. "Yes, Chevakia is not a cheap place." He also thought that the family was rich enough to support her, but it could be a matter of principle or teaching her to be independent.

Tamerane let her shoulders sink, as if she didn't want to be here.

"What about you, Tamerane?" Isandor asked. "What is your reason?"

Tamerane looked up, her cheeks red. "I would be most pleased if you would like to hire me."

That was not really an answer.

"You want to go to Chevakia?"

"It would be nice." She flitted a quick glance at her mother. Her cheeks went red.

"What would you study?"

"She would be a healer," her father said. He sounded a bit peevish.

Her mother said, "She studies the stars and makes notes of her observations."

Her father countered, "She would study diseases like the wasting sickness to stop them."

By the skylights, what was going on here? Isandor held up his hand, silencing them. "Tamerane, do you like animals?"

Her eyes met his, wide, petrified. "Yes . . . I think so."

"Then let us go upstairs and let me show you the eagles." He rose.

"Er . . ." Tamerane looked at her parents. Her mother had already donned her shawl.

"Just you." Isandor turned to her father. "I would really like to speak to your daughter alone."

Her mother nodded.

Her father nodded, too, and shifted back in his seat, his face prim. He clearly didn't like it but, well, that was the advantage of being the king.

Isandor shepherded Tamerane to the door in the meeting room and out into the corridor. Tamerane followed quietly. They went up the stairs without speaking a word. Isandor listened to her soft footsteps behind him, not sure what to say. From the exchange downstairs, he figured she didn't want to do this at all, and if that was so, he would not go through with it.

They entered the stables, where the birds were still asleep. One raised its head and glared at Isandor with an orange eye. He led Tamerane to the open mouth of the stable from where you could look out over the lower part of the city and the bay. He took a deep breath of fresh air.

Tamerane had come to stand next to him, looking very prim.

Isandor turned sideways so that he could see her face. "Please, be honest with me if you don't want to do it."

"Do I have a choice?"

"Yes."

"No." Her eyes burned with anger.

"I say you have a choice."

"But my father doesn't. He is all about duty to your country. He says—" She froze, her cheeks red. "I'm sorry. It's not appropriate to say this."

"But it is."

"You're not going to want to want to hire me now."

"I'll hire you if *you* want it. Not your parents."

She stared over the city and the bay. Her mouth worked. She seemed to make an effort not to meet his eyes. Her nose was big, that was true, but her mouth was nice, and her hair was thick and full and curly. She raked a strand out of her face. Her chest heaved with deep and nervous breaths.

"Hey, I'm not evil. I won't push you to do something you don't want, and I'm clear that you don't. We'll go downstairs and—" He reached out to touch her shoulder.

She whirled around. "I have no choice!" Her eyes glittered.

Whoa. Isandor withdrew his hand.

"You don't understand. My father, he controls everything. He heard a rumour that you were looking, and he's been *waiting* for this, keeping me to be sold off—"

"I'm not buying anyone, and I would pay the money to you."

"He has access to all my accounts. He would give me some money, but he would keep most of it."

Isandor stared at her, dumbstruck. "You're twenty-nine."

She nodded. Tears welled in her eyes.

Even when he was much younger, and worked as butcher's assistant in his uncle's shop, he had enjoyed quite a lot of freedom. His friend Carro had less freedom, because his family felt they needed to keep up certain appearances, but even he had the freedom to choose what he wanted to do with his life. Neither Isandor's mother nor Carro's family had been too happy when they joined the Eagle Knights, but they never tried to stop them either.

"So, if you had the freedom, what would you really want?"

She took a shuddering breath, wiping her eyes with the back of her hand. "It's not appropriate for me to have this discussion. I'm sorry."

"But it is, because I'm not in the business of forcing you to do this. We abolished all that when we rebuilt the city."

"Then you have not grown up in my family."

No, of course he hadn't. He'd grown up in the Outer City, looking at the rich nobles with a feeling of envy, because he had no money and they had more than they knew what to do with.

"Tell me what *you* would want."

"I would study the stars and the sky."

"Not be a healer?"

She snorted. "No. He just says that because it's the only kind of study he finds acceptable. He actually means *nurse*, not healer. That's what he usually says when it comes up at dinner. Because being a nurse is a respectable thing to do for a woman of noble birth."

"Studying the skies is not?"

"No, because it's a *men*'s occupation, and a frivolous one at that, because it makes no money and has no importance."

"Well, I don't agree with that at all. It has importance."

"None that he can eat or sell."

True. But he thought nobles didn't care so much about things they could eat or sell. Some obviously did, and maybe those nobles were most successful in building up business empires, as her father had obviously done.

The picture she painted of her father was of a hard-nosed businessman, who cared nothing about the typical noble pursuits like the arts, theatre or music. As such, he valued financial independence and probably taught his daughter that "life is not free." No doubt he was tight-fisted, and he might even want to manage his daughter's money, because he thought she was frivolous with money. Maybe because she wanted to study.

"All right. So what about this: if you would help me and give us an heir to the throne, my payment will be that I will buy you a small but nice apartment that I will put in your name."

She stared at him. Her mouth fell open. "Would you do that for me?" Her voice was no more than a whisper.

"Of course I would. I believe in study, and we may need your study soon enough."

"Really?"

"Yes, really."

Her face split into the most beautiful smile he had ever seen. It caught him completely by surprise and he could not help but smile in return. Jevaithi did not yet know about Tamerane, but surely, after hearing this story, she would agree to this arrangement.

"So I gather you're happy with my proposal?"

"Very happy." She hesitated. "But my father might not agree to it. He'll be furious."

"Hey." He reached out and stroked her cheek. "It's not his decision to make. I will write up the document, and you can sign it. It's not his life."

They went back downstairs, where Isandor announced that they had reached an agreement. Ledor smiled. His wife raised her eyebrows at Tamerane, who kept her expression blank.

Isandor wrote out a statement that Tamerane would receive "benefits to the value of five thousand gold eagles". Her father said that it wasn't enough, so Isandor allowed himself to be talked up to five and a half thousand. He'd expected this.

Tamerane's father was happy with this, but that happiness would only last for as long as he didn't realise that he was not to be paid in coins, by which time it would be too late for him to renege on the agreement.

CHAPTER 9

"YOU SAW a windwalker?" Arukat said, his eyes wide.

Javes had made it back into town, dropped off the broken cart, the salvaged equipment and Pashtan's donkey in the back yard, and returned to Arukat's house with the borrowed cart and Arukat's donkey. The man seemed mildly amused that he'd been able to do all this on his own.

"I don't know what it was called, but it was creepy," Javes said. He inserted his hand in his pocket and took out the metal globe. "He gave me this. It seemed some sort of exchange for taking the money and jewellery off the body."

Arukat nodded. "The windwalkers exchange objects. They rob the dead, but they always leave something that they think might be of value to us."

"Is it?" Javes held up the globe. "What is this thing?"

"I don't know, but the metal could be worth something." He had that glint in his eye that told Javes not to give up his prize too easily.

"By rights, this thing now belongs to Pashtan's family. I need to contact them about what happened. Do you know where I could find them?"

Arukat spread his hands. "Pashtan never mentioned his family. To me, that says that he walked out on a wife and children somewhere and was afraid that his wife's brother would come and beat him up for leaving his sister without income."

Javes shrugged. He didn't *think* Pashtan would do anything of the sort, but then again, what did he know?

"How much do you think you could get for this thing?"

There was the glint in Arukat's eyes again. They were standing in the metal yard by the dying daylight. "One, maybe two hundred foxes?"

"That's not very much."

"For you in the city, it isn't, but for around here, it is. There are entire villages that live from this metal trade. They go into the desert, trade with windwalkers or find their own, come back, sell their stuff and live well."

"Wait—they *find* these things?"

"Yeah, but the best places are secret, and they're in windwalker territory, and they will kill you if they find you there. Really, it's a good thing to be given something by a windwalker. It means that you don't have to risk your own life to go and get it."

Javes *had* wondered why Arukat had a sand cart. He thought he'd found the reason.

"But I can sell it for you, seeing as I'm in the business. I can help you out."

Javes almost gave him the metal globe. The thought of having money was very attractive, even if it was such a piddly amount for what was clearly considered to be a fairly valuable object, if a mysterious one. Also, Arukat had done him a favour by lending him the cart and donkey. It made sense to repay the favour by letting him sell the thing.

But . . . he glanced at the scrap metal pieces around the yard. "Do you have a lot of other pieces like this?"

"Have? No. I don't keep that type of stock. I sell any that I get."

"Who buys it?"

What was up with that a shifty look? Was he afraid to divulge his customers in fear that Javes might steal them from him and go direct to these people?

"There's a man who comes into town. He doesn't make any noise about buying these things. The only people who get to see him are his trusted suppliers."

"Where is he from? Where does he take the material to sell? What do those people do with it?"

"That's entirely too many questions for a young grasshopper like you."

"What does that mean? You don't want to tell me or you don't know either?"

He laughed. "Bit of both, bit of both. The things I know you're better off not knowing, and the things I don't know . . . well, who really cares why people in some other place want this stuff and who they are?"

Javes cared, but maybe his caring was a product of living in luxury in Tiverius. If he got stuck here for long enough, he'd ask no questions either, and he'd be glad if someone offered him money for something that was of no use to him anyway.

He slid the globe back in his pocked, having decided to hang on to it for a while. He could keep it for when things got really desperate. He thought Arukat was disappointed with that decision.

Javes went inside Pashtan's house and lit the lamp. By its feeble light, he took off his disgusting clothes and hung them over the back of the chair.

The warm evening air stroked his naked skin. He poured some water in the washing bowl, just enough to wet the washer, and wiped himself clean. The cloth came away orange with dust, even after several wipes. He should also do something about his dirty clothes.

Pashtan had a young man who came in to do his cleaning, but Javes had no idea who this was or how to contact him, and that thought made him feel miserable.

At home, he would soak in the bath, but here, water allocation was barely enough for cooking.

Javes took the bread and jam out of the cooler box. He poured a glass of goat's milk, drank it, and then poured another. He was exhausted, filthy, smelly, sweaty and utterly alone in his misery.

Another thing he should do: write to his family and his tutor. Maybe they could do something.

Then he remembered the measurements he had taken. He should file a report with the meteorological office tomorrow morning, but in order to do that, he had to compile the data.

He collected the box with his equipment, which still stood in the back yard. The folder with all the readouts sat tucked along the side.

He opened it and laid out all the barygraph papers underneath each other.

The first one had a strong spike two days before the end of the roll. So did the second one, and the third one. In fact, all of the measurements showed a distinct spike in sonorics at the same time. That's when the dust devil had struck. Pashtan had known about it.

He remembered the mud monster he had seen in the dust. He'd written the sight off as hallucination, but maybe . . . The sonorics level had, very briefly, risen to thirty motes per cube, a mildly dangerous level. From memory, sonorics could mess with people's minds as well as killing them.

He went to Pashtan's bookshelf that hung above the bed. This contained the usual meteorological texts, basic books that Javes also had at home. There were also some strange storybooks and one book with—good heavens did men and women do those things? His ears burned.

He found nothing about dust devils.

When he was in Tiverius and he didn't know something, he would go to the Scriptorium's library, but as far as he knew, there was no library here. Maybe he should ask someone at home to go to the library on his behalf.

Pashtan's desk contained one drawer with various pens and a small stack of paper. He took out a sheet, a pen and sat at the desk. Who was he going to write?

His parents didn't have the knowledge to answer a meteorological question, and his father would only scoff at his suggestion to go to the Scriptorium to ask. His father didn't think he should have started his studies at all. He said Javes would have been much better off becoming a merchant like him.

His tutor Viki was much too busy with important things to be bothered with trivial things such as a visit to his parents to tell them their son was fine, if for now stuck in the hellhole.

The fellow students . . . would only laugh, because that's what they always did where he was concerned. They thought he was stupid. They thought he didn't belong there.

No, he was not from one of the major families, but did that mean he couldn't study?

Lana han Chevonian.

That was who he should write. She was the proctor's daughter, but the proctor had been a meteorologist, and she was in his class.

She never laughed at him. She was quiet and studious. She talked more often to other students than he did, but she never took part in their games.

Javes went to mail his letter the next morning. The clerk at the telegraph office insisted on payment, even if Javes said that he worked for the doga and therefore should get the service for free. He began to see why so little news came from this region. There was no way of notifying people unless you had money, and many locals did not. Not only that, but they didn't care about Tiverius and Tiverius had not shown them why they should report any trouble to the capital.

After the telegraph office, he went to the bathhouse.

It was a simple affair, nothing like the luxurious establishments in Tiverius, and unlike in Tiverius, there wasn't actually a lot of water inside the bathhouse.

The main feature of the establishment was a dark, dungeon-like room with change rooms feeding into it, but with no openings to the outside.

One got undressed in the change rooms and then entered this room, where you sat on hard benches while the attendants poured water over a bed of glowing coals. Clouds of steam billowed into the room. The air was searing hot and burned the inside of his nostrils.

Most of the bath patrons were old men, and most of them were much cleaner than Javes was. They watched him with curious glances until he wondered if it had been appropriate for him to come here.

A woman in a long white robe offered to wash him. He lay face down on a table while she rubbed his back, and then he had to turn over, which made him very self-conscious.

A couple of old men in the room were talking. They sounded like they were village elders. They mentioned that dust devils had twice closed the road to the next town.

"Excuse me," Javes said.

The two men looked at him.

"I'm sorry, but can you tell me what you think dust devils are?"

"I would have thought you knew all about it, having gotten close to one yourself."

"Well, yes, but I always thought they were vicious whirlwinds."

"That's what they are."

"I think they're more than that."

The men gave him strange looks.

"Has no one ever spoken of seeing things in dust devils?"

"What sort of things?"

"Faces. Eyes. Other hallucinations?"

They frowned at him.

"I saw those things."

"You must have been dreaming."

"I thought so, too, but the devil coincided with a spike in sonorics."

This was met with blank looks. They didn't even know what sonorics was, Javes realised. And why should they, living so far from the southern border, where sonorics used to be a problem years ago?

IN THE NEXT FEW DAYS, Javes traded milk for a chicken. The chicken laid eggs, and he traded eggs for another chicken. Then he told Arukat's daughter next-door that she could sell the eggs as long as she came in to milk the goats. That was one problem solved.

He fixed the cart. The local carpenter did a so-so job on the wheel, and Javes cobbled the tray and the two halves of the axle back together, but every time he went out, his hatred for the cumbersome cart increased. He'd seen people travel with camels. They walked faster than donkeys and carried more than he'd ever needed to bring.

But camels were expensive. He'd stood watching the animal pens, where there were usually one or two of the beasts for sale. Few people in town owned a camel, but all the travellers between towns did. That was enough of a sign for him that he wanted one. If worse came to worst, he could get on the camel's back and ride all the way to Tiverius, because Pashtan's broken and fixed up cart would never make it that far.

Yes, that was a comforting thought.

At night, he studied Pashtan's maps. Surely, during his field trips to take measurements, he would have come across windwalkers or the places where they might find their treasures.

If he could find enough of those strange objects, he could afford to pay for someone to collect the field data, and he could get out of here.

Every day, he went to the telegraph office to check for a reply from Lana, and every day that the reply didn't come he felt more certain that everyone in Tiverius hated him.

He adjusted his plans. He needed money most of all. It meant finding windwalker treasures and selling them for a decent price, not to Arukat, but to the buyers direct. It meant he had to find the treasures first, or meet windwalkers in their settlements to trade with them. They wanted jewellery or coins, so he collected all of those that he could find in the house. There were some strange coins amongst them, tiny gold coins the size of a shirt button with glyphs that he couldn't read stamped on them. There was even a headdress made out of them, a metal chain with strings of coins hanging off it. The assembly fitted neatly over his head, but, looking in the reflection of Pashtan's cracked mirror, he guessed that it should be worn by a girl.

He put all those treasures, including the metal windwalker globe, in a leather bag that he wore underneath the *temuz* that he had borrowed from Pashtan's wardrobe.

On Pashtan's map, he'd found an area marked *DO NOT GO HERE*, which was one of the northernmost points marked on the map. That seemed the most likely area for encounters with windwalkers.

He was still thinking and planning when one day, in town, on his way to the telegraph office, he ran into a commotion in the marketplace. A large camel had broken out of the animal pens and was running around the markets, insofar as camels can run. The ropes that trailed off the saddle and headgear became tangled around the legs of tables, and the beast pulled the stands clean over. It kept going, even when the stall owner seized one of the ropes.

Wow, that was a strong animal. A bull, visibly excited by the prospect of—ah yes, there were two female camels in another pen.

The man in a dark *temuz* running after the animal was a merchant Javes had seen in town before. He yelled, "Stop, stop, you stubborn piece of meat!"

And the camel, clearly, had no intention of doing so. It was almost comical to watch.

Eventually, the beast found a stall which sold incense sticks and proceeded to eat those. And when it stopped running, several men closed in and grabbed the ropes.

The camel grumbled and bellowed when being dragged back to the sales pen.

Javes went to have a look.

A couple of men stood to the side of the pen in agitated discussion, waving hands and calling out swear words, probably discussing damage done to stock for sale and compensation to be paid. The incense seller was one of the men.

Javes stuck his hand into the pen. "Come here, boy."

The camel gave him the side-eye, but took a step towards him, and then another step. Javes had been on his field station round already, and his arm was sweaty. The camel nosed his sleeve with its flubbery lips and then licked salt off his skin with a wet, slimy tongue. Javes rubbed the animal's neck. The fur crawled with fleas. Well, that was one way to irritate an animal. That someone had neglected to castrate him was probably another. On the shelf in Pashtan's shed was a bottle with anti-flea oil. Castration . . . well there was sure to be someone in town who knew how to do that.

The merchant had noticed Javes' attention to the animal. "What is it, city boy? Want to buy a camel for eating?"

"How much?"

"You're kidding, right?"

"I might be, but for now, I'm asking, so you can either answer me, or I'll walk away for certain. I notice that you and this beast don't get along very well."

The merchant's mouth worked. He eyed the camel. Maybe he'd hoped to sell the beast quickly for a good price as a breeding bull. Maybe he didn't have the time to put into looking after it.

"He's an amazing animal," the merchant said. "Look at those strong legs. Have you ever seen a camel taller than this one?"

"He's flea-ridden, cranky and should have been castrated," Javes said. "So any price needs to come less the cost of castrating an adult animal. Besides, this is probably not the first time that he's played up. Camels are smart. They hate certain people."

The merchant's mouth worked again. He sighed. "A hundred

foxes. But only as a special price, and don't tell anyone I've offered you that."

"That's still too much for an animal I'm going to have to pay to be castrated."

In the end, the merchant settled for seventy-five. Javes dug up the last of his money and walked his purchase home, watched by many curious villagers.

In the back yard, he gave the camel hay while he rubbed the fragrant oil into the fur. Big chunks of wool came loose, and the animal leaned into him while he rubbed its back and sides, pulling loose big wads of hair.

Wool. Another thing he could trade.

His plan was progressing well.

A week later, at his round of the weather stations, he replaced the paper in all of them, so he would not *need* to come back for another two weeks. Tiverius appeared to care little about the data he sent anyway. The figures disappeared into the telegraph line and he never received as much as an acknowledgement that they had been received.

Maybe the link to Tiverius didn't even work, or else Lana hated him so much that she didn't even want to write him the shortest of replies.

His parents had evidently forgotten about him, too. They were probably too busy admiring his brothers' successes.

In short: he was on his own, and he was not going to sit here for the rest of his life.

When he came back from his round, he traded the irritating, badly repaired cart for a camel saddle, a couple of shirts and a length of linen. He put the saddle and headgear on the camel. It seemed a little irritated by the thing on its back and head, but Javes judged that it had worn a saddle or pack before, and he gave it some carrots to sweeten its temper. Clean, and without fleas or its male tackle, the camel was easily bribed.

For the next few days, he put the saddle on during the day and took it off at night. Three days later, he climbed on the camel's back and when he pulled the reins, it rose, first on its hind legs and then the front. Oh, wow, it was really tall. He slowly walked the beast around the yard. The goats bounded out of the way, bleating their protest.

He leaned down to pull the gate open, and walked the camel through the streets of the town. People watched him from the roadsides, from their yards and doorways. Children ran after him.

Javes felt like he was on top of the world. Yes, he would get out of here.

When he came back, he went to Arukat's house.

"I'll be away for a bit," he said. "You can use the donkey, your daughter can milk the goats and sell the milk. Keep an eye on the house."

Arukat frowned at him. "You *will* be back, right?"

"Yes."

"Where are you going?"

"Checking something out."

Arukat looked suspicious, but said nothing. If Javes had to make a guess about his thoughts, he might have guessed that Arukat hoped that Javes would find a source of metal artefacts to sell that didn't require going through windwalkers, and without running any of the risks himself.

Which was probably close enough to the truth.

CHAPTER 10

ISANDOR NEEDED to wait a few days before Tamerane was receptive to a man's seed.

During that time, he made several more attempts to speak to Jevaithi, but each time he got close to the subject of succession, she announced that she had a very good candidate picked out.

"I've been seeing a woman who is affiliated with the Brotherhood of the Light. She deals in spirit healing and she says that for a child to mature in the womb, there must be love between the parents. That's been the problem all along. I could never have *your* child because I love you but you're my brother, and all the other men we've tried I don't have any love for. Using just the seed made it even worse. A child needs to grow from an act of love."

"So who is this ideal man going to be then?" He'd never known Jevaithi to fall for any man.

Her cheeks coloured. "Someone I respect and appreciate a lot, and someone who respects me and has done so for all of my life."

"And this person is?" Isandor had a bad feeling about this. It sounded like someone from the upper command in the Knights.

"Rider Barton."

He closed his eyes and blew out a breath.

"What? Why are you pulling a face like that?"

"Does he know about this?"

"Not yet, but I'll tell him about the honour."

"Jevaithi, Rider Barton is a . . . he doesn't get excited by women."
Like many of the Knights.

"I know that. Surely he'll make an exception for me?"

"It doesn't work like that."

"It always did in the past. I'll ask him. He won't refuse."

Isandor sighed. He didn't argue because arguing was pointless
when she was in this mood, but he could just about imagine the
awkward conversation. Would Rider Barton comply? Isandor even
hated the thought of him being put under this kind of pressure. This
was the main difference between him and Jevaithi. She had grown up
in the palace and he in the Outer City, and even if much had changed,
she *still* thought that the Knights lived to attend to her every whim.

Maybe he needed to speak to Rider Barton and tell him to refuse.
He just could not bear this kind of behaviour anymore.

So when he walked out the palace entrance to the waiting coach,
he still hadn't told Jevaithi about Tamerane. It was stupid, he knew
that, but he also hoped that the conversation would be easier once a
child was on the way, and he also knew that it wouldn't be easier. She
would just be more upset with him. He got into the coach anyway.
This issue had already taken up far more of his valuable time than it
should have.

Jevaithi acted like he was married to her, and it was starting to get
on his nerves.

Tamerane lived in the old part of the city, so the ride was very
short. Her house was one of the stately mansions that had survived
the icefire explosion much better than the tall buildings on either side
of it had. The coach stopped in front of the gates, and the guard, who
had evidently been told to expect him, opened the gate for him.

Isandor pulled the hood of his cloak over his head and climbed
down the coach steps. He had chosen a plain coach with horses
instead of the royal coach with the white bears. He did not want
people to see him coming here. He wanted no talk until such time
that not talking became a worse option than talking. Hopefully that
point would be after a child had been born and people could be
happy that there was finally a princess heir.

He went up the steps to the porch. A servant of the family opened
the door for him, with a deep bow. "Your Majesty. Let me show you
to the family."

Isandor followed the man down the hallway. He wasn't sure why he needed to see the entire family, but it was probably polite to let them know that he was here.

Someone had put a lot of effort into decorating the hallway with vases of fresh flowers that must have cost a fortune. It was autumn. Where did they even get the flowers?

The servant led Isandor to the formal room, where a fire burned in the hearth and a rich selection of food stood on the table.

Both Tamerane's parents sat there, in the company of a woman Isandor didn't recognise at first, but then—by the skylights, was that really Tamerane? She wore a bright red dress with so many frills on the shoulders and the skirt that all he saw was gauze. The dress' bodice was tight, pushing her body into a shape it didn't normally have with a narrow waist and broad hips. Her breasts, too, appeared larger, pushed up.

She wore her hair piled up on top of her head, held by many pins and her cheeks and eyelids had been painted.

Isandor stared. "What . . . You look . . ." *Like a sausage.*

"Isn't she gorgeous?" Tamerane's mother said.

"Yeah," Isandor said, totally horrified.

He sat down in the chair pulled back by a servant.

She offered tea and cakes, while Tamerane's parents chatted about unimportant things like the weather and building projects in the city. Apparently also, the family had recently invested in steam ships.

Tamerane stared at the table. She ate nothing and said nothing. Isandor finished his tea and was offered more tea, and the conversation seemed to drag out, while Tamerane's father laid out all the problems he had in his business and what he thought the Council should do about it.

After the third cup of tea, Isandor had enough. "Look, I'm sorry to interrupt this gathering, but I have a lot of things to do."

"Oh yes, yes, Your Majesty. Why don't you do what you came for."

Like, make my daughter pregnant. By the skylights, this was embarrassing.

"Do show your guest upstairs, dear," Tamerane's mother said.

"Yes," Tamerane said. She rose quickly, bumping the table so that the cups danced on the saucers. She met Isandor's eyes. "Shall we?"

"Of course."

"Do make sure to use the front bedroom," her mother said.

"Yes, yes."

She led him out of the room, up the stairs. Her dress was so big that it brushed the walls on both sides of the staircase. She had to lift up the front, and still almost tripped. Isandor had to steady her so that she didn't fall. The fabric around her waist was as tight as a Knight's rolled-up sleeping bag.

She preceded him into a large bedroom that was probably not hers, judging by the large double bed that stood against the far wall. The bedspread was folded back to reveal rich satin sheets and luscious pillows. Everything with pink frills. A fire burned in the hearth.

"I'm sorry about this." She gestured at the room. "It was my mother's idea."

"This is not your room?"

"No." She shook her head. "My mother said that my own room was too embarrassing."

"Why?"

"Because it has books, and instruments and anything except frilly dresses."

"That dress looks uncomfortable."

"I'll take it off." She reached for the buttons.

"Wait." Isandor put his hand on hers.

She froze.

"Calm down. I want you to take the dress off, because you don't look comfortable in it."

"I look terrible, don't I?"

"No, the *dress* is terrible. Put on your comfortable dress and show me your room. I don't like frilly dresses. I don't like frilly cushions, and if we are going to do this, I want you to be comfortable."

She gave him an uncertain look. "Are you sure?"

"I'm interested in the things you study. I want to hear about them."

She led him to the room opposite the frilly bedroom.

This room was about the same size, but looked much smaller because the walls were hidden behind bookcases. It was also quite cold in here.

"This is my room," she said, unnecessarily and nervously.

"This looks much nicer. Put your comfortable dress on. I won't look."

She disappeared into the wardrobe.

Isandor looked around. Save for his own library, he had never seen this many books together. He read the titles. Some were books from the Thillei kings that had been forbidden until recently. Some were Chevakian, some even Aranian. There was a desk in the corner and a round table in front of the window with on it, a variety of instruments with lenses.

Isandor went to the table. "What is all this for?"

"It's a spyglass," Tamerane said, muffled inside the wardrobe.

"What do you use it to look at?"

"I watch the skies." She came out of the wardrobe wearing a sturdy and very plain brown dress.

"That looks much better." Isandor reached for one of the pins in her hair and pulled it out, and then another one. Locks of black curls tumbled over her shoulders. "Your hair is very nice. You shouldn't put it up."

"Tell my mother that."

She sat on the chair at the desk while letting him have the armchair by the dark hearth. His breath steamed with the cold in this room. "What is there in the skies to look at?"

"Sky gazing is an Aranian pastime, and while they are mostly about star signs and future-telling, there is a lot we can learn from the sky."

"What, other than that the stars revolve around us? You can't do anything with the sky."

"You can't? Then look at this." She rummaged on the desk and held up a picture with many circles.

"What is that?"

"I went out at night to the mouth of the bay, where it is dark. I put a light plate on the ground so that it would catch the light from the stars. And then, because the stars are very very weak, I left it there until early morning. Then when I processed and fixed the plate, this was what I got."

All the concentric circles made him dizzy. "Why did you do this? It shows that the stars turn around us."

"No, it doesn't."

Then she rummaged on her desk again and pulled out a sheet of paper that she unfolded. "On the same day, a friend of mine in Tiverius did the same thing. She went out of the city, she put a light plate on the ground and left it there for most of the night. This is what she got."

She held up the paper. It showed a pattern of lines that were barely curved.

Isandor frowned. He looked from one paper to the other. "Why would the stars make circles here and lines in Tiverius? Aren't they all the same stars?"

She shook her head. "I got into Aranian astrology a while ago—my father was furious when he heard how much I spent on this book—wait." She let the sheets of paper slide to the desk and turned to the bookshelf. She pulled out a heavy tome which, when she opened it, turned out to be full of curled Aranian script and hand-coloured illustrations in blue and gold paint. "These are Aranian constellations: the Duck, the Donkey and the Mother's Child. They are supposed to have special significance for luck. My friend in Chevakia can see them, but I searched the sky for days and days, and I can't. When I describe our sky to them, they are baffled. *We each see different parts of the sky.*"

"Yes, because they're in Chevakia and Arania. There are different stars above those lands."

"No, but *they* are seeing the same part of the sky, despite being far from each other."

True. Isandor stared at the page in the book, really a magnificent work. He had looked at the stars at times, and could honestly not remember if he had or hadn't seen any of the constellations. Astrology was the domain of future-tellers, and everyone knew how much their knowledge was worth.

"So, what do you think this means then?"

"Well . . ." She suddenly looked quite hesitant. She raked her hair behind her ear with her hand. She wore a ring on her pinky with the Brotherhood emblem on it. He didn't think they usually accepted women at their meetings, but this woman was . . . something different.

"I think it could be like this." She lowered her voice. "In the City of Light, we get days and nights, but sometimes we have only days and at lows we have times that the sun doesn't rise at all. That doesn't happen in Tiverius. It doesn't happen in Arania either. There is one way that we can explain it." She got up again and fished a ball from her desk. It was painted red with big white spots, the type that children used to play. She set it on the table and twirled it like a spinning top. The white spots in the middle of the ball blurred into stripes. The ones on the top of the ball blurred into circles.

Isandor stared. "How does that prove anything?"

"It doesn't, but it does make you think, right? Because if the world was a ball, and we were here . . ." She pointed to the top of the ball. "And if Tiverius was here . . ." She pointed to the middle. "Then it would make sense. And if the sun was here . . ." She held her fist an arm's length away from the ball, a little bit higher than the table. "And I think we all agree that there is only one sun, then it would explain why we are getting times that the sun doesn't set and times it doesn't rise. Because we're here." She tapped the top of the ball.

Isandor scratched his head. "Is this all your idea?"

"Not *just* mine. There are a group of people in Chevakia talking about this, but no one listens to them because there is always so much urgent stuff to be addressed."

That was the whole problem, he agreed. For the past fifty years, maybe longer, the world had floated from one disaster to the next, with big recovery efforts in between.

"But if the world were round, you would see the curve."

"And you do see it, especially when you go up high."

Did you see it? He should know as ex-Knight, but again, it wasn't something he had paid much attention to.

"The curve is not strong, but if you know it's there, you can see it. You can measure it. With this." She extracted a metal rod on a stand from the mess at her desk. "You need to go to the peninsula or anywhere you look out over the ocean and it's very obvious. Of course when you were a Knight, the ocean was misty and full of big icebergs and it would have been hard to see the horizon on most days."

He nodded. He should try this. Then he had another thought. "But then, if the world is round, you should be able to travel all around it."

"Yes."

"What's on the other side?"

"Who knows? Maybe another land that the Aranians don't want us to know about, or maybe sea. No one knows."

Well, that was . . . interesting, worthy of consideration. It was certainly not what Isandor had come here expecting to hear.

A female voice sounded in the hall downstairs.

Tamerane gave a nervous laugh. "Oh. Those are my parents. They probably wonder what we're doing."

Yes. There was a reason he had come here. That was a sobering thought.

"Maybe we should . . ." Her cheeks were red.

"I think all this stuff is interesting," Isandor said. "I would like to talk about it again."

She nodded, suddenly much more nervous. "Yes. But my parents are going to be disappointed if we don't . . ." Her hands went to the top button of her dress. She fumbled with it either because her hands trembled.

Isandor rose. "Let me do that."

He faced her and stepped inside a perfume-scented bubble that surrounded her. She was half a head shorter than he, and he looked down on the top of her head.

He slowly unbuttoned the top of her dress. It fell open in the middle and the gap showed pale skin and the hint of the mounds of her breasts. He placed both his hands on the soft skin on either side of her neck and slid his palms over her chest, pushing the dress off her shoulders.

She didn't wear any undergarments. Her skin felt cold and was dimply and pale. She broke out in goosebumps that made her nipples dark and hard. Her breasts were very small, and had started to lose the firmness of youth.

She clamped her arms around her soft stomach, looking at the floor. "I'm sorry." Her eyes glittered.

"I can go home if you'd rather—"

"No. My father would kill me."

And he would have to come back again, and the more he put this off, the harder it would become. He did want to talk to her again, but not like this. "Maybe if you come to the palace instead—"

"No. My father would still kill me. When you leave, he's sending my mother up here. She's going to check me over. She's going to sniff the bed. She's going to yell at me that I let you in this room and didn't use the other."

"You're old enough to make those decisions for yourself."

"Tell her that, because she won't listen to me."

She pushed the covers aside and sat down, pulling her legs up onto the bed. The hair between her legs was as black as the hair on her head.

"Just do it. I'm cold in this room with no clothes on."

She pulled the blanket over herself while he took off his shirt and then his trousers, and then he had to take off his wooden leg. He didn't meet her eyes, but could feel her gaze on the stump of his leg. From the moment he had first met her, she had spoken frankly to him, none of this *Your Majesty* grovelling that he so disliked.

He respected her. He even liked her courage. She did this so that she could move away from those horrible parents. He was helping her.

He hung his clothes over the back of a chair and awkwardly climbed into the bed with her. The sheets were clean held a whiff of a female smell: soap or perfume.

He'd been afraid that the cold and the awkwardness would stop him becoming aroused, but once under the warm covers, the deed came naturally. It wasn't what he'd call amazing, but it served as a painful reminder that he had not been anywhere near a woman for a long time. So it was satisfying, and it quenched a thirst that had lived inside him all that time, and he hadn't been aware that he possessed. He even lingered in her warmth for a while afterwards, and she simply held him, not saying anything, not stroking him, but not pushing him away and hurrying to wash herself and get dressed either.

She might have enjoyed it, or at least not felt terrible or hurt.

He blew out a breath. "I better go. It's getting dark."

Although at this time of the year, it hardly ever got really light. The house smelled of cooking and he should return to the palace and the disasters that would face him there.

He rolled out of bed, put his wooden leg back on and got dressed, leaving Tamerane in the bed, lying on her back on the pillow, watching him wordlessly.

He wormed his one foot and then the end of the wooden leg into his boots and looked around if he'd forgotten anything.

"Your cloak is downstairs," she said.

"I know." His gaze roamed the room and came to a rest on the desk with all its instruments. "I'd like to talk to you about the stars again, without this performance." He spread his hands.

One corner of her mouth moved up. "That would be nice."

She didn't say what would be nice, having a talk or not having to sleep with him. Both, probably. He left the room, not sure if he wanted to face the comments he would get about this.

Both of Tamerane's parents waited downstairs. Her father handed Isandor his cloak. "We'll let you know," he said.

Isandor said, "Tamerane is old enough to let me know. My contract is with her, and she knows what she needs to do."

"Sure, sure," the man said. "Just making sure, you know?"

No, Isandor didn't know, but as he left the house and walked into the misty air, he could only think that if he lived in a family like that, he would hire himself out, too, because he'd want to leave home fast.

The coach waited at the bottom of the steps. He climbed in and settled in his seat. Tamerane had come to the upstairs window. She looked at him while the coach jumped into motion, a sad face behind the glass.

By the skylights, why should the Knights laugh at the customs of the Aranian nobles while this sort of thing was going on right in their town?

While the coach rattled over the streets, Isandor leaned back on the bench. He felt good, better than he had felt in a long time. His mind was calm, and he felt ready to face any problems.

The coach turned into the palace garden and stopped in front of the entrance.

A guard came to open the coach door. Two more guards stood on either side of the palace entrance. Both bowed to their king.

"Your Majesty," one of them said. "My excuses, but you're wanted in the small audience room. The Supreme Rider is waiting for you."

Isandor's heart did a little jump. Rider Barton would never be this formal unless something important had happened. Disasters indeed.

Isandor made his way to the room in question as quickly as he could. He had recently had a newly made Chevakian wooden leg with a fake foot fitted that allowed him to walk almost like a normal person, but *running* was still out of the question.

Rider Barton and Jeito were sitting on the couch and had already been supplied with the mandatory tea and cakes. Isandor came into the room, grabbed two cakes off the plate—amazing how certain activities always made him hungry—and sat down.

"All right. I'm here. Give me the news."

Their faces were serious. Deadly serious.

Then Rider Barton said, "The patrol we sent to Arania hasn't returned."

Isandor was going to say things like *Maybe they were held up by the weather*, but it had been days. Bad weather wouldn't hold for that long. So he said, "There has been no news at all?"

Jeito shook her head. "This is one of the best patrols I have. They should have been back days ago."

"Something happened."

"Obviously."

"Maybe they found something that they wanted to investigate further."

"They would have sent a gull."

True. "So what could have happened?"

Rider Barton sighed. "There are several potential scenarios and I have to add that none of these are particularly good. Firstly, they could have run into the icefire source, which might have been a lot stronger than they anticipated. In this case, the team will probably be dead; and if they managed to send a gull, it would have been blown off course and be wandering around somewhere else in a state of daze."

Jeito said, "But if that was the case, the earlier patrol's measurements would have shown a much more concentrated and clearly defined source of icefire, something truly on par with the Heart."

Rider Barton nodded. "And we might have recovered one of the eagles at least."

Eagles did not easily become affected by icefire.

"So, the next option?"

"They, and their birds, ran into trouble with a human enemy. They were killed or captured."

"They carried an innocent message to the Aranian king, written in Aranian," Isandor said. "They would also have taken peace offerings."

"They did indeed," Jeito said. "One of the team members speaks Aranian."

"We might wonder if the king didn't like the message," Rider Barton said.

"I'm more of the opinion that they never reached Kadrish," Jeito said. "For all his other faults, King Orik is not an idiot. If he was really unimpressed with our message, then he would have sent at least one eagle back so that we were aware of that fact."

Both Isandor and Rider Barton agreed with that.

"So the most likely option is: they never reached Kadrish and got waylaid in the mountains."

Isandor thought about that for a bit. "So we're back to those mountains. But who lives there that could take out an entire Knight patrol without even a single bird able to return to us?"

"No one knows," Jeito said. "The roads used to be trade routes and there is a ghost town on this side of the foothills. The Chevakians used to come through the pass to deliver their goods there so that they didn't need to wear the suits when going as far as the City of Glass."

Rider Barton said, "I've seen that place. No one lives there. The road is still there, if terribly eroded."

Jeito pushed the tea things aside and unrolled a map onto the table. It showed the latest layout of the land, including the new farming communities and the tiny fishing harbour that had sprung up on the western coast, to the south of the Aranian mountains. If anything, this map showed how quickly the land had changed after the destruction of the Heart.

"The last we heard from the team they were here." Jeito pointed. The spot was the end of the road through the mountains, at the ghost town from where sleds with bears used to take produce into the City of Glass.

It lay at the end of Peria's first telegraph line, an ambitious project that had met with no end of trouble, because somehow the telegraph signal didn't work as well as it did in Chevakia. Some days it was great and others the machine was dangerous to use, with sparks issuing from the connectors. No one had the time or knowledge to try to understand why this happened.

"The team used the telegraph station to send their message. After that, they went into the mountains."

Isandor let his gaze roam over the area. In his mind, he saw the terrain of high peaks and deep crevasses, and the road that wound its way through them. There were no towns and no other sign of habitation.

"It would be advisable to send someone after them," Jeito said. "This is not a team likely to panic, and they're not likely to all fall in the same trap at the same time, so I can only conclude that whatever has happened was catastrophic and it would be a good idea to check it out."

Isandor nodded. He looked at Rider Barton. "Do you agree with that?"

Rider Barton nodded, slowly. "Much as I hate to commit more people to this. Maybe we're waking a problem that's going to blow up bigger than we can handle. But to attack a peaceful mission is effectively an act of war. We can't let it pass. Yet we need to be careful. It might be dangerous."

"Considering Arania considers the mountains as part of their territory," Jeito added.

No one had settled on the exact position of the border. They had just assumed that no one had much interest in the mountains, and accepted the entire region as de facto border. And with Arania having gone quiet, that could be a problem.

Isandor said, "I would like to think that we're discovering a problem before it becomes so big that we can't do anything about it."

"Fair enough," Rider Barton said.

They stared at the map on the table for a bit. Then Jeito said, "So, what and who do we send?"

"We need to send a much bigger team," Rider Barton said. "Better armed, for one."

"I'd like to send a different *sort* of team as well," Isandor said. "Sure, we can send more Knights on Eagles, but they have certain disadvantages. They can only carry light weapons, only one person to a bird, and they're highly visible. I'd like to send a ground team."

Both Knights frowned at him. Knights might ride horses in town, but this was a very new development; mostly, they rode eagles. Knights didn't *do* ground teams, but, having seen the Chevakian army in operation, Isandor could see that not having people on the ground put them at a disadvantage.

"What sort of ground team?" Jeito asked, although her tone betrayed disapproval. "How is a ground team even going to get there?"

"There is the road."

"But all the way stations are gone. And the snow is mostly gone as well."

"Wheels don't need snow."

"But the animals need feeding, and then one of the main reasons why the eagles can't investigate a lot of the mountains is that it's too high and the air is too thin. How are the animals going to cope with that?"

"We won't use animals. We'll use trucks."

That ended the discussion, and Jeito left, but Isandor held Rider Barton back. The Knight raised his eyebrows.

"Has Jevaithi spoken to you?" Isandor asked.

"About what?"

Isandor cringed. "Apparently, she has her sights set on you as the father of her next try for a child."

A brief look of horror flitted in Rider Barton's eyes. "Has she told you this?"

He nodded. "Some spirit woman has told her that a child needs to be conceived out of love."

"Well . . ." Rider Barton said. He took a deep breath and then said nothing for a while, before repeating, "Well . . . if that's what she decides, I'll do it."

"No." Isandor said. "She is destroying herself. We're up to over twenty failed attempts. She can fall pregnant, but her body doesn't hold onto the child to let it grow. She's killing herself. When she asks you, I want you to say no."

"But . . ."

But she's the queen, and what the queen says goes. Yes, Isandor knew, they had *all* grown up with that mantra, including Jevaithi. "Someone needs to stop her. I can't stop her by myself. I need help from others.

You, Carro, people dear to her. We need to stand up and tell her: enough."

"Yeah. All right." But he looked dubious. "What about an heir, though?"

"I've visited a breeder."

He flicked his eyebrows up. "Is she pregnant yet?"

"Not that I know, but I'm happy with her and I will continue to go back to her until we're successful."

"Who is it? If I may be so rude to ask."

"Tamerane."

Rider Barton sucked in a breath. "House Mara?"

Isandor nodded.

"By the skylights. They're not friends of the royal family. I hope you know what you're doing." Rider Barton had often spoken at the council about the unwillingness of the old nobles to cooperate with the new council.

"I've got a good contract with her. Don't worry."

CHAPTER 11

"Oy!" SOMEONE called on the quayside. The sound was loud in the fog that so often blanketed the harbour.

Zaina jumped. There he was. That was sure to be Nayek and she wasn't ready for this. No, not at all. She didn't have the information he wanted. None of the noble families had responded to her letters yet and her new plan—to observe boats—had not been successful either.

She straightened from where she had been, bolting shut the panel that gave access to the back end of an engine's boiler, a little trap door with a narrow ladder that led into a room full of gears and pistons. The engine was idling, drowning out all but the loudest sounds from the quay.

Zaina walked to the ship's railing, mentally preparing for the excuses that she had figured out over the last few days. *I've been busy, I haven't had the time to go and see any of those people yet.* Because she hadn't, and she was not the type of person who knew how to weasel her way into socialite parties, and didn't own dresses that would allow her to come into those parties anyway.

But when she came to the ship's railing, the person on the quay was not Nayek. It was an Eagle Knight. Well, that was . . . different. She wasn't sure if it was better. Could be worse. Certainly different.

"Uh. I'm not the captain of the ship. If you want him, you'll have to go into the meltery."

"No, I wanted to talk to you."

"Me?" This wasn't good. It really wasn't. This meant that they'd already discovered her side business as informant for Nayek. She was not suited as spy.

Zaina stuck her hands in her pockets and sauntered down the gangplank. The Knight stood between the ship and her truck. That was annoying should she choose to make a quick exit. Not just that, her gun was in the truck, too, because one did not normally need guns in the commercial harbour district. Compared to, say, the northern Aranian port city of Curack, the City of Glass had a strangely naive and innocent commercial sector.

"I gather the truck is yours?" the Knight said.

He was typical for his ilk, straight-laced as hell, formal, his body devoid of any features that would distinguish him from the next Knight. Crew cut, clean-shaven, perfect uniform, glittering buttons and decorations. They were all the same. And they could not be bought. She knew; she'd tried. It had not ended well.

"Yeah," she said. "The truck is mine. You want to see the papers?"

"I believe you."

She wanted to joke, *That'd be a first*, because no one believed her, ever. Not a woman who owned and fixed trucks, not a woman who looked like, and clearly was, a foreigner.

"Would you come with me to my command?"

"Well . . ." What the hell was going on? "Is there any guarantee that I'll be able to leave again?"

The Knight laughed.

Zaina got angry. "It's easy for you to laugh. I've got work to do, so why don't you just tell me what sort of trouble I'm in before I agree to go anywhere. Whatever is wrong, I can fix it, as long as I know what it is."

He laughed again. Normally, if men treated her that way, she would have pulled a knife and held it to their throats. That usually stopped them laughing, but she couldn't do that with a Knight. For one, he'd be faster and stronger than she was, he had the law on his side, and she would regret it deeply as well as having to deal with injuries other than the ones on her face. Secondly, her knife was also in the truck. And that thought made her angrier than the first. What was wrong with her?

"There is no trouble that you're in. You wrote a letter advertising your skills. We have a proposition for you. A job."

Shit, the letter she'd left at the palace. It had ended up with the Knights. And then, *Shit, Nayek*. No, she couldn't take this job.

But she'd be able to give him really good information.

But she *wasn't* ready to betray a place that had been good to her just because Nayek was a first-class bully and jerk.

She asked, "Does it pay?"

"Yes."

Damn it. She'd hope to be able to refuse. "How much?" The Eagle Knights would pay well, wouldn't they? They usually got repeat contractors, didn't they? And if she got this money independent of Nayek, she could use it to get out of here and would never have to deal with his sordid business again. Or . . . she could hide from him. Maybe, if they allowed her to stay in their compound.

"You will hear everything about it if you come with me."

Suspicion rose again. "It's not a trick?"

He stood his head. "It's not a trick."

"Your word?"

"My word." His face was utterly serious.

The word of a Knight was worth something. Over the past two years that she'd lived here, Zaina had found the Knights to be petty, pedantic, meddling and arrogant, but always consistent and honest, even if what they had been ordered to do was total nonsense.

Zaina collected her tools from the deck of the ship, because she didn't trust that captain as far as she could throw him. He was very big and fat, so that wasn't particularly far. She put the tools in the cabin of the truck and locked the door. She would have to finish work on the ship's engine later. It had been an interesting job for a well-known merchanting company, with a lot of potential for information-gathering.

The Knight waited for her. He did look very dapper and handsome, if quaint and old-fashioned, with his red tunic, his oiled and polished riding harness and shorthair cloak. He carried a dagger and a crossbow rather than a sword and gun, and a baton. He was lean and muscled and well trained as they all were, and when the breeze wafted past him, it carried a tang of leather and oil.

Zaina jumped off the step to the truck's cabin, aware of her own dirty overalls, her too-long, too-messy ponytail and her broken nails and grease-engrained skin on her hands. She'd skinned her knuckles while messing in a truck's gearbox a few days ago, and the scabs were black with grease.

In other words: she was the perfect picture of feminine nobility. These Knights usually consorted with painted noble ladies, right?

They set off through the streets of the commercial district in an uneasy silence.

Zaina noticed how people gave her sideways glances. Some people would know her, and would wonder what sort of trouble she was in. Maybe the news that a Knight had come for her would even reach Nayek. Maybe he would come to visit later when she was back, and get her to tell him everything she would learn. She hoped the job would be simple and boring. Maintaining the heaters or the trucks—did the Knights have trucks? She'd never seen any. But something that would keep her far removed from important people, or Nayek would force her to share her knowledge. He had very convincing ways of getting her to talk.

Maybe she should have told the Knight to fuck off. But one did *not* tell Knights to fuck off, or at least not without getting in trouble.

They walked up the incline and then turned left into the palace gates.

Zaina had never been inside the garden. You could see the clipped trees, the flowers and the neat grass through the wrought iron gate. Sometimes you saw guests arriving or deliveries being made. She had looked at those things, dismissing them as things she would never have anything to do with. Well, guess what?

The guards at the gate stepped aside for Zaina's companion. She wouldn't have judged him as such, but that meant he was some sort of hot shot, right? Oh, she was so incredibly out of her depth.

They walked up the drive between the clipped bushes to the entrance.

The Queen's coach with the white bears stood there. The driver was taking the tack off and attaching the headgear, presumably to take the animals to the stables. He greeted the Knight and said something she didn't catch. The Knights were said to speak an archaic dialect amongst themselves, and Zaina was only familiar with the language of the street.

They went up the steps into the foyer.

The hall was made entirely from sheets of glass mounted against one another. Some of the sheets were as thick as her hand was wide; others were thin. Some were clear, others were blue, green or brown. Some were transparent, others had patterns carved in or had been rubbed with sand so that the surface was cloudy. Some even had mirror paint applied to the back, so that they reflected the low light from the sun back into the hall, sometimes via directing it onto other sheets which added their own hue.

It was the most amazing thing she had ever seen. She craned her neck to look at the vaulted ceiling, with its hundreds of planes and angles, spots of light and reflections.

"Excuse me?" the Knight called from the other side of the hall.

"I'm sorry." Zaina ran to catch up with him. "I was looking at the glass. It's incredible."

"Yes, I've heard that remark before from first-time visitors." The way he said it grated on her. It sounded like *you poor bumpkin*. In Arania, the high-class people just yelled at you, or they hit you. They didn't pretend to be polite and then let you know that they were so much better than you through words.

The Knight turned into a corridor.

Even here all the walls and the ceilings were made of glass. Similar to that in the hall, the tall ceiling sloped sharply to catch most of the sunlight and reflect it into the building. There was a gallery level upstairs with open doors and warm light.

So different from the dank guesthouse that must have been built by a Chevakian using the Chevakian principles of architecture: small windows, thick walls.

They followed the corridor all the way to the end. Two more guards opened double doors to let them through into a large room.

About twenty people sat around the table in the middle. Many of them wore uniforms similar to that of the Knight who had come to get her, and whose name she probably should have asked. But she'd been overwhelmed, and names didn't mean much in her experience.

She did know Rider Barton, who was easily the oldest person at the table, and whose uniform was positively blinding from all the glittering decorations.

And that man at the very end of the table, with the blue eyes and sleek black hair, was that really the king? And the woman next to him, with honey-coloured hair, was that the queen? They looked no older than she was.

Zaina bowed because she didn't know what else to do. There had to have been some mistake. There was no way she had anything to offer these people, and what was worse, whatever she heard here would reach Nayek's ears.

"Rise and sit down," a pleasant male voice said.

Zaina wasn't sure that it was the king who had spoken, but it seemed so.

She raised her head, again looking around the table.

A servant came and pulled back an empty chair for her.

Zaina hesitated. "Thank you, but I'm not dressed nicely. I will make your beautiful furniture dirty."

"Not a problem, lady." The servant pulled a cloth out of his pocket and spread it over the seat.

That had to be the first time ever that someone had called her "lady".

The cloth was white, and her overalls would still leave greasy stains, but Zaina guessed the cloth was worth less than the uphol-stery, so she sat down, because they were all waiting for her to do so, all those important people with their sincere faces.

"Welcome," the king said. "These are the men and women of the Knights' Council of the City of Glass."

Zaina looked around the table at all those clean and noble faces. Her injured eye was throbbing from embarrassment, not pain.

She met the cool eyes of a wiry Knight seated two places from the king. Was that the legendary Jeito? The Knight who was her own Jadan's role model, who was a woman and looked, dressed and acted like a man, and who could kill any opponent in a knife fight.

The king said, his voice bemused, "This may be a little bit different from what you are used to, but rest assured, each of us has, at some point in our lives, stood in your shoes. When I was young, I worked as a butcher's assistant. Rider Carro here used to do the books in his father's fabric business. We lived in the old Outer City, which was destroyed by fire and has thankfully never been rebuilt. We were poor, it was cold, and we were always hungry and dirty. We know how this must feel for you."

No, they knew nothing. Because they knew nothing about Nayek.

"Well then, let's get to business," said another Knight. He had a hard face far more typical for the type of Knight she knew, ones where you were never sure where you stood.

"Yes. We may have a need of your skills with trucks and engines," the king said. "Your solicitation for business came at an opportune time. We ask if you would like to provide support for an expedition."

"An expedition? One that would take me out of the city?"

"Into the mountains."

"The *Aranian* mountains? What is the expedition for?"

"There used to be an overland path that leads to Chevakia and Arania. It has not been used for many years, since the Knights closed the borders, and the road has fallen into disrepair. I would like to re-open the land route, because it is a quicker route to the western half of Chevakia, and the slope to Chevakia is mild enough for trains to negotiate, without the need of a cable train and all the unloading and reloading necessary at the cable train station at Bordertown. I should also like to open trade with Arania." He gave her a searching look. He *did* realise what her background was, right? With her light eyes and big nose, she could only be Aranian.

He continued, "But all of this is just background information. This expedition wouldn't do any of those things yet. We want to investigate the current state of the road and the investment necessary to repair it. The expedition will include an air division with eagles, and a land division on the ground. They will take all kinds of measurements regarding slopes and soil types and air composition. You would be required to look after the trucks: their maintenance, their repairs and any modifications that may need to be made prior to or during the trip. The mountains are high, the air is thin and environment is taxing for vehicles and people alike. The expedition needs to carry its own fuel."

"It would pay?"

"Certainly. We pay a hundred Eagles. You get twenty after committing to the agreement, so that you can buy personal supplies. You get fifty when we leave and the rest when we get back. Any supplies related to the vehicles will be at our expense."

"Sorry . . . a *hundred* Eagles?" She had never seen that much money.

"That's what I said. In return, we ask for your service and confidentiality. This project is . . . well, not exactly a *secret*, but we don't want everyone to know about it, especially since the expedition will be going into sensitive territory and may run into Chevakian or Aranian patrols. We are aware that the border region is sensitive, and I have notified the relevant Chevakian and Aranian authorities of our peaceful intentions, so I would prefer not to start a public fear campaign about it. This is not about war; it's not about exact position of the border. It's about the benefit and safety of all of us."

She looked into his eyes to find any sign that he wasn't as naive as he sounded, but all she could see was his sincere expression. This was something she had found a lot in the City of Glass: people who genuinely didn't know that they were being ripped off and spied on, because it had never happened before, she guessed. He would *have* to understand that sending a group of people, including Eagle Knights, to the border region would be considered an act of war by Arania, wouldn't he? Especially with Prince Nayek looking over her shoulder?

"So what do you think? Do you have any questions? Would you like to come?"

Zaina hesitated. She very much wanted to say yes, even if it would only take her away from Nayek. But Prince Nayek never gave in and never let his prize go. And if he found out that she'd escaped him, there would be hell to pay.

The king said, "You are welcome to think about it. I understand that it may be hard for you to get away from your workshop."

Yes, it would be; there was that, too.

"But we would appreciate your help, and I'm willing to negotiate about the price. Come back here tomorrow or the day after if you want to sign the agreement, if you want to know more. But the team will have to leave early because of the coming winter, so don't think about it for too long."

ZAINA ENDED up giving the council her tentative agreement, and was allowed to go. But the further from the palace she got, the more she doubted her decision. The mountains were the border with Arania. Nayek would *not* like her leading an expedition there. What was it for, anyway? Apart from "checking the road", that was. Just look after the engines, we will pay. Our people will do the rest of the work. That had been the reply in various forms over and over. Why did they need to go into the mountains if Arania was easily reachable by sea and they had the train line to Chevakia?

But she could use the money to start anew somewhere else. She could ask Jadan to keep the workshop running so that Nayek would think she was coming back, and then he would wait forever and she could escape—and be forever on the run.

How long would the job be for? Would it be possible for her to leave the expedition in Chevakia? All questions she should have asked while she was in the room. That determined what sort of excuse she could use to fob off Nayek, if she was going to use any excuse at all. Maybe it was best just to disappear quietly and hope he would be too busy to look for her. But damn it, she *liked* it here.

Should she then tell the Knights about her situation with Nayek? No, that would definitely cause trouble. Because even if they could catch Nayek, he hadn't actually done anything that warranted arrest, and so he would just turn around and punish her for telling the Knights about him. And so her thoughts went from one problem to another.

By the time she got back to the harbour, the ship's captain had turned up to find his engine unfixed. He stood, glaring, on the deck while Zaina rushed to get her tools and go back to work. She took her toolbox from the cabin, shoved her knife in the top of her boot—she wasn't going to make that mistake again—picked up her toolbox and walked up the gangplank of the ship, ignoring the man.

"It's not done," he said. "You promised it would be done by start of business. It's not done."

"I needed to get something from the workshop," Zaina said, again without looking at him.

"The workshop is that way." He hooked a thumb to his right. "I saw you coming from over there."

"Look, something came up. Stop talking and I'll fix it right now. See? I'm getting to it."

"No, I don't think you will," a lazy male voice said.

Another man came from the cabin. He carried a mug of cider and leaned against the doorframe. It was Nayek.

CHAPTER 12

"A LETTER, for me?" Lana han Chevonian came into the kitchen where the maid Myra was kneading bread. Her mother sat in her chair in the corner, a blanket over her legs, even if it was quite hot in here with the oven blazing in readiness for the bread to go in.

"A telegram. It's on the table," Myra said.

Lana looked between the pans and bowls and baskets of vegetables standing on the table. Oh, there it was. Her name was written in neat letters on the front. In the corner there was a stamp from the telegraph office, so this had not been written by the person who had sent it, but rather by an employee of the office.

She unfolded the paper.

It said Ysherra at the top. Where even was that?

It said,

I'm sorry to bother you with this request. I have an urgent need to know all information there is in the Scriptorium library on the subject of dust devils. I may not return to class when tutoring resumes. Please inform Viki that a meteorological assistant would be greatly appreciated.

Yours,

Javes

"Who's it from?" her mother asked.

"Javesius han Demerian."

"You mean the son of Ledelius? Do you know him?"

125

"He's in my class at the Scriptorium. He's . . ." But she didn't say anything else, because her mother advocated to never say nasty things about people, unless they were based on the other person's actions, and not on your own likes or dislikes Javes was one of those weird kids that no one liked or understood. The other students would play pranks on him a lot, which he tended to bring upon himself. Sometimes, Lana felt like slapping him in the face and yelling at him, "Why do you even think that's a good idea?" but mostly, Javes was just . . . Javes. Socially awkward, quiet, in the back of the class.

"Why does he write to you?"

"I don't understand it either. He wants me to look up something in the library. What are dust devils?"

"I don't know. Ask your father. I can hear him in the hall."

Ill as she was, there was nothing wrong with her mother's hearing, because a moment later, the kitchen door opened and Sadorius han Chevonian, proctor of the Chevakian doga, came into the kitchen. He discarded his cloak over the back of the first seat on the table, kissed his wife at the top of her head and sat down in his usual seat facing Lana.

"Why aren't you working hard in the archives?"

"Dad, seriously, I've finished work."

"Good jobs are never done."

"I wanted to go home. It's so boring."

"Boring work has to be done. The quicker you do it, the sooner you can do something interesting."

"But all the jobs in the archives are boring." Why had she been landed with this boring field assignment while others in her class had gotten placings in interesting locations? Even Javes had been placed in a field station.

"You can't do the interesting work if you don't accept the mundane—thank you." He accepted a cup of tea from the cook.

"Yeah, Dad, I've heard that so many times before."

"Then why are you still complaining?"

"I'm like the *only* one who didn't get a placement out of town."

"And you don't think there might be a reason for it? I don't control Viki's decisions, but he's a smart man, and I have no doubt that he has matched the students to their best abilities."

Lana rolled her eyes. She bet her father had asked Viki to keep her in Tiverius, because she was never allowed to do anything. And Viki listened to him because he was the proctor. She'd been looking forward to travelling to an unfamiliar place all year. Some place like Solmeni, where veil-like waterfalls cascaded down from the cliffs that surrounded the town on three sides, or a place like Fairlight, where goods were transferred from the main train line to the vertical train so that they could be taken to and from the City of Glass on the southern platform. Mother was even from the City of Glass, and had not been back there for almost twenty years.

She would have been happy even with Ysherra, wherever that was.

"Second lesson in life: be happy with your lot, not because you should never aspire for anything better, but because you might as well enjoy it while you're trying. It makes you a more pleasant person to be around."

Yeah, yeah, she got the message. Maybe she'd go and see Mari or another friend after dinner. She would understand. Or at least commiserate, when she wasn't talking about her upcoming wedding. Or she would sigh and say, "You'll speak differently once you're out there using your education."

Bah, people. She was really grumpy today.

"What's that?" her father asked, nodding at Javes' letter.

"A classmate wrote to me."

Father's eyes narrowed. "Ysherra?"

"Yeah. That's where he was placed." And she still had no idea where it was. "He wants to know what information the library has about dust devils."

"There is your task. That's what librarians do. Answer questions, put answers together into a bigger picture."

Easy, just like that. As if she didn't have anything else to do in the archives, boring as those tasks were; but the librarian would be angry if they weren't done. "I don't know where to start. I never heard of dust devils. What are they?"

"When the ground gets very hot and the air is even hotter, you may get whirlwinds that pick up dust and turn into little self-contained pressure cells that rip a path through the land."

"They're whirlwinds with dust in them?" She'd seen a whirlwind once, a scary funnel that reached down from the clouds and that tore through a field pulling out crops and scattering them in a wide path. It had destroyed a shed, too.

"That's what I understand."

Lana surmised that Ysherra had to be on the edges of the northern desert. Wow. There were a few northern people in Tiverius. They were very dark-skinned and wore loose robes and lots of coloured beads.

That was where Viki had sent Javes? That wasn't fair.

But, she decided while the cook put dinner on the table and the conversation moved to other things, she would look up dust devils in the library and she would write to Javes, even if it could only help her share some of his great adventure. No wonder he was going to sign up for an extra job after his placement finished.

AFTER DINNER, Lana did something unusual: she went back to the library.

The nights had finally acquired enough of a bite to require a cloak, and she walked quickly, and already dreaded the comments she would get from tutors and lecturers.

She wasn't particularly studious, but she wasn't frivolous either. She did the work and passed her courses.

Sometimes Dad would comment that she had little passion for the work, or he would say he hoped that she would find it because it was hard to survive in the competitive study of meteorology without that passion.

She knew that. It was just . . . hard. There were so may other things that she was interested in, like astronomy. With some money she had saved, she had bought a spyglass. Father had been angry because it was just a fad, he said. Stars didn't look any different through a looking glass than without, even if the moon had looked interesting when it was closer. You could clearly see that it was a ball by the way the light fell on it. More than anything, Lana liked the group of students who would gather once a week to look at the skies, but so many had now gone to their placements, leaving Lana to look at the skies alone.

The library was very different at night from the buzz during the day. Gone were the chattering groups of first year students and the tut-tutting librarians shushing them while wheeling trolleys around.

With both first year students and librarians absent, the tables were filled with older students, who talked, but didn't yell and giggle so much. No one was there to stop them talking, so the place was noisier than it was during the day.

In the meteorological section, a large group of third year students sat around a table, talking about some project they had to do. They gave her strange looks that said *Shouldn't you be on field placement?*

On the shelves, Lana found a book called *The Northern Fringe* and another about *Phenomena of Weather and Wind*. She also found a map of the north of Chevakia and took the big and well-thumbed copy of *Seasonal Barygraphic Patterns of Chevakia*, a book she would probably have bought herself if not for the fact that it would have burned a considerable hole in her study allowance.

She took the books to a table in the corner.

Lana had brought her notebooks, too. She opened up a new page and wrote *Dust Devils* across the top.

Then she started reading.

Apparently, the seasonal fluctuation in sonorics pushed bands of rain depressions into and out of the northern desert.

The town of Ysherra was marked on the map because it had a measurement station. It was the northernmost field station of the department of meteorology, and its measurements were hugely valuable for that reason.

Wow, the average temperatures were really something. It didn't rain much either. She imagined a hot and dry landscape. She'd seen pictures of hills of orange soil with rows of olive trees.

In another book, she found some sketches of the main street of the town. It looked . . . really bare with its blocky buildings and the absence of large trees.

All right, maybe it wasn't such a wonderful place to spend a couple of months. That made her wonder: why had Javes signed up for an extension?

In the most recent edition of *Phenomena of Weather and Wind* she found a section on dust devils that described exactly what her father had told her. They were whirlwinds that contained dust. They could damage houses and crops. Mention of dust devils was strangely omitted from an older edition of the same book.

She made notes of all this, and was about to close the book when she took notice of the extensive scribbles that someone had made in the margins.

People who scribbled in books annoyed her. So what if they were academics and didn't agree with the author? They could write their own book. For students making notes, the behaviour was even worse. Why write and underline words in a library book that wasn't even yours to keep?

But someone had underlined the world "whirlwind" and written in the margin in capital letters: RUBBISH!

Underneath it said,

Dust devils are semi-autonomous constructs of sonorics that can be mistaken for eddies. People getting really close—not to be recommended!—often sustain burns to exposed skin similar to those sustained by travellers to the southern platform that are caused by sonorics. If they survive, they often suffer continuing illness. They also speak of having seen "things" inside the devil when it passed them. This could range from monsters to animals to armed soldiers, often dependent on the individual's fears.

Someone else had drawn a couple of clouds, with the text *What are you smoking, ha, ha?*

Lana stared at the first note. It was written in a neat hand, not the scribbles of someone uneducated.

She went back to the shelves and found a book on sonorics. She had to look really hard, because since the machine under the City of Glass had been destroyed, no one thought they'd need those books anymore.

She had heard of what sonorics did to a person not resistant to it: the skin peeled, the eyes became blind, wounds developed into weeping sores that would not heal.

The same happened inside the body. If exposure was bad enough, the person died.

Ew. She could really do without the detailed description.

Sonorics was limited to the south. The book even had maps to show when and where flare-ups happened and what to do about them. That was until the barrier had been built and southern Chevakia became a little safer. Sometimes older people still spoke of the sonorics alarms, but most people who remembered that time had died now. Although plenty of people still remembered the explosion and the tide of refugees that had washed over Chevakia.

There was nothing written on the subject of sonorics in the last twenty years, and nothing about it occurring in the north at all.

Then she retrieved another book on the northern desert. In the front, it showed a map of the northern half of the continent that had Peria in the very south, Chevakia in the east and Arania in the west. The north was a vast wasteland. The shoreline had been mapped, and early cartographers had written landmarks across their maps like "Big Rock" and "Dogshead Peninsula". There were no settlements marked on the map at all. The coastline was said to consist of sheer cliffs with occasional beaches. No rivers drained into the ocean.

Of one place, an explorer's report said,

There was a small beach where we went ashore. The cliffs receded in this area, and we managed to find a path that took us up to the top of the platform. At the top, we found nothing but barren rock, orange in colour to reflect the content to iron and the magnetic irregularities we had observed earlier, but otherwise without feature.

The view down both sides of the shoreline was desolate, with red cliffs disappearing in the mist of sea spray.

Nothing grows here. There is no rain. There are no animals and no people.

Lana tried hard to imagine such a world. The desert was incredibly vast, and the habitable part of the continent took up less than half.

Another section of the book was devoted to the question of whether people had ever lived in this area. The author posed that since the City of Glass dated from an ancient civilisation, there might be other traces of this civilisation, which probably *wouldn't* be found in areas with lots of vegetation, areas where natural decay of materials was fast. He wrote,

Metal rusts and, given time, will fall into dust. Even the artificial rock that we see in the City of Glass must decay. In places like Chevakia and Arania, decay is helped by nature, by plants extending their roots into crevices and making them bigger, by trees dropping leaves over things to bury them, by water seeping into cracks and helping the rust to grow. In places where there is little nature, there will be less decay.

Underneath, he had made the off-hand comment,

Of course, the task of actually mounting an expedition to this barren place would amount to suicide, and may well be impossible to achieve. I do not know that any kind of pack animal would lend itself to walking through such heat, and the expedition would need to carry so much water as to make it impossible.

Of course in that time the people didn't have trucks.

But even after trucks were invented, no one had seen the necessity of exploring that part of the continent. Although there were a couple of known routes to places like Red Hill, where it was said there was an oasis and where astronomers travelled to see celestial events.

Then again, no one thought much of astronomers either.

Although there did appear to be at least *some* people living there. Some reports spoke of *windwalkers*, people who rode camels and wrapped themselves in cloth, presumably to minimise loss of water through the skin.

None of the authors elaborated on who they were and where their towns were, if they lived in towns at all.

It was strange that none of the early explorers' reports mentioned dust devils. They sometimes mentioned sand storms, which was a rather more widespread phenomenon. One book had a coloured drawing of a wall of orange clouds rolling over a town. That looked scary. Could you breathe inside that cloud?

"Lady han Chevonian, I'm afraid I'm going to have to close up for the night," a voice said behind her.

Lana gasped and looked over her shoulder. It was one of the older librarians who had spoken, a man whose name she didn't know, but whom she had seen working in here.

"Oh, I'm so sorry." Lana got up and put her books in a pile.

"Don't worry about them, I will put them back for you."

"Thank you so much." She stuffed her notebooks in her bag.

The librarian collected some other books from tables where students had sat when she came in, but that were now deserted. When had all these people left?

"I am really sorry to keep you here." This was so embarrassing. Likely he'd been waiting to leave so that he could go home.

"Not at all, Lady. I love seeing the mark of a true academic. Study and science above all."

Lana walked back through the dark streets of Tiverius clutching her notebook.

She came home and took a cup of tea with her father in the kitchen. Mother had gone to sleep already. The fact that she was getting worse did not need to be said. Lana understood that she would probably not live long. Maybe that was another reason why Dad had asked Viki to keep her in Tiverius. The thought of losing her mother disturbed her, because then there would be just her and Dad in this big house.

She had little enough family already. Uncle Milleus had two sons, but both were quite old and their children had long since married and left home. Lana had met them, but didn't really like either of the families. They always seemed to want to compliment her on her "exotic" dark hair as if constantly hammering home the point that she was different.

Her father poured tea and they talked a bit about the library and dust devils, and Lana told him about the note.

Then Dad asked, "What do you think about dust devils? Why does the older edition of *Phenomena* say nothing about them?"

"Because no one goes there to check. People can travel a bit further into the desert with trucks now, and therefore they come across more of the desert phenomena."

"Yes, that could be one reason." Not the one he was looking for, obviously.

"Or people know more. In the old days of the explorers, the reports came from people who lived there, and they might not have seen dust devils as something you needed to write about. Everyone knew what they were. Or at least everyone they ever talked to."

"Yes, maybe." Her father leaned his chin on his hand. How she hated it when he did this, when he knew the answer but was just teasing her.

"Or they just weren't around. It seems to me that if they were frightening enough and they killed people, someone would write about them, so if there are no old reports, it could mean there weren't any. After all, the climate has changed a lot in the south, it may have changed everywhere."

"Yeah," he said, and then he stared into the distance for a while.

Little references to this fact had been sprinkled throughout her course. Tutors were always saying that this was how it used to work twenty years ago, but those patterns hadn't been seen since then.

She met her father's eyes over the rim of her teacup. These days, his face seemed set in a permanent frown.

She asked, "Is this a thing that worries you?"

He blew out a breath through his nose. "Not the dust devils in particular. There is probably some local mythology involved. That handwriting is in the northern style. But we've been missing rain seasons for a second year in a row. A lot of people in the north are afraid and they want to come to Tiverius, because they think that we live in riches. I guess that compared to some people, we do, but that doesn't mean that we'll have riches to share with them, if they don't farm the land and sell their crops to the cities and towns."

"And they can't farm the land because of the drought."

"Precisely. We don't know when or even if rain is going to fall. All the weather patterns across the continent have been turned upside down."

"Just from the destruction of one thing?"

Dad sighed. "I don't know anymore. It doesn't look like sonorics has died with this machine. Some people think there may be a second machine somewhere, maybe in the Aranian mountains. Arania is stirring."

"But they were defeated in the war." The war led by her uncle Milleus, whose stories of victory she remembered. They had always represented safety for her. Arania was ruled by mad kings, but those bad guys were well and truly defeated by her own family.

"Much time has passed since then. The old king of Arania has passed the crown to his oldest or most favoured son, Orik, who is reported to be impatient, with a temper that is not improving with age. He would be somewhere in his fifties now. He's power hungry, and said to have a great need to prove his worth to his great number of sons, all of whom are vying for the most favoured status. They're probably waiting for him to make a mistake, at which time the fastest will kill him and grab the throne. It would be lucky if that happened soon, but if not, he might start doing something stupid."

Lana felt chilled.

After her life had been happy, and Chevakia had been prosperous and no longer threatened from the south or the west.

She climbed the stairs to her room, where she lit a lamp to write about what she'd found out to Javes. She'd send it tomorrow morning before going to the archives.

135

CHAPTER 13

$\mathcal{N}$AYEK SPRANG FORWARD and grabbed Zaina by the arm.

She protested, "Hey, what's going on?"

But he didn't reply. He dragged her down the gangplank, pushing her in front of him. There were a number of people on the quay, but none of them spoke up. In fact, most of them looked away in the manner they had done when Zaina had turned up with bruises on her face. Because matters between a man and his wife were *his* business and one didn't interfere.

Nayek pushed her up the road to the *Silver Gull*. People in the street gave them a wide berth, again without attempting to help. Zaina wasn't sure *she* would help. Everything about Nayek's appearance said trouble.

He dragged her through the alley, devoid of hookers at this time of the day, up the stairs, through the corridor to the end, where two fearsome-looking guards stood. They opened the door into a large room that overlooked the harbour. It had to be his room.

It was not until the door had shut that he let Zaina go.

She rubbed her arm. "What was that necessary for? You know I'm busy doing stuff for you. I took that job on the ship only so that I could give you stuff on the owners."

"You went to the palace." He spat out the words. "Why didn't you tell me that you were going to the palace?"

"Because I didn't know until the Knight came for me this morning."

"You went to the fucking palace!" He yelled in her face. His breath smelled of alcohol.

Zaina didn't speak. She had no idea why he was so angry or what he expected her to say.

"You went to the Knights and told them about me, didn't you?"

"No, I didn't!"

"You did. You fucking lying minx."

"I did not. They offered me a job."

He frowned at her, taken aback. "A job? Why would they do that? Huh, why should I believe that?"

"Because I know about engines and they do not."

Again, a frown. He rubbed his upper lip with the back of his hand. "That true, huh?"

"Yes."

"Their engines, huh?"

"Yes."

"They don't have any engines!" he screamed in her face. "They're backwards. They use *swords, knives, bows and arrows.*" With each word, he shouted louder and closer to Zaina's face.

Zaina did her best not to retreat, but his breath was foul, and he sprayed drops of spit into her face.

"I know they don't have engines. They still asked me."

He stared at her for a moment, then retreated while uttering a disdainful grunt, and spat on the floor. "What's the job then?"

"They said they needed someone to maintain engines. I presume they are trucks, but they could be ships. They didn't tell me."

"And you didn't ask?"

"No."

"You call yourself a knowledgeable mechanic and you didn't ask?"

"They said they'd tell me later, when I turned up for work."

"When you turned up for work, huh?"

"Yeah." She hated how he always mockingly repeated part of what she said.

"And when you 'turn up' for this supposed work, I am guessing that this supposed work is not trucks or ships—because they don't have any fucking trucks or ships!" He shouted in her face again. Then took in a deep breath, and continued, "It will be about the palace heating, and maybe about their pitiful lights since those pathetic icefire bulbs don't work anymore. And such a job is a caretaker position, which means, you'd live in the palace. Which means I can't get to you."

Oh shit. "No, it's not like that at all!"

"It's not?"

"No."

"Then you do know what it is about, and I'd advise telling me, because I'm not known for my patience. I can tell you that had you been male, I would have killed you after your first lie, and I would have dumped your body in the street and by now, it would probably be cold. The only reason you're alive is because I am looking forward to listening to your screams while I fuck you. So. Stop it with the games. Don't lie. Don't think you can outsmart me. Don't think I don't know what you're doing. I *know* you delivered that letter to the palace. You *asked* them for a spot where I can't reach you. Know this: you are not safe from me *anywhere*. Not even in the palace." He took another deep breath. He reached out and ran his finger along the line of her jaw in a mock tender gesture.

"Now. The truth, or I'll give you a bit of a prelude to what I will do to you."

A drop of sweat trickled between her breasts. She had to get out of here.

He crouched so that his face was level with hers. With his pale eyes, dark skin, red tattoos on his skull, his oiled plait and rings in his nose, he was terrifying.

"Who did you meet at the palace?"

"I was asked in the King's Council." Being vague would not help her.

"The king was there?"

"Yes."

"And Supreme Rider Barton?"

"I don't know him. He might have been."

"The queen?"

"Yes."

"Rider Farey?"

"I don't know him. He might have been."

"Farey is the Aranian traitor." As if that was supposed to help her remember him. There had been twenty people at the table. She hadn't gotten a close look at all of them.

"Rider Jeito?"

She nodded. Jeito had been there.

He snorted. "And they asked an Aranian woman to come and help them? Do I have to believe that?"

"That's what they did. I'm telling you the truth."

He lashed out and hit her in the face. "Stupid woman. You don't know anything."

Zaina's head reeled. Her nose tickled. She wiped it the back of her hand, and it came away covered in a smear of blood.

"What was that good for?"

He drew her up by the collar of her overalls. "Because you're stupid. I asked for information. The information is staring you in the fucking face. And you are too stupid to report it to me. I will forgive you this once, but you're going to have to do better than this."

He let her go.

Zaina drew in a shuddering breath.

He took a counter out of his pocket, an old Aranian device that looked like a medallion. It had a little window in the front. A metal disk sat inside a slot in the side. You could turn it so that it would display a number in the window.

In Arania, men would use it to determine deals and favours, mainly the men who went to tobacco houses and who would discuss business over a small table filled with empty tea cups and an over-flowing ash tray.

Nayek moved the fat tip of his finger along the recession in the counter's housing, so that the disk turned and the window said *one*. He held it up to Zaina's face.

"See that? It says 'one'. I will use it to record the number of times you disobey me. When it says 'three', I'm going to fuck you. You could rack up three strikes just today. You will have noticed that this is my room, and there are guards at the door. The inn owner is a friend of mine. The rooms next-door are my men's. No one will hear your screams."

He sat down. "With that in mind, let's restart this little talk, shall we?"

Zaina told him everything: about the king, about the expedition to the mountains. That it was to open the road, and that there would be an air and land team. She hated herself, but she could do nothing else if she wanted to get out of the room alive. Her mother had always told her to be meek. She knew why—because these men cared nothing for the life of a woman, and if you struggled, the man would just hurt you more.

"Hmph," he said when she finished. "It seems that little king is smarter than he looks."

He thought for a bit. Then he met her eyes. "I want you to go on this expedition. I want you to report on the people who go on it, what they say and what they do. I don't think they're really interested in re-opening the road to Chevakia. They have the trains which are much faster than trucks. They will be going into Arania, and they will be spying on us. They will be looking for the group of spies they sent recently and that we intercepted. Either they're dumb or they misjudge my father's power."

Zaina licked blood from her upper lip.

He held a finger to her face. "Don't make their mistake. Don't misjudge my father's power. Don't think you can get away with disobedience. Don't think you can hide. We see and know everything. Is that understood?"

Zaina nodded.

"Good then. You can leave, for now."

Zaina rose. Her legs trembled so much that she almost fell sideways. He smirked at her, watching her as she walked to the door.

Zaina couldn't believe it. She was actually getting out of here unscathed. But fear was a very powerful thing, and the fear of what he would do to her was almost worse than the thing itself.

He'll keep you dancing as long as you're afraid, her mother would have said. Then again, her mother had submitted to her lot, and see where it had left her: dead at the age of forty-nine with a child in her belly.

She reached the door, put her hand on the doorknob, turned it . . .

"It occurs to me that I forgot to give you a demonstration," Nayek said behind her.

Damn it. *Demonstration of what?* Zaina slowly turned around, because anything else would be disobedience, half-expecting him with his pants down.

But he was fully clothed, standing in the middle of the room holding some sort of metal wand with a gemstone at the top. What the hell was that?

He came towards her. As she backed into the door, he swung the wand. It trailed a crackling beam of golden lightning.

Zaina was too slow. It hit her in the side, paralysed her, pinned to the door. Pain exploded through her.

Nayek laughed. "You like it?"

Zaina would have screamed expletives at him had she been able to speak. Her mouth was frozen and her arms were frozen and she couldn't feel her legs.

He pointed the thing at her. "I can do it again."

No, no!

"Then again . . ." He lowered the wand. "They said it would probably kill a person, and I'm having far too much fun with you. I don't fuck dead things either." He stuck the wand in the inside pocket of his jacket.

"Come on, you're free to go."

But Zaina couldn't move.

He shoved her aside. She lost her balance and fell to the floor.

Then he opened the door and dragged her into the corridor. "I don't fuck drunk girls either."

He stepped over her, went back into his room and shut the door.

Zaina was left motionless on the floor, with her face pressed into the disgusting runner. The guards on both sides of the door to Nayek's room pretended she didn't exist.

It took a while before Zaina was able to raise herself onto her hands and knees and crawl to her room. There was a guard in front of her door as well, who also ignored her struggle.

Damn, what was that wand he had used on her?

Zaina opened the door and dragged herself inside. She sat on the floor, looking around the room which had for the past two years been a safe haven for her, but nothing was safe anymore. As soon as she had recovered enough, she was going to get out of here. She didn't care if it killed her. She could *not* go through the suffering that her mother and her mother's friends had been subjected to. Nayek would play with her until she was so broken that she'd beg him to rape her, if only to be rid of his constant taunts. If she was lucky, he would leave her alone until she gave birth. He might demand one of those horrible birth ceremonies and watch her agony, accompanied by his Counter, who officially tallied up everything in an important prince's life: how many wives, how many children, how many enemies, how many disobediences.

Once the child was recorded against his name, he might give it a favoured place, if it was a girl or if it was a boy by a woman he liked. He didn't like her, so if she gave birth to a boy, he would probably kill the child before her eyes, while she was still bleeding.

And then he would do it again, and again, and again, until she was spent and died.

She would rather die in a knife fight than in the way her mother had died.

Her legs wouldn't support her weight yet, but at least she could feel them, and she managed to sit on her knees so that she could reach the water jug. She drank deeply and washed dried blood from her upper lip and her chin.

Later, she dragged herself on top of the bed so that she could look out the window. The freedom of the street seemed impossibly far away. She lay on the bed staring at the ceiling in the darkness. Her head was still ringing from the hit, and her side itched where the beam had hit her. She slept a bit, but the itching grew worse. Whenever she ran her hand over that side, she could feel lumps of growing blisters. The hand mirror was on the cabinet on the other side of the room, and she didn't think she could get that far.

Zaina woke up long before daylight, but the sounds of carts rattling through the street betrayed that it was morning and merchants were arriving for the markets.

She struggled out of bed. Everything hurt and all her muscles were stiff, but at least she could walk, although she still felt clumsy. She took off her overalls and found her travel gear: leather trousers, leather jacket. The skin at her left side had blistered and was peeling. She dabbed some of the ointment that she used for cuts from machines on the skin, pulling a face. It stung like blazes. She covered the weeping sore with a clean washcloth, put her shirt on over the top, and then the jacket. She put on her leather pants and her boots—with the knife inside.

Then she packed her most important possessions in a small bag, slung it over her shoulder, draped her overalls over her arm and left her room. The guards were still outside the door, and still ignored her. She hoped she looked like she was going to work.

Zaina went downstairs, paid the owner, loudly proclaiming that she was paying the weekly rent and walked onto the street. Of course, the street wasn't as free for her as it was for all the other people. She would be watched. Maybe that man over there, or the woman just coming out of the bakery, or maybe there were spies on the roofs or the upstairs windows of houses. Nayek had many people watching out for him.

Zaina walked aimlessly around the Harbour District in the dark, past the ships that had just arrived and the fishing boats that were leaving.

Her workshop workers were good people, and she didn't want any of them mixed up in this mess. But she had to tell Jadan at least the practical matters of what was happening, and it was too early for Jadan to have turned up for work yet.

She bought some food and forced herself to eat it, while sitting on the steps of the harbour master's office, which was also not open yet, but it was within view of the guard post. It was another cold and misty morning, perhaps even with a bit of frost, and Zaina's breath steamed in the morning air.

By the time Zaina had finished eating, she judged it late enough to try the workshop.

A light was on in the main room. Jadan was walking between two trucks with a candle to light the lamp in the office. She gasped when she saw Zaina's face.

"Who keeps hitting you all the time?"

"I met an unfortunate acquaintance." She looked around the workshop. She knew she could trust Jadan, but wasn't sure of anybody else, including the neighbours. There could be spies here, too.

She gestured Jadan into the office where Jadan took a cloth and wiped Zaina face.

"This is the second time now in three days," Jadan said. "These cuts will probably leave scars."

Nayek's rings had made cuts over her brow that were still weeping.

"I'm not terribly worried about the cuts," Zaina said. "Ouch, that stings. I'd like you to look at this." She took off her jacket and lifted the shirt underneath.

Jadan winced. "What by the skylights is that?"

"It hurts."

"Yes, I believe that. It looks like an icefire burn."

Zaina stared at her. The gold beam—was that this thing called icefire that she had heard people talk about? What was Nayek doing with it?

"I have something for that." Jadan crouched at the desk and opened the little door at the bottom of the drawer compartment. She took out a stone jar, unstoppered it and poured a gooey, oily substance onto her hand that spread a rancid smell through the room.

Zaina pulled a face. "Ugh, that smells."

"Yes, it's not the prettiest of smells. It's made from the blubber of tusked lions."

Zaina had seen those creatures a few times, giant brown beasts that swam in the ocean but came up to the surface to breathe. The males were much bigger than the females, and they had long, downward-pointing tusks.

The oil helped a bit.

"I'll buy some more of it, if you like."

Zaina said she did.

Jadan rebandaged the wound. Zaina shivered under the touch of the soft and gentle hands. Often, she had lain in bed, wondering what would happen if she took Jadan's thin, boyish hands in hers, if she pulled Jadan closer, lifted up her shirt and ran her hands over the firm skin. She wondered what those lips tasted like.

If a woman dressed like a man, did that mean she was agreeable to this sort of thing? Or would she be hit in the face, called names and lose a valuable employee?

An awkward silence hung between them.

"Look, I'm going to be away for a bit," Zaina said. "I'll try my best not to abandon you, but in case I don't come back, the workshop is yours."

Jadan's eyes widened. "What . . . what happened?"

"Trust me, it's best that you don't know. You're a nice, hard-working mechanic. You'll do well." Zaina put a hand on Jadan's shoulder, pushed herself up and limped out of the workshop.

It was not until she was outside that she noticed she was crying.

Those barbarians destroyed everything.

"I'll kill him," she whispered to herself. "I'll kill the bastard and his father, and all his vile brothers."

CHAPTER 14

ISANDOR WAS DEEP in financial reports when someone knocked on the door to his study.

"Come in," Isandor said.

The door opened and a gate guard entered the room. Isandor frowned at the man. He might have expected the mail boy or the maid who had gone to get some tea—which he had almost forgotten about.

"There is a visitor for you," the guard said.

Isandor wasn't expecting anyone. Puzzled, he went with the guard through the breezy hallways. It had now become dark enough that the domestic staff kept the oil lights burning even during the day.

A slight figure waited in the relative darkness of the guard station, sitting on the bench where the guards would sit during quiet times.

It was Zaina, and she rose as soon as she saw him coming.

Her face was bruised, one of her eyes almost swollen shut, there was a nasty gash above her eye.

"By the skylights, what has happened to you?"

"I should know better than to get involved in bar brawls." She tried to smile, but it looked more like a grimace.

"I can let a healer look at it," Isandor said. Those bruises were impressive. That *had* to hurt.

"It's all right. I'm fine." She didn't look fine to him. "I'm here because I decided to go ahead with the trip."

"Oh. Well . . . the expedition won't be leaving for a few days yet." He noticed the bag on the ground next to her feet. Sturdy materials and efficiently packed, the mark of someone who travelled a lot.

"I'm ready to go."

"But the expedition is not. We need some days to get organised."

"I can start today." Her voice sounded very insistent.

Isandor looked her up and down. She held herself tall, with her back straight and her chin up, but those bruises spoiled the effect.

"Are you all right?"

"Yes, I am."

"Have you got money to survive for a few more days?"

"Yes, I do."

"Have you got somewhere to stay?"

"Actually, I was wondering if I could stay in the barracks, because . . ."

"Boyfriend trouble?" He looked at her bruises.

She grinned. "Yes."

"Had a fight?"

She nodded, visibly relieved that he'd breached the subject. "Yes, a big one."

"He was drunk?"

"I think so. He got very mad."

"And now you're afraid of him and you have nowhere to stay?"

"Yes." She attempted another smile. Her stance relaxed visibly. He recognised her behaviour from his youth. She was relieved to be asked this question and not to have to volunteer a lie.

Isandor felt sick. He had seen women abused by their husbands with words much more often than with fists, but he knew that it happened, especially when there was drink involved.

He was also sure there was more to the story. An extortion attempt on her business perhaps, or a violent dispute with a customer.

But he remembered his life as a young man in the Outer City, hunted by Tandor, when he had done things that might not be terribly legal because he had to survive. When the fact that he *existed*, as Imperfect with his wooden leg, was not terribly legal. He'd escaped with Jevaithi into Chevakia, and people there had accepted him despite the lies he'd told them about himself and Jevaithi. The old man Milleus at whose house they had stayed had known that there was more to his story.

"All right. Come with me," he said.

He preceded her into the hallway. She followed him, but kept shooting skittish glances over her shoulder.

"Whatever you're fleeing, you are safe here," he said. He knew that type of glance, given every time a man sought to be alone with her. Maybe he should ask the guards to ask around the bars to check that she hadn't murdered anyone. "I will take you to the baths. You can wash, and I'll seek out some clean clothes." He might have to ask Jeito to share some of hers, although getting Jeito to share *anything* was a major feat. Maybe he'd ask Jeito to check her out as well. She might talk more easily to Jeito.

They went to the service quarters, where he explained to the guard on duty what he wanted.

"She can stay in the female room," the guard said.

Zaina was happy with that. "I can work and fix things until we leave," she said. "You won't be disappointed."

Isandor walked back with the guard. "There is something going on there," he said, when they were in the hallway out of earshot of the service quarters.

"Do you want me to keep an eye on her?"

"Just to see that she's safe and that her boyfriend doesn't come in here."

"He's probably some drunken sailor type."

"Probably. But keep an eye on her anyway."

When Isandor came back to his study, the mail boy had been in and a letter was on his desk.

It was plain and businesslike, but the hand was clearly a woman's. By the skylights, Tamerane.

He ripped open the paper. It was from her indeed. It said, *I'm sorry to inform you that we were unsuccessful. I am ready to try again.*

That was . . . a disappointment. No, it wasn't. It gave Isandor another chance to talk with her about her interesting gadgets. He wrote a quick note in reply that he would be in later and called the mail boy to deliver it.

Then he walked around the study, pulling out a couple of books he wanted to discuss. He felt strangely excited about the prospect of seeing her. Her discussions reminded him of the excited discoveries he and Carro used to make in the old and forbidden books. Now that the knowledge was no longer a secret, he'd delegated knowledge-gathering to academics, and rarely did any of it himself. It had been so long that he could discuss wild theories with someone. Jevaithi wasn't interested in the sciences, and Carro was very practical and always busy.

He went into the bathroom, washed and shaved himself, daubed a few drops of perfume on his chest, and dressed in clean clothes. He stood before the mirror, changing his earrings when Jevaithi came in.

"Where are you going?"

"Into town."

"Do you need to dress up for that? Look at the weather."

Yes, it had been raining since this morning.

"Official business."

She raised her eyebrows. She probably knew him well enough to figure out that he was lying. He felt terrible, but he'd still not worked up the courage to tell her about Tamerane.

Isandor finished dressing, then he went to the kitchen and filled a tin with cakes, he asked a maid to put a ribbon around it, and went to the greenhouse to pick some flowers which he fashioned into a little bunch.

When getting into the coach a little later, there was a spring in his step.

Tamerane opened the door to her house and let Isandor in.

He held the tin with cakes and the flowers out to her.

"For me?"

"I didn't do a very good job last time. I guess, I'd forgotten how to be nice to a woman."

Her smile was worth having come here through the rain. What was more, he was already getting excited about what was going to happen upstairs, and not just the academic part. She took his cloak and shook the raindrops from the fur. "The weather is awful. Just as well it's warm upstairs." She cast him a quick look from the corner of her eye. One corner of her mouth moved up.

They walked through the hall. The sound of voices drifted from somewhere else in the house, but by the time they were going up the stairs, no one had come to look.

"Your parents not here?"

"I told them I can look after my own visitors."

"Good."

"They're very busy anyway."

"It must be a lot of work, running that many businesses."

"Yeah." She started up the stairs. From the tone in her voice, she didn't want to talk about business or about her parents. Both probably.

That was fine by him. Business didn't interest him greatly either.

The room smelled of tea and cakes and a good fire burned in the hearth.

Tamerane said, "Tea first, or business first?"

He couldn't help laughing.

"What?"

"I can't believe you have agreed to this. You're just not a professional breeder."

"No, I'm not. Would you like to be?"

"No. I saw my foster mother do that for many years. I believed that fertility was a curse for many girls."

"It is indeed."

"You had one child?"

She sighed. "Yes. I was very young. I thought I was a big girl taking part in the Newlight festival. I went to the bars and I danced and got drunk and I had fun. Then an older noble son offered to take me home. I took his offer. It turned out his family was out. He dragged me to his room, ripped the ceremonial feather from my neck and . . ." She clamped her arms around herself. Her voice lowered to a whisper. "He hurt me a lot. He pushed me with my face into the bed and did it . . . from behind. It was like all my insides were on fire. I bled for days and was too ashamed to tell my mother, because . . . I thought it was my fault that it didn't go as they had told me. And then I started growing and my parents went to him to negotiate. I couldn't even look at him, I hated him so much. As soon as the child was born, I refused to have anything to do with it. I don't even know if it was a boy or girl. He was about to leave the country. I presume he took the child and left."

She shuddered.

"I hope I haven't hurt you."

She shook her head. "I was afraid, but it was quite nice."

Isandor closed her in his arms. She smelled nice and her body was soft and warm. It pleased him to feel her arms around his waist.

He stroked her back and ran his hands through her bushy hair. Then his fingertips found the fastening to her bodice. He pulled the laces.

From one thing came another. It was very, very pleasant.

Afterwards, Tamerane poured tea and they sat in bed under the comfortably warm blanket drinking it.

Isandor showed her the books that he had brought, old dusty tomes compared to the splendid volumes in her collection.

She opened the first book, and her mouth fell open. "Wow, these are incredibly old."

Isandor explained how he and Carro used to scour the market stalls in the Outer City, a settlement that was burned to the ground and that no longer existed. "We risked our lives for these books, back under the regime of the old Knights. Somehow we believed that the act of acquiring knowledge is not something that should be controlled by anyone. It sounds rather pompous when I say it, but as a boy I would never have thought of it that way."

"Your youth sounds a bit like mine. I found a lot of all these things in old collections cast aside after people die. My parents never liked me hoarding all this stuff, but it was one thing they could never stop me from doing."

Isandor nodded. That was how he had obtained many of his books. "Why did you become interested?"

"Because my father said that girls shouldn't." She grinned, and he laughed. That was the best thing about her: that wicked smile.

He couldn't resist reaching out for her cheek. "You know I like you much better when you smile?"

She smiled again.

They spoke of the shape of the world, and the function of the stars and the moon, which would be big and fat, and then fade to little more than a speck and would then disappear for periods of time before coming back as a speck that grew into a mottled disc.

She set up a looking glass in front of the window and they gazed, stark naked, at the few stars that were visible during the day. There was a group of wandering stars in the sky, and Isandor could see them clearly: a large dot and three smaller ones in a row.

"They move quickly," Tamerane said.

It was cold near the window, so they got back into the bed for more warm tea. He was enjoying himself more than he had during the past years.

It was as if it had taken him this long to realise that his life had been empty, a string of important but soulless meetings, drinking a good deal too much with his advisors afterwards, then coping with Jevaithi's comments about it. There was no purpose, no future. The queen ruled officially and he was an afterthought. His official function was still to be determined, as it had for the past twenty years, since there were always more important matters to be attended to. Nothing excited him . . . until now.

He took the tea from her hand, and set it on the bedside table. Then he turned to her, cupped her face in both her hands and kissed her on the mouth.

She gave a surprised squeak, but then sank back into the pillows and replied. The tea was forgotten as he entered her a second time, slowly, languidly, watching the expression of bliss on her face.

Isandor left with reluctance, hoping that once again their task would be unsuccessful. She was interesting, intelligent and had provoking ideas. Talking with her took his mind off more depressing matters: worries about icefire, about Arania and about what he was going to tell Jevaithi.

Over the next few days, Isandor watched the expedition prepare. Trucks were delivered to the Knights' eyrie and drew a lot of attention from the public. They needed to be adapted to run on firebricks, because the City of Glass had no supplies of wood. There was a firebrick making machine, too, that compressed grass and leaves into fuel. Zaina did a lot of this work.

Isandor was sending Jeito on this expedition. Jeito had a passable command of the language, and her companion, Farey, was half-Aranian. He was also sending Rider Tomason, a Senior Knight of the new guard. He wished he could go himself. It had been a long time since he had travelled out of the city by any means that didn't involve taking a complete entourage, with guards and servants.

But he was too busy in the City. There were laws to be rewritten, meetings to be held, people to speak to, and that was just without a potential icefire emergency. He couldn't leave all of those things to Jevaithi. For one, he wasn't sure how well she'd do them.

Life had been hard as apprentice Knight in the Outer City, but sometimes he cherished the memories of the freedom he used to have.

Zaina worked hard and gave no one any reason to suspect that she might cause trouble. After she finished adapting the trucks, she looked at the palace's pipes and water tanks. She did maintenance on the lift mechanism; she looked at the hot water boiler and the heating. She groomed and fed the bears, and cleaned and oiled Jevaithi's coach.

All this while Isandor spent a lot of time staring idly out the window.

He remembered when he and Jevaithi had been on the run, and how he'd even learned to milk goats. How lazy and decadent had he become, with people seeing to his every whim? Maybe he needed to fly more often.

Yes. Once they were on top of this icefire issue, he would shove aside all the administrative jobs once a month and travel to one of the regions.

He turned when the door opened and Carro came in. He came to stand next to him and they watched out the window while Zaina worked in the garden.

"Hard worker," Carro said, nodding at her. "I worry a bit about her background."

"Is there anything about her that we don't already know?" Isandor looked at him, and gestured at the couch. They both sat down. Isandor nodded at the drinks cupboard, but Carro shook his head.

"She flatly refuses to leave the compound. Whenever we have any jobs that require travel into the city, she finds someone else to do it."

"You did see what she looked like when she came in, right?"

"I did."

"Did anyone find out who did that to her?"

"No. Jeito said she was tighter than a noble's arse."

Isandor laughed. Only Jeito would say things like that.

"The patrol compiled a file on her," Carro continued. "She came into the City of Glass in the wave of immigration with the rebuilding. She came from Kadrish. She sold herself as a mechanic."

"She *is* a mechanic. A good one."

"Yes. But no one can track any of her history in Arania."

"I don't necessarily see that as a problem. It's not like we have ready access to Aranian records. So we don't know where she comes from, which means she is not from any of the influential families and she hasn't escaped from any of the princes' harems. I see that as a good thing. On top of that, she's familiar with the land and language."

"Yes." Carro sighed. "That doesn't mean I have to like it. In order to be a mechanic, she would have received some training. It's rare for Aranians to educate their women, because all of them are needed to make babies for the powerful men—"

"By the way, is there any evidence that the wave of infertility is hitting Arania as well as us?"

"If it was, would they tell us?"

"No, but we might notice, like back in the days when the Knights abducted Chevakian girls, before they knew that icefire would kill the women, and brought them to the City of Glass because the Chevakians are far more fertile."

Carro said, "I understand what you mean, but no, there is no evidence of anything of the sort happening. If anything, they wouldn't allow a woman to leave the country if that was the case."

"They might still not allow women to leave. She might have just left regardless, and that might be why you can't find any record of her being in contact with Arania. I suggest you might try treating her well. She might be amenable to parting with useful information."

"Milking her like a spy?"

"If that's what you want to call it. I have to admit that I'm a bit concerned over all these Aranian interests in our city."

"They're all refugees," Carro said. "We've got a long list of Chevakians and Aranians who live in the Harbour District as result of the forms we distributed after the alert."

"Make sure that someone runs checks on who these people are," Isandor said.

"I'm not sure that's necessary, or that they will appreciate it, but if you wish, I can do that."

"I do wish that."

Later, Isandor had dinner with Jevaithi, who had fully recovered, and had been quite cheerful for the last few days, suspiciously so, in fact.

He asked her about it.

"I'm seeing Rider Barton," she said, her chin in the air. "I asked him and he said yes."

"Of course he did!" Isandor probably sounded more indignant than he should, but oh, how he hated it that his sister used her status to force people to do what she wanted. Being old school, Rider Barton had obedience to the queen rammed into his head, no matter what Isandor told him. Back in the day when he came up through the ranks, being asked to father the queen's child was the ultimate honour for an Eagle Knight. Except, to Isandor's knowledge, Rider Barton had a male lover, and had been with this man for many years. Jevaithi would know that.

"Isn't that great?" she said.

"No, it's not. Jevaithi, I wish you would stop this charade. You're not going to have a child—"

"Why do you hate me so much?"

"I don't hate you. I love you. I just hate to see you suffer. We've tried—what?—more than twenty-five times. It's not going to happen. The midwife says that you might die next time. I don't want that to happen."

"We need an heir."

"Yes. And I'm seeing a breeder." There. He'd said it.

"You—what?" Her eyes were wide.

"A breeder. You know. Someone who will have a child for us."

"What? Who is this woman?" Her voice was full of suspicion.

"It is someone I respect as a person—"

"How can you do this to me?"

"To you? What does that even mean? How can I help you so that you don't have to die for an impossible wish?"

"How can you visit and share someone's bed and not tell me about it? After all the things we went through together."

"By the skylights, what has gotten into you?"

"You slept with her!"

"Yes, that's what generally happens with these arrangements."

"You didn't tell me."

"She is a *breeder!*"

"Did you enjoy it?"

He stared at her, suddenly understanding her problem, and he couldn't believe how he hadn't seen it before. "You're jealous."

And yes, Jevaithi probably had every reason to feel that way, if she wanted to act like a jilted spouse.

Tamerane was *not* just a breeder. When he thought of her, his heart sped up and his face glowed. He'd had some *thoughts* about her that he considered too secret to even admit to himself.

Before he knew that they were brother and sister, Isandor had slept with Jevaithi, many times. He remembered how she used to cling onto him when making love and how, when he found out she was his sister and stopped sleeping with her, she had become distant.

Because she still wants me to sleep with her. Because she depended on him. Because she loved him and had no one else. Because she was lonely and afraid.

Look at her sitting across the table from him, pale-faced, desperate, broken. Even when the land became prosperous, she had never found happiness in the palace, never had a lover, never had a child, never cared much for any of his rebuilding projects.

The fear has broken her.

The fear of the first fifteen years of her life, living in fear amongst the Knights, constantly watching out for that one Knight who was going to rape her. Try putting a happy face on that situation, as a fifteen-year-old girl, living utterly alone in an opulent room in the top of the palace.

By the skylights, Jevaithi.

Isandor rose and pulled her into his arms. She cried with wracking sobs into his shoulder.

CHAPTER 15

IT WAS EARLY morning and the streets were shrouded in pale blue light when the convoy of trucks left the palace. There were five trucks, two with trailers full of tents, mats, fuel, food and other supplies. Once they left the city, they would be joined by three eagles.

Zaina sat in the cabin of the second truck with the driver, a young man named Daro, who, like her, had been employed by the Eagle Knights for the duration of the expedition. He was a young local man, not a Knight and not an Apprentice either. Zaina had learned that there were no people in the City of Glass who got fewer perks than Knight Apprentices, so they would not be allowed to come on this expedition.

While they were going through the streets, Zaina stuck to the back of the cabin, worried that Nayek might see her if she sat in the front. He would probably have his men on the lookout for her.

She had not left the palace since getting there, and had not seen any sign of him or his men in the palace. He'd probably been bragging about being able to get into the palace. She didn't think he really could.

But now she was outside again, and Nayek would be watching. He had to be furious that she had escaped him.

The trucks travelled through the streets at walking pace.

People in the city went out of their way and lined up along the

159

side of the road to watch. Some of them waved and cheered, although Zaina had no idea if they knew where they were going or what they were doing.

The leader of the expedition was a Senior Knight by the name of Rider Tomason and he was in the front vehicle with the maps. The back tray was full of packs and boxes and machines. She had been wondering what they were for, and had been told that they were to measure the weather and the incline of the terrain, and to make detailed maps.

As mechanic, she was interested in how this would work. The Chevakians were very keen on measuring things, and those disciplines seemed to have spread to the City of Glass.

She liked measuring things.

Once they left the city behind, the trucks picked up the pace. The terrain was surprisingly uneven, with grass tussocks and unexpected channels and holes. The first truck was following trails made by farmers with carts, and those tracks didn't always go anywhere. Rider Tomason would use the mountains for navigation, and would take directions from the birds that flew above. Zaina could see the riders on the birds sometimes. Rider Jeito was one of them.

The terrain was without trees and the low grass made for good visibility. All Daro needed to do was follow the first truck across the bumpy ground. A stack of three cages with messenger gulls inside swayed ominously, and their occupants flapped and squawked at each other.

After having lived in fear for the past few days, Zaina finally relaxed. She was out of Nayek's influence, at least for the duration of this expedition.

For most of the day, the trucks bumped over this plain, which looked deceptively flat, but was full of sinkholes. Twice, they had to rescue a vehicle sunk to the axles in the mud. There were no trees for a winch, so they strung several other trucks together as a counter weight. Everyone got very muddy.

Rider Tomason stopped the truck several times to get out and take positions from the sun.

The compass was behaving strangely, Zaina picked up from a snatch of conversation that she picked up during the midday break.

Tomason and Jeito discussed the implications. Tomason said that the pass was ahead; Jeito said that they were too far to the west.

Tomason argued that he could see the saddle in the snow-covered mountain, and though they might *seem* to be too far to the west, there was a swamp to the east and they needed to go around it.

Jeito said that there were many tracks through the swamp and it hadn't rained much recently.

"Seriously, who knows this land best?" She spread her hands and walked off to tend the eagles. Jeito had two mounted companions, silent clean-shaven, stubble haired men who appeared nameless and faceless. One of them would give Zaina a penetrating look that chilled her, but as long as those riders followed the group, she was free from Nayek.

One of the eagles had caught a deer.

The Knights cut and gutted the animal and strung it up on the back of one of the trucks. The eagle could keep the head and forelegs, and while the travellers ate and drank hot aromatic tea, it ripped the meat off the bones in long threads.

They continued in the afternoon, when the sun vanished behind the mountains. By the time it was starting to go dark, the convoy had arrived at the bottom of the mountain slopes. They were, as Jeito had said, off course. She was angry about it, and Tomason was angry about it. Darkness was fast falling and they had to track east, where the ruins of an abandoned settlement stood out against the meagre light.

The ground was rough and it took them until it was almost dark to get there, which made Jeito even grumpier.

They parked the trucks in a circle. The ground was barely thawed, and muddy. They had to unload the luggage from the truck beds and roll their mats out up there.

Two Knights made a fire, while another strung up the deer and hung it to roast. All the travellers brought drums and buckets to sit on around the fire, while the meat cooked and the wonderful smell spread around the camp.

The men told tall tales, mostly from competitions and games within the Knighthood. Zaina listened, alternating between enjoying the careless atmosphere and despairing that when she came back to the City of Glass, and Nayek came back to her, she would have very little to tell him that he would find of interest. These Knights served their king and queen. They had little contact with business and noble interests. For all that she could see, the nobility in the City of Glass was considered quaint. They had their own secluded lives and did not mingle much with the citizens and the rulers of today. Was there a way to explain this to Nayek that wouldn't involve her getting punished for being lazy?

The fire died down and, one by one, people retired to their mats. Zaina climbed into the truck bed next to Daro, who told her good-night and did not as much as blink an eye or make the slightest suggestion to her. Damn it, these people were honourable. Whatever they were doing in the mountains besides investigating the state of the old roads, their aims served the people.

It got cold.

Zaina lay on her back, looking at the sky.

The sky was clear, showing a multitude of stars, and even showing the twin bands of stars that stretched across the sky. Zaina had learned some astrology, because every Aranian learned it, but she must have forgotten all her star signs, because she couldn't find any of them. The moon was a small crescent shape in the southern sky, casting barely any light.

The sky over the mountains showed an unusual green band. She watched it glimmer and move through the northern sky like a snake. Was this was people called the skylights?

It was an eerie green light that made the mist rising from the ground look ghostly.

And then it got very cold.

Even after living in the City of Glass for the last few years, Zaina still didn't handle cold very well, and she couldn't sleep. She was shivering too much. She would have to find a way to make a warmer bed. Find another blanket, or open the sack that made up her blanket and fill it with warm things, like hair from the next deer they caught, or feathers.

She crawled out of her bed, dropped herself off the back of the truck and walked across the campsite. The moon had long since vanished over the horizon and it was really dark. She had to be careful to avoid rubble and clumps of grass and could see the outlines of the ruined walls only where they blocked starlight.

There wasn't much left of the town that had once stood here, just some ruins and even fewer walls that still stood upright. None of the buildings still had a roof.

Zaina had learned that, before the rule of the Eagle Knights, this had been a reasonably lively place. Trucks would come up from Chevakia and goods were exchanged here, because they were far enough away from the City of Glass that Chevakians could come here with minimal protection against icefire. The people who lived here would put the goods on the train. They had come across the old rails several times during the day. Most of the track was overgrown with grass. Sometimes there were old telegraph posts, too, but the wires always lay on the ground.

What had happened to these people, she asked, and it turned out that the Knights had closed the borders and the town had slowly died when the reason for people to live here had disappeared.

Nearby stood a tall wall with the chimney still on top. The roof had fallen in and the inside of the house was a treacherous ground of rubble, but it was perfectly dark for a piss. Ugh the air was so cold on her backside.

She had finished and was threading her way out of the rubble-strewn ground when something rustled nearby.

Zaina froze and held her breath. She squinted at the grotesque shapes of bushes and rocks and jagged walls. It was too dark to make out anything on the ground. It could have been an animal, or maybe the eagles had stirred.

No further sound came so Zaina continued.

She could already see the trucks ahead when someone grabbed her from behind, clamping a hand over her mouth and holding her in a strong grip. Zaina recognised the smell of leather and sweat.

How had Nayek followed the group without getting noticed?

Zaina struggled, but he was much too strong, dragging her through the shrubbery to the back of one of the ruins.

He pushed her up against the wall. "This is your second disobedience." His voice was a sibilant whisper.

"What do you want? I'm doing your work for you. If you leave me alone, I can actually do it, instead of having to be nervous about you hanging around."

"You never came back for the most important task I was going to give you to complete during this expedition. I could go on about your continued disobedience, but we'd be here all night. This expedition is going into the mountains. Once you're at the top of the pass, you're in Aranian territory."

Zaina didn't know about that. She always thought that the location of the border was a matter of disagreement, but that the closest land to the southern plain that Arania could claim to be theirs was in the middle of the mountains.

He continued, "This expedition must not reach Arania. You must stop them."

"I'm a junior member of the group. How can I stop them? I make no decisions."

"I'll let you figure that out. But once you cross that pass, you're dead. When you tell your pathetic Knights about me, you're dead, too."

He let her go and vanished in the darkness. She heard no horse's footsteps, no rustling.

Zaina did not sleep for the rest of the night.

PEOPLE STARTED MOVING around the camp before daylight, and since it was dark until midmorning, that was easy to do.

Zaina joined the others around the fire for breakfast and then helped to pack up the trucks. Every bone in her body ached, and she shivered so badly that she thought she would not get warm again. Standing at the top of the truck bed, looking over the campsite and surrounding ruins, she couldn't spot any sign of Nayek or his transport. Yet, she was sure that she hadn't dreamed about his visit, because dreams usually made no sense at all.

Nayek's words made far too much sense. Frightfully so.

The column started before daylight, zigzagging up the steep mountainside. Sometimes their path crossed sections of the old road, mostly eroded away, with missing sections of paving. Carting goods up here must have been hard work for those Chevakians. The engines they had back then were really primitive and this area would have been covered in snow.

Low clouds rolled in, halfway through the morning, taking away

Zaina's view of the plain below. She'd been keeping an eye out for anything that indicated that Nayek followed, and the mist made her feel trapped. Even the eagles were gone from view.

They climbed higher and higher. The trucks found it hard going in the thin mountain air. They were now mostly following the old road, but it was uneven, eroded by runoff water, and they often needed to stop and fill in holes. They didn't break out of the cloud cover until the end of the afternoon, when suddenly all the mist was gone and the view behind them consisted of a bath of fluffy clouds.

"Wow," Daro said. His breath steamed even inside the cabin.

Zaina hid in her jacket. Up on the mountainside, she could see the saddle of the forbidden pass not far ahead.

She was meant to stop the group reaching the position where Nayek declared the border to be?

If either Supreme Rider Barton or the king got wind of this, they would consider his declaration an act of war. No one had ever considered the pass as the border to Arania. Certainly, the old road to Chevakia was never considered to cross Arania back in the days before the war. What was Nayek's game?

It turned out it wasn't really the pass she had seen from further down, because when they got there, the passage descended into a small valley before rising to a higher level. There, in stark black and white against the low light of the sun, was the saddle of the pass with a giant glacier crawling down, like a hammock filled with snow.

The trucks picked their way down the slope into the valley. The ground was treacherous here, slippery, with loose stone beds and patches of icy snow. They had to cross many streams of icy water. Twice a truck got stuck, and Zaina had to wade into the water to restart the engine.

Zaina had to put snow chains around all the truck wheels before they could get back to climbing, slowly zigzagging over the face of the glacier.

When the first truck reached the saddle, it stopped on the gently sloping snowy ground and the passenger door opened. Rider Tomason got out and disappeared over the rim of the ridge.

Zaina's heart jumped.

This was where Nayek said the expedition could not come. Maybe there were guards, or an ambush.

But when she and Daro arrived up there, Rider Tomason sat on his knees in the snow taking measurements with his box of devices. The view to the north from the pass showed more mountains poking out of fluffy clouds. The last pink tinge from the sunlight gilded the cloud tops with purple. The sky overhead was deep blue. The first stars were about to come out, but the sky at the western horizon was still pink.

"Time to stop for the night," he said when Zaina joined him.

She turned her face into the icy wind. "Here?"

"The downward slope could be dangerous. There might be avalanches."

True. Ahead, a Knight on an eagle soared over the clouds. It was a strange sight to have a view of him and his bird from any other position than below.

Zaina studied the steep slope into the mist, the ill-marked path they would have to take tomorrow, into the territory which Nayek considered part of Arania. It felt strange standing here with the leader, this highly ranked Knight who probably considered her no more than a speck of dirt. Sometimes she was surprised that these men spoke to her at all.

She asked, "Where *is* the border, actually?"

Rider Tomason rose. He waved his hand to the right. "That side over there is all Chevakia." Then he waved to the left. "That side is Arania. Most rulers consider the mountains no man's land."

"Most?"

"Most. At any time in military history, any country that has occupied the mountains has done so in preparation of a war."

Zaina's heart thudded. "Why is that?"

"Because this region is by far the most vulnerable of all the borders. Few troops patrol the area, and in time of peace, no one starts disagreements about the position of the borders. This land is harsh, remote and holds few resources. It is simply not worth fighting over, unless one is looking for a reason to fight."

He spread his hands. In his right hand he was holding a device with a round dial.

"What is that?" she asked.

He held the device up. The dial had a little red needle that pointed to the middle of a scale marked with Chevakian characters.

"This is a barygraph," he said. "It's a device to measure what the Chevakians call *sonorics* and we call icefire."

"I thought it was supposed to exist only in the City of Glass."

"Supposed to. The device that existed there was so strong that it masked all other sources. Now that it's gone, these other sources become visible."

"Is that dangerous?" She nodded at the dial. These people were strangely obsessed with those devices.

"At this level, no."

They joined the others by the fire and ate a very plain meal of dried meat and salty soup.

Zaina had thought that once the wind died down, it would stop being cold; but, if anything, it got even colder. The fire went out and people started going to bed.

Zaina climbed onto the truck bed next to Daro, who was already asleep. She hadn't been able to do anything about her insufficient blanket. She shoved some of her spare clothes into the sack, and kept her jacket on, but she was still cold. And she worried about Nayek.

She wanted to scream *Watch out, we're being observed by spies*. But that would certainly get her killed.

What had Rider Tomason said about war?

Did this mean that Arania was looking to create trouble? Attack peaceful groups in the mountains and insist that the mountains were theirs? What was the point of that anyway? Nobody would be stupid enough to spill any blood over these stupid, cold mountains. They were useless. That was why no one had bothered to make an agreement about them.

Her mind churned. She heard Nayek in every little sound. Snores and bumps from her fellow travellers became footsteps in the snow. The cracking of the ice became the clopping of horse's hooves. If this expedition never returned, it would be her fault. Several times, she strained her legs to get up, wake Rider Tomason to tell him about Nayek. But if she did that, they would be dead anyway and then maybe two countries would go to war over it.

Nayek had done this to deliberately put her in a difficult position. She could not stop the expedition without sabotaging the vehicles, and if she did that, she'd endanger everyone's life, and the Knights would punish her. She did not want to betray these people, because they had done nothing that deserved betrayal.

She sat up on the bed of the truck, her knees pulled up to her chest with the blanket wrapped around her, staring at the sky while the others slept. The green flashes she had seen the previous night returned, long filaments of green and pink that reached over the pass deeper into the mountains.

The night was as still as death. The light from the sky was strong enough to make the snow glimmer. The other trucks sat like square boxes in the snow.

One eagle sat on a rock and two had ensconced themselves on top of the trailer. Daro said eagles didn't get cold feet, but she thought they did. The two sat pressed up against each other, their feathers all fluffed up.

She was shivering uncontrollably.

In Arania, riders would sleep against their horses when traversing the plains in winter. Machines were useless for warmth when they weren't running, and the fire had long since gone out. She was so cold and so incredibly tired. She just wanted to be warm and she wanted to sleep.

Zaina gathered up her inadequate blanket and dragged her mat through the snow to the trailer where the eagles sat. The animals only stirred briefly. She had heard that they could be aggressive, and that Knights didn't like other people interfering with the birds, but these birds remained quiet, even when Zaina climbed up on the trailer.

She stepped between the feathered bodies, put her mat down and snuggled up. A wing reached out and half-covered her. Underneath the feathers, the eagles were incredibly warm. Zaina drifted off to sleep. Her last thought was that if Nayek attacked during the night or early morning, it would at least happen while she was asleep and she would suffer only briefly.

CHAPTER 16

ON THE DAY of his trip, Javes got up before sunrise.

He carried all his packs into the back yard and set them next to the camel's pen while the camel ate. Then he put the saddle on the camel, filled up all the water skins and tied them and his packs to the saddle. He checked that he had everything; then he climbed into the saddle. The camel rose with a groan.

The sun was just coming over the horizon as he left town. The camel cast a long shadow over the stubbled hillside. The light was still soft, the sky above pink and the landscape orange. It was pretty, in its own strange way.

For the first half of the morning, he headed west, until he picked up the path to the area that was marked on the map as a place where people from the city sometimes came to watch the stars. This was a rock-strewn outcrop called Red Hill. He found a little oasis at the bottom of the red cliff, a dark, still pond that reflected the rocks perfectly. A little patch of real vegetation grew around it, with tall palm trees and grass so green that it hurt his eyes.

Javes took a break here, giving the camel a rest. He tied it to a post that someone had driven into the ground long ago, maybe for this purpose, and left the camel to attack the green grass on the bank of the pond.

Javes climbed the hill. It was coming up on midmorning, and the air was already hot. The hill wasn't particularly high, but at the top,

169

he could see over the surrounding undulating terrain. The wind, hot and dry as furnace, cooled the sweat on his skin.

He sat in the shade of a rocky outcrop, eating some dried fruit and drinking water. There were signs in the little shelter that other people had visited here: a piece of a wrapper, an empty bottle. Someone had stacked a pile of stones.

From up here, the view was as impressive as it was desolate: red hill after red hill stretched to the dusty horizon. The land here was rockier than it was to the west, and this probably made it more suitable for travel.

He descended to the pond, where he poured some water over himself and made sure his water bags were all completely filled up.

Before he was ready to continue, he completed the final part of his disguise. First he found the nail paint and turned his fingernails blue. Then he took the length of linen from his bag and started wrapping himself. He'd practiced this in the living room of Pashtan's house and had cut the pieces at the right length. The trickiest bit was the head, but he had also worked out how to position the fabric so he could still see and breathe.

So disguised, he approached the camel, but it merely gave him an indifferent eye and continued grazing.

Javes got back into the saddle.

This was where all paths stopped and navigation became important. As meteorology student, he had learned to do this by the sun, stars, sextant and compass.

He also left markers of paint on each landmark he passed. Later on, once he hit the sand plains, this might well become impossible.

The sun rose, casting its shadows in front of him. Having grown up in a place where the midday sun hung in the north, having it in the south was a novelty.

It was hot in the valleys, and on the ridges the oven-like wind buffeted him. He stopped every time he came to a place with a view to check for sand devils. He would also check his pocket barymeter. The needle remained, fortunately, glued to the left side.

Whenever he reached the top of a hill, he looked around for signs of other people. He couldn't shake the feeling that someone was following him, but it was probably just his fears speaking.

When the shadows grew long, he stopped at the bottom of a hill by a clump of straggly, leafless bushes. He hobbled the camel and it wandered around tearing branches off those bushes. They looked dead, but he didn't think they were.

Javes climbed a little way up the hill to look at the valley he had just traversed. You could see the vein of ground water going through it by the winding path of what passed for vegetation.

A little thrill went through him. He'd learned about this as part of his studies: recognising the signs of weather and the movement of air and water on the land.

Had *anyone* ever charted this land? Had anyone been here? There was not a sign of civilisation to be seen anywhere.

He went back down before it got too dark to see, because one thing he had brought only little of was lamp oil.

He rolled out his mat and ate biscuits, dried fruit and salted meat, watching the camel graze. It finally gave up and lay down. Javes dragged the mat over to where it lay, and used the camel's hairy flank as a backrest while he watched the stars come out.

Some people in Tiverius held great stock by the star signs. They assigned good or bad luck according to the position of the wandering stars and your month of birth. Tutors at the doga would sometimes poke fun at these people. The point of star signs, they said, is purely to know where you are. Wandering stars are useless for that, because they move around too much. Wandering stars were very good for counting months and years. They did not determine luck and misfortune and those who put too much stock in studying the stars and reading meaning into their positions were wasting their time. That's what the tutors said, at least.

When asked, Chief Meteorologist Viki had said that he agreed somewhat, but that he also didn't want to discount any discipline that made an objective study of natural phenomena. No one was exactly sure what the stars were. Other suns, people said, or other worlds, seen from very far off. His favourite theory—albeit thoroughly discredited—was that the stars were pinpricks of sunlight that peeped through a black cloth that was drawn across the sky every night.

The official position of the Scriptorium was that the stars were very far away. They surrounded the world to help people find their way at night. Also, the further you were from Tiverius, the more important the stars became, and that was why there were so many of them in the sky here.

And look, there were even streaking stars, and the pale green glimmer returned to the northern sky.

Javes eventually went to sleep leaning against the flank of the camel. He had to move in the middle of the night, because he didn't know that camels snored, but it did so, loudly.

Then it got up and started tearing at bushes again.

Daylight came much too soon.

Javes travelled north for two days. He marked his position on the map. The land remained rocky, rugged, with occasional veins of vegetation. Once he dug into the ground and found water. It smelled foul so he didn't drink it, but the camel had no such qualms, and it gave him confidence because he knew that he could survive if he needed.

He was now deep into the territory that Pashtan had marked *DO NOT GO HERE*, and he had not found out what had prompted his tutor to write that. He could travel for another two days before he had to turn back to Ysherra to look after the weather stations.

On the morning of the third day, he climbed a hill as he usually did, and spotted sunlight glinting off a shining surface to the west of his intended route. He'd heard of people having spyglasses that allowed you to see in the distance, but he thought that those were limited to the captains of the balloons in the army. He wished he had one of those.

He made a note of the direction and marked the spot on the map where he thought the glimmer was. He plotted his course in that direction and included details on how to get back onto his intended course.

For much of the day, he found himself traversing a hard, dry plain. Occasionally there were lower areas where salt had risen to the surface and sometimes there was evidence of cracked mud.

So, clearly, it did rain here, or it had done so in the past, probably infrequently, because there was no evidence of vegetation.

The glinting surface had been on the other side of this floodplain, but when he got there, the terrain rose steeply, he couldn't see it anymore. It could have been a smooth rock face or an illusion of the light. The light was turning golden, so he decided to set up camp here before turning back to his intended course. There were few bushes for the camel to nibble on. Javes ate dried fruit and salt meat, and had to admit to himself that he was getting thoroughly sick of the menu options, and also that he should probably turn back tomorrow, because the land was too vast, and he would need to get a better idea of where to look for these metal artefacts. Maybe the windwalkers had to dig for them. Anything exposed to the air would stain.

He still held the globe in his pocket. Seated on his mat, he took it out and studied it yet again. It was the size of a large marble and wasn't as heavy as one would expect a metal object of that size to be. He judged it to be hollow.

The wire loops were most curious. They protruded from one end and bent around the curve of the globe and re-joined at the other end. There were six such wires. When he dropped the globe, it bounced over the ground on these wires until it came to rest on one of the two spots where the wires joined and disappeared into the globe. Whatever was this thing for? Why was it worth so much? What was more: who had made it?

He had by now been trekking through the desert for four days and had become used to sleeping in the open. Also, he had been walking a fair bit to give the camel a break and at night he was exhausted. He slept so well that the first sign he had that something was wrong was a snort from the camel.

Javes sat up—

—staring into the sharp point of a dagger, held by an arm wrapped in cloth. A set of vicious eyes glared at him from a slit in cloth wound around a man's head. One eye was dark brown; the other, light blue.

Windwalkers. Three of them, one holding the dagger and two watching silently. They had come with three camels. Those animals, with the magnificent leather side-plates and headgear, nosed his camel. The animals *knew* each other. Stupid, stupid. That was why the merchant had been so keen to get rid of the beast. And the camel had needed little guidance and had given him little trouble because it knew this country.

"I'm sorry," he said, holding up his hands, staring at the dagger. "I don't mean to cause you any harm."

The windwalkers spoke to each other. Their language was strange, full of rattling sounds.

Two were men, the third was either a young man or a woman. It was hard to see under all the layers of cloth, but he was going to go with a woman, because her figure was slight.

Eventually, one of the men gestured for Javes to get up. The sun was just clearing the horizon and shone straight in his eyes. The three seemed fascinated by them. The colour, probably. His eyes were very light brown, while theirs were much darker. The woman took his hand and ran dirt-engrained, callus-hardened fingers over his skin. Javes' skin had become a lot darker in the weeks that he'd been out with Pashtan, but he still wasn't as dark as she was.

She rubbed the skin as if she suspected that he wore paint.

One of the men pulled at the cloth with which he had hoped to disguise himself as windwalker, but he looked ridiculous next to them. Yes, they wore cloth wound around their limbs, but there was a pattern to it, with pieces of cloth wrapped around so that the top looked like a hair plait. That would have to involve more than one piece of fabric.

The men made Javes get onto his camel, and tethered it onto the back of the saddle of the leader. Then they set off along a narrow track uphill. The camel made no protest, plodding after the leader's camel, its head held low, occasionally trying to make a detour while reaching for dry bushes.

The track zigzagged across the bare mountainside. Occasionally, they had to traverse shale fields, where the camels' footing was treacherous because of the many loose stones.

It was close to midday when they reached the crest of the mountain pass, and Javes could see the thing that had made the glint that he had spotted. It was a . . .

He had no idea what it was. A giant bowl-like structure pointed at the sky, the size of a city block across. It sat atop a pedestal many floors high. The bowl was covered in a thin, translucent, cloth-like material, held up in the middle, that made the structure like a tent. The inside of the tent was misty with humidity.

A group of regular tents of the dark and thick fabric Javes had sometimes seen in town clustered at the base of the pedestal, in the shade cast by the giant bowl. A great number of camels stood tethered on what looked like a section of a metal fence, from which hung food troughs and water bowls.

The surrounding hills were bare, covered in sharp rocks and jutting outcrops.

What a strange place for a camp, and what was that strange bowl thing anyway?

As they came closer, the bowl appeared even bigger than it had from a distance. Javes judged it to be made of either wood or metal, with many supporting struts. A ladder led from the pedestal into the bottom of the bowl. A steady stream of young boys and girls were climbing up with baskets containing what appeared to be mud and coming back with the empty baskets.

What in all of the heavens' name were they doing?

The leader stopped and waved for Javes to get off the camel. He tapped the beast on the leg to make it sink to its knees.

He let himself slide from the saddle, aware that people stopped walking, stopped talking and turned around. Some came closer, but most watched, silently, from a distance. Most wore their coverings of cloth, although only few covered their heads as well. The windwalkers had mostly dark hair, but a number of them bleached random parts of their hair white.

The terrain was exposed in this desolate mountain pass, and the tents, made from thick material, flapped and strained against the wind. Clouds of dust and grit blew across the ground.

Javes' companions set off into the camp. The walkways between the tents were narrow, cluttered with thick guy ropes and stacks of supplies in bags or bales or crates, many of them under nets that were also tied down with metal tent pegs.

They had left the camels behind with the others. Javes was afraid that he'd never get his camel back. Without it, he couldn't return to Ysherra. What about his job, what about the people of the town?

You should have thought about that before you came here, a voice in his head said.

They progressed into the camp, coming closer to the base of the pedestal. It was made from a large square piece of stone many paces across. You could fit at least four of five Tiverian mansions with their gardens in that space. The base consisted of a single slab. Javes boggled to think of how many people and carts they would have needed to shift that piece of stone. And where had it come from? Not locally, because the desert stone was orange.

The captors led Javes into a tent that stood at the bottom of the pedestal. It was quite a large tent, but the pedestal stone dwarfed it.

Two windwalker men—without face coverings—stood on either side of the tent's entrance. One of them held up a spear with a serrated blade. The other carried a . . . whatever type of gun that was. Javes was familiar with the powder guns, but this silver metal thing was nothing like the heavy and clunky weapons that some of the guards carried. He also wore a curious belt with a silver buckle and many metal boxes that sat snugly at his waist.

He and his fellow guard opened the tent flaps.

Javes followed his captor inside. It was dark and it took Javes' eyes a little while to get used to the sudden drop in light.

The group had entered a small room with a large mat in the middle. All three of his companions unwound the cloth from their heads. They were, as he suspected, two men and a woman. All three had black skin but with unsightly white patches. The face of one of the men was half dark, half pale. One of his eyes was black, the other blue. The woman's face was reasonably normal, but her neck was covered in white patches, which extended to her left arm.

The other man was the least affected. His white skin only covered his hands.

Javes did his best not to stare.

A couple of low benches stood around the perimeter of the room and this was where his companions left their shoes and gestured for him to do the same.

They wore thin, cloth-like shoes, but Javes wore heavy boots and his feet smelled of dirty socks.

Ew.

A young boy scurried from further into the tent and brought him a cloth. It was wet, cool and fresh.

He asked, "What am I supposed to do with this?"

But his companions were already wiping faces and hands, and he did the same, relishing the coolness of the water on his skin. He wondered if it was considered a bad thing to wash his feet. They really smelled very bad.

But none of his companions washed their feet. The boy collected the cloths in an empty bowl and the three led Javes into the tent, where about ten people were gathered. They all looked similar to Javes' captors: extremely dark-skinned with patches of milk-white skin. Sometimes the patches were on the top of their heads, and then their hair was white in that spot, too. If a white patch coincided with an eye, that eye was blue.

In the middle of the tent, on a bed of cushions surrounded by low benches, sat an elderly man. He wore a loose *temuz* of the khaki type that Javes also wore. He didn't wear any of the covering cloths that windwalkers wound around their bodies. Maybe it was because he didn't go outside.

His arms and legs, or at least the part of them that Javes could see, were free of white-skinned patches. His eyes were dark and his skin dark and wrinkled. Neither were as dark as those of the others, but that could be from lack of sunlight.

"Welcome to the home of the patchwork tribe. I am Tiraa, whisperer of the wind." The man looked at Javes with sharp eyes, nodding at the cloth still clumsily wound around Javes' legs and body.

"You're smarter than the others," he said. "You've taken a camel, not a useless horse that only dies in the desert. You've copied our disguise. Badly so, and for no reason at all, but you've thought about it. You have followed our path all the way here. You are very determined. What is your name?"

"Javesius han Demerian. Javes. I'm from Tiverius. I'm a meteorology student."

"Hmmm." He pressed his lips together. "It is a long way to Tiverius."

"I know. Have you been there?" He didn't *think* that this man was a local. His skin was lighter, his eyes were lighter and he lacked the patches of white skin. But maybe his ability to speak the common Chevakian language meant that he dealt with visitors on the tribe's behalf.

"Ha. I have not. But I have heard of the place. Too crowded for my liking."

"I take it that you are originally from further south?"

He snorted. "Young man, learn this about us: you do not ask a windwalker about his place of birth or his family."

"I'm sorry. I'm just curious." Javes guessed that Tiraa was not his real name either. Maybe he'd fled from the south. Maybe he was a criminal. A murderer.

Javes shuddered.

A young girl came to bring a tray with earthenware cups and a large terracotta jug. She poured water from the jug into the cups and handed them out.

The water was fresh but tasted rusty.

Tiraa put his cup down. "Anyway, what you want to trade with us must be worth a lot of money to have gone through all this effort to come here."

Javes said, "I'm not trading anything. I'm only exploring. I'm not a local. I'm a meteorology student from Tiverius. I study the weather."

Tiraa laughed out loud. "The weather, eh? You find much to study here? One day it's hot and windy, and the next day it's hot and windy. I need no study to tell me that. Don't be shy, tell me what you want to buy or trade."

Well, if he was going to be like that . . . Javes took the metal globe out of his pocket. "I was given this by a windwalker, but I don't want to sell it. It made me curious and I wanted to know where the wind-walker had found it." The light caught the polished surface of the globe and the golden threads that encased it.

Everyone in the tent—Tiraa, the three who had brought Javes here, and the young boy who looked after the water—stared at the object in Javes' hand, eyes wide, mouths open.

CHAPTER 17

PROCTOR SADORIUS han Chevonian of the Chevakian doga drew a hand over his face. He desperately did not want to appear uninterested, but the day had been very long and arduous, and he didn't like being yelled at by senators half his age with far less experience.

Not that the senator from the Ensar district didn't have the right to be angry. If Sady represented a distinct—which he did not—and the district was under as much pressure as Ensar, then he would be angry, too. He just wasn't sure that yelling in the doga and accusing the doga of his district's misfortune was the right way to go about it. In his experience, yelling had never been the best way to get help. And today, he was tired of yet another young and keen senator who had to learn this lesson.

Sady signalled to the doga's Speaker, a tall and broad woman from Fairlight, and she brought her hammer down on the bell.

It made a loud *binggggg!*

The senators in the tiered rows of seats in the assembly hall quietened.

"Sit down everyone," the speaker said, her voice prim. "The Proctor will speak."

Sady rose and slowly crossed the floor to the dais. His right knee hurt with every step. He was already looking forward to going home and sitting by the fire with a nice cup of tea. Seriously, he was getting too old for this.

He put his hands on the dais, looking at all those faces of the doga, all those eager representatives who came here from their districts full of hope. All these people who adored him almost like a god.

There were times that he wished that they put together a challenge, voted him out, and gave the job to a younger person with new views.

"We have heard the Ensar senator's plea. We have accepted his request for assistance with drought relief. We are aware that if the doga elects to give Ensar the assistance they have asked for, other districts may be equally entitled to the same. We are unable to promise anything right now, but we will investigate and report within the next few days. I adjourn the meeting for today. The sitting will resume when the necessary information has been collected. This sitting is now closed." He brought the hammer down on the wooden surface of the dais.

And that was it for today.

Senators got up from their benches and made for the exit in groups. As viciously as they had attacked each other in the meeting, they were now chatting as if they were best friends. On odd occasions they even were best friends.

Tomorrow was another day in which to argue.

While Sady collected his folder from the table, the doormen opened the large double doors, letting in the golden sunlight that fell through the windows in the foyer. The members of the assembly streamed out. Sady met up with the doga's Chief Meteorologist, Vikius han Maronian, on the floor of the hall. Viki nodded, and a look of understanding passed between them.

A warm breeze met both men when they entered the foyer. It was autumn, but still very dry and warm and that dry weather was a big part of Sady's problems. If only there was significant rain across Chevakia, so that the crops could be planted and people could stop moving into the towns looking for relief and housing and work and a host of other things which weren't available.

The two set off in the direction of Sady's office walking through the airy stone corridors in amicable silence. Occasionally a waft of warm air drifted in, reminiscent of these passages in summer, when the biting dry air would remind people how fragile their existence was.

"Busy?" Sady asked.

"You don't say." Viki shook his head. He was doing the job Sady had held before becoming proctor; and Sady was well familiar with the many claims on the time and attention of the Chief Meteorologist, especially by the northern districts, along the edge of the desert, where towns lived and died with rainfall which many saw as the Chief Meteorologist's to distribute. He could only imagine what it was like during the drought.

They entered Sady's office, airy, well-appointed, situated above the building's entrance. The windows looked out over the assembly hall's forecourt and the many senators who were streaming through the gates on their way home.

"The problem is much bigger than just Ensar," Viki said when the door shut. "The entire air streams are upset. Nothing is as it should be at this time of the year." He sat down. "I've never seen anything like the current patterns before, and it affects the entire continent, wherever we have measurement points. It would even show up on other points where we don't have measuring devices."

"I guess it probably takes a while for the atmosphere to settle into new patterns after the destruction of the sonorics source."

"Agree, but the disturbance is getting worse, not better. I came to show you this." He opened a folder in the stack of books he carried and took out a piece of barygraph paper, which he handed to Sady.

A wiggly line ran across the paper, so familiar to him, that had been drawn by a barygraph over a period of two weeks. Most of the line sat at a perfectly acceptable average of eight motes per cube. But in the middle of the line were a couple sharp spikes to over a hundred.

"What's that? A mistake, certainly?" A barygraph could return these false readings when insects or mice got into the housing.

"I would normally say so, yes, but we've been seeing this pattern a lot, becoming more frequent all over the country, especially along the northern and western borders."

"Northern? Where is this reading from?"

This particular one is from Ysherra. I have a student there. He sent it to me, and I admit to being remiss and leaving it on my desk while we were dealing with the loudmouths in Ensar. It's not the only reading that's like this. My student told me that the locals call these dust devils and they're extremely destructive."

Sady gave him a sharp look. "Lana asked me about those. She has been looking in the library but can't find anything more significant than that they're a dust whirlwind. There is no specific information known about them other than an obscure note made in the margin of a book. I told her that I thought it was a myth. She . . . tends to get easily discouraged. I wish I hadn't said that now." He sighed. "I'm not doing this father thing too well."

He couldn't even comprehend how Viki coped with having ten children. Lana had an ever-increasing arsenal of ways and comments that seemed designed solely to step on his heart. Viki would say, "The problem with you is that you care too much."

He looked at the paper again. "If this is a real phenomenon, it's something we haven't dealt with before. There was never any sonorics this far north of the platform. What could be the cause of it?"

Viki shook his head. "I don't know. I really don't know what this is. We were supposed to have eradicated sonorics and now we find it coming back in all the places where it hasn't been previously."

"Getting stronger, too."

Viki nodded, and was silent for a while. Then he said, "I was wondering how much you need me here for the next two weeks or so."

"Are you thinking of going up there?"

"Yeah. This worries me more than Ensar. I'll send someone else to Ensar to talk about the drought. It's not that I can offer anything that hasn't already been said."

"They won't be happy."

"Nope, but they'll get their hearing. Given the situation, we're doing the best we can."

SADY FINALLY WENT HOME when it started to go dark. The life of a proctor was never easy, and never without pressing issues to be attended to.

His personal driver dropped him in front of his house, where he had lived for many years. He went through the gate, up the path through the front yard, the steps to the veranda. He greeted Farius who was on duty at the door and went into the hallway.

The sound of voices drifted from the kitchen, where he found Lana and Myra at the table. A cloth lay spread out between them with a heap of dry bean pods on it.

Lana and Myra each had a bowl in front of them and were twisting each pod, pulling apart the halves and emptying the beans into the bowl. The beans hit the metal with a rattle, bouncing over the bottom.

"There he is," Myra said. "Let me get you some tea. I'll reheat dinner." She rose.

Sady sat at the table. Reheated dinner was the story of his life.

Myra set a cup of steaming tea in front of him, and then busied herself with a pan on the stove. Lana ripped apart bean pods, a look of concentration on her face. By the sound of the beans hitting the bottom of the bowl, it was filling up.

"Daughter, I don't normally see you doing domestic tasks."

"Does that mean I can't do them?" Her blue eyes met hers. She looked so much like her mother when she said that, it hurt him inside. It hurt him that he was losing both of them.

"It doesn't mean that at all."

Another lot of beans hit the bowl. These were all red and white spotted. When Lana was a little girl, she would collect all these different colours of beans and stick them on pieces of cardboard. She'd give them names, or she would shape them into patterns.

"How was your day, daughter?"

"Same as yesterday, and the day before, and the day before that."

Sady sighed, trying to push aside the feeling of hostility implied in her words. If only she could be a bit more patient and be happy with her lot. If only she would spend her time on appreciating the opportunity she got in working in the library, and not spend so much time on the balcony watching stars and reading Aranian astrology.

Myra set a plate in front of him holding cooked potatoes with a rich sauce made from meat and mushrooms, typical autumn fare. The smell that rose from it was heavenly.

Sady ate, while Lana continued shelling beans. Their father and daughter gatherings always ended up being like this: silent and awkward, as if neither knew what to say.

Sady was tired and wanted to see Loriane before she went to sleep, so when he had finished eating, he rose, poured a cup of fresh tea and left the kitchen. Lana's eyes met his when he was at the door, almost accusing, as if wondering about those times that she had spent enjoyable afternoons with him going to the gardens and learning to name all the plants.

Yes, what had happened to those times?

Loriane sat in the big bed in the bedroom at the top of the stairs. Myra had been in to close the curtains and light the lamp, and Loriane was reading a book by its gold glow.

She looked up when Sady came in.

"I brought you some tea."

"Thank you." Her voice was soft.

He handed her the cup. Her hands and arms were thin as sticks. There was no meat on her bones, and her hands trembled so much that she needed help to hold the cup. He had intended to find an infant's bottle with a straw, and reminded himself to do that tomorrow on his way to work.

Taking just a few sips of lukewarm tea exhausted her.

"How was the doga today?" she asked.

"Same as always. Everyone is complaining and wants more money." This was a variation on his usual answer. He didn't like talking about his problems. Compared to hers, they were insignificant. But lately, the tone of discussions in the doga had changed, and he didn't like hiding his concerns from her.

So he said, "Viki has measured a number of sonorics flares."

"Oh. Bad ones?" Because she was from the City of Glass, sonorics didn't affect her at all. She frowned. "But I thought, with the Heart destroyed, there would be no more sonorics."

"Yes, we all thought that."

"But you thought wrong?"

He closed his eyes.

"Is this what has been worrying you lately?"

He sighed. There was really no way of hiding anything from her, sick as she was. "That, and other things."

"Is this about Ensar?"

"Who told you about that?"

"Lana did. She says the senators are all afraid their districts are going to be affected by drought next."

"That pretty much sums up the feeling."

"But? There is always a but with you."

"Yeah. I don't think it's that simple, especially after what I heard today. It appears there are manifestations of sonorics along the entire western border, even in the north. It looks like Arania might be doing something."

"Maybe they discovered a second machine."

"That's one of the options. The most easy one."

"What are others?"

"I fear that we are missing a vital piece of knowledge that may change everything about our understanding of the world. Things are changing so rapidly, I feel we need to hurry, or we might reach a point where whatever is happening to the world is not reversible."

"You should put some people on it to investigate."

"We're doing that, but the doga is more concerned with immediate aid. Understandably, but it doesn't help the long term vision."

"Why don't you put Lana on that project? She is really terribly bored in the archives."

"How can I put her on exciting projects when she doesn't appreciate the opportunity I'm giving her to work with a top academic?"

"He's an old man. She doesn't feel at home with him at all."

"She doesn't need to feel at home with him. She needs to learn from him."

Loriane shook her head. "Sady, Sady. It was all so easy for you. You were from the right family, you were a boy, you didn't get your education in a time of great uncertainty."

"My brother went to war while I was getting my education. I didn't have the luxury to complain about what I got."

"Times are not the same, and even if they were . . . how many girls were there in your course?"

"Two."

"Did they get the same treatment as everyone else?"

"That's not a fair question." Back then, of course they didn't. They were trained to become someone's assistant.

"Yet, it is, because you are expecting an old man to teach her the things he taught students of your generation who were still convinced that girls couldn't be educated. Don't you think that doesn't affect his thinking today?"

Sady sighed. Yes, it probably did. It was just that . . . he didn't see the point of all this. Times had changed. Many Chevakians had died in the sonorics explosion or in the years afterwards. They needed everyone to pull their weight. What did it matter if the student was a boy or a girl? It mattered nothing. To make a distinction was just stupid. "All right. I'll think about it."

"She'll think you're the best father ever."

"Nah. I think I've failed irredeemably on that front already."

Then Sady's attention fell on the book that Loriane was reading. It was written in Perian, a language he hadn't often seen written. In recent years, Loriane had collected these books, especially the ones to do with the old Eagle Knights and the establishment of power in the City of Glass. Those people had mostly died in the explosion or the chaos afterwards.

She had many of these old books, and more, including hand-written lists, would arrive every day.

She said she was making a list of people who had died in the explosion so that their names could be included in a memorial. It was a noble cause, except Sady didn't understand why Loriane cared so much about the old Eagle Knights who had been so cruel to her and her people.

Meanwhile, her list had grown very long and spanned several books. She was talking to authorities in the City of Glass about it, and hoped it would be a lasting contribution to the homeland that she would never visit again. It gave her a sense of worth in these dark days.

"You think too harshly of yourself," Loriane said, and Sady had to remind himself what they'd been talking about. "Lana loves you very much. She is just itching to do something for herself. She's old enough."

Yes, she was. There had been plenty of offers of marriage already and Sady felt somewhat proud that Lana had refused them all. Maybe he should give her a project—or better, he should tell Viki to give her a project.

He left Loriane in the bedroom to spend some time in the library reading. But when he walked down the stairs, the door to Lana's room opened and she came out. "Dad, can I speak to you?"

See, there was something going on. Lana never did domestic work without wanting something in return.

Sady gestured at his library. They went inside without speaking a word.

The room was well-appointed with rich red carpet and big armchairs. It was dark outside, but normally the library looked out over the courtyard with its clipped bushes and fountain that had lain dry since the start of the drought.

They sat down in the armchairs on either side of the fireplace. The house retained both heat and cold well, according to classic Tiverian design, and it wasn't yet cold enough to light the fire.

"I was wondering . . ." Lana began. She looked so much like her mother when she did this, and oh, did Sady know that this kind of humble question could lead to anything from going to a party to the most outlandish requests.

Sady raised his eyebrows.

Lana's cheeks coloured. "I heard that Viki is going to the northern districts. I asked him if it was all right for me to come. He said yes, but I had to ask you first."

"To the north? Viki is going to Ysherra. Do you know where that is?"

"I looked it up. Someone from my class went there for his field work." There was that pointed tone again, the tone that said *everyone got an interesting placement and I didn't*. And Sady was *not* in the mood for petulant children. "You've rarely even left Tiverius. What makes you think you can travel that far?"

"It's not for my lack of trying. I put down on my fieldwork application sheet that I wanted to go somewhere, anywhere, into the field. Other students were really picky. They wanted to go here, not there. I wasn't picky. Anywhere, I said. So who is the only student who gets placed in the archives in Tiverius? Me!"

"How can you say this when you don't even appreciate what you've been given? It's an honour to be working with Loran. He is one of the most distinguished academics Tiverius has ever known."

"*Was* maybe, but he spends most of his days asleep and the other half drinking. How can anyone expect me to learn from him? He barely even speaks to me."

"Whose fault is that?"

"Not mine! I tried."

"You are ungrateful. Loran worked hard on the restoration of the land after the sonorics ravage. Without him, we would not have rebuilt the railway to Fairlight and the southern region would still have been a wasteland."

"Dad, that was twenty years ago, when I was born." Her face was red from arguing. "This is now. Things have changed."

"I have noticed."

"Argh! You always do that, trying to turn everything I say into a joke. This is not a joke and I am not a child. I want you to take me seriously."

"I do take you seriously." She was so young and still so inexperienced. The world was a dangerous place. He didn't like how she went out into the dark with her viewing glass. There were wild animals and strange people. "People in the north have some very curious customs. People here are used to seeing young women in the position of meteorologist, but Viki didn't choose a boy to go out to Ysherra for no reason. It's not a nice place. It's hot; it's unfriendly. Viki will be looking at dangerous situations. There will be plenty of other times for you to travel."

"You always say that. Is there anything you will allow me to do?"

"Your best."

She snorted, turned on her heel and left the room, slamming the door behind her. In the hall, she called out, "How can I do anything while he's treating me like a child?"

Sady sat down, leaning his head in his hands. He wished he could muster the courage to tell his daughter that her mother would be dead before the end of winter. It would break her heart. He so desperately wanted her to be happy where she lived and with what she had. She could do all she wanted, but he did not want to lose her to a distant place, or a young man in a distant place.

Sady no longer felt like sitting in the library. The only thing he would do there was dwell on his shortcomings and despair about how no one, not in his family, not in the doga, had seen these shortcomings for the last twenty years.

Not even the doga wanted to get rid of him. Maybe the makers of political schemes were waiting for the best opportunity to use him as a scapegoat for all that was going wrong in Chevakia. Not just the drought—which they could pin on Viki—but the failures of the past twenty years, for example, that northern railway that had been promised but had never been built. They'd done so many costings on it, and every one of them said that it would be a money sink, because the north didn't have the population to sustain it, and it had no potential for further development.

To be blunt, the region was hot and dry, and if anything, people looked for ways to leave the region, not to move to it.

Promising railways was one thing, making them viable was another altogether. Lately, though, the doga sessions had been a string of non-decisions. Sady didn't think that the senators had ever been as decadent and lacking in strong motives as they were now, and that reflected on him. He could not get out of the doga what the senators didn't bring in. Back in the time of Milleus, the proctor would have been challenged a long time ago, but instead these senators worshipped him like a god, "carrying on the legacy of the han Chevonian family." He had not done anything special, not even during the sonorics emergency when Chevakia was flooded with refugees from the south. He'd bumbled through the best he could. He had not done anything that deserved this status.

He was tired. He wanted someone to take initiative, but he appeared to be stuck with this monster called reputation.

He went back into the bedroom.

"I heard Lana slam the door and yell in the hallway. What was that all about?" Loriane asked.

Sady told her of what Lana had asked him.

"I gather you said no."

"What else was I supposed to say?"

"I think it's a good idea. All her fellow students went somewhere."

"But they went to a position where they'd be looked after."

"Not this student she was talking about. She found out from the department that his tutor was killed and he's been forced to run the meteorology outpost by himself."

"That's . . . outrageous." Lana didn't tell him about that. "That's the meteorology department's responsibility."

"I guess that's one of the reasons that Viki wants to go there. I can't see why Lana can't go with him. How much danger would she be in, going with Viki? I don't know anyone who is more cautious than he is."

That was true.

"Go and talk to her a bit later. She has thought this over carefully. Our daughter is not silly and won't walk into trouble with her eyes closed."

"Did you have anything to do with this?"

"She asked me. I said she needed to discuss it with you."

"What do *you* want her to do? Do you want her to go to Ysherra? Certainly not."

"Sady, it's no longer about what we want. Lana is an adult."

CHAPTER 18

*I*SANDOR STARED at the letter in his hand. A guard had delivered it to his room where he had been staring out the window, worrying about the lack of response from the expedition.

The letter bore the seal of House Mara and Isandor's full name and title was written in calligraphic letters on the front. Written by a professional scribe, dictated by Tamerane's father.

That was not the type of response he had wanted to his informal message to Tamerane, asking her if she wanted to take up rooms as the palace's resident academic.

He pulled the ribbon and read the short message,

The option of my daughter living with you was not included in the agreement and is not normally considered part of the breeder contract. I am happy to renegotiate, but it will increase the price.

Isandor threw the letter down. What was the man thinking? He had asked *Tamerane* if she was interested. Why did he think he could control his daughter like this?

Rider Barton, Carro and his other advisors would tell him to push his case by saying: "I am the king and what I say goes." They would even offer to say it on his behalf. But things weren't quite that simple. Existing laws made plenty of provisions for the queen, but said nothing about the queen's family. The people wanted him to rule and organise. The law did not quite allow him to do those things.

He bet Ledor *knew* this, and was trying to play out his power against Isandor's over his daughter's head. It made Isandor feel sick.

"What is it? Bad news?" Carro had come in.

Isandor handed him the letter. Carro read, raising his eyebrows. "You offered her—what?"

"She is twenty-nine, petrified of her parents, who control much of her life. She has brilliant ideas that should be able to flourish. She should study. I *want* her to study."

Carro gave him a strange look. "She is a breeder."

"She is also a human being. I want her to be treated as one. I want her to be able to study and do what she is good at without her parents having any say in it."

"Is there any sign of a child?"

"That's irrelevant. I want her to study these ideas. She leads a miserable life."

Carro dropped the letter on Isandor's desk. The expression on his face disturbed Isandor. "Back when you asked me to hire her, you agreed to just use her as a breeder. I warned you about House Mara ties—"

"You did, but those ties have nothing to do with her father treating her like a slave."

"Maybe not, but your attachment to her definitely does."

"My—" He stared at Carro.

"You've fallen in love with her, haven't you?"

"Well, I—" Isandor was going to deny it, but every night, he'd gone to sleep thinking about losing himself in Tamerane's soft embrace. It was a physical attraction, compensation for the fact that he hadn't touched a woman for so long, he'd told himself, but she wasn't that attractive, except when her smile set his entire body on fire. He took a deep breath and blew it out. "I guess."

"Any chance of breaking off the agreement?"

What? Isandor gaped at his friend. Leave Tamerane with that bully of a father? While she could be pregnant with his child?

Carro got up, walked around the desk, opened a drawer, took out paper and the box with the official royal stamps and seal and plonked them in the middle of the desk.

"What's that for?" Isandor asked.

"You should write Ledor an entirely different letter: one asking for his daughter's hand in marriage. Do it now, before there is any sign of a child."

Isandor stared at his friend. Marriage? Him? But oh, how he burned with desire all of a sudden. What a brilliant, brilliant idea. Imagine going to sleep in her soft arms every night. Imagine setting up her spyglass on the top of the tower in the palace—

But Jevaithi would be devastated.

He pulled the paper towards him. One part of him wanted to write that letter immediately, but he couldn't do this to Jevaithi.

A voice inside him said, *But what has she done for you?*

Without Jevaithi, he would have been a butcher in the Outer City, and when the Outer City had gone up in flames, he would have died with it.

"Well," Carro said when the silence lingered. "That's what I would do. Mind you, I'm not interested in getting married, so what do I know?"

Isandor pushed the paper away. "I . . . have to think about this." No, he was lying. He didn't need to think about it at all. He needed to work out what he was going to say to Jevaithi.

By the skylights, how was it ever going to work?

He'd intended putting up Tamerane in the guest quarters and going to see her occasionally. But he couldn't do that to her either, making her the subject of gossip. No, he deeply and utterly *wanted* to ask her to marry him.

But Jevaithi . . . But Tamerane's crazy smile . . .

He needed to think.

After Carro had left, he went to his room, opened the wardrobe and took his riding harness off the hook on the inside of the door. He hadn't worn it for several months, and the buckles and clips felt familiar, but a little . . . unused. He put on his shorthair cloak and left the palace.

The guards at the door asked him if he needed the coach, but he told them no. He walked out the gates into the Knights' Eyrie next door. The building was five floors tall and the entire top two floors were taken up by roosting stables.

Isandor no longer had his own eagle. The poor beast had been retired several years back, but the Knights kept several animals ready for riding for both Carro and him. Carro had marked on the slate on the wall that he had taken one of the animals out this morning. The other, its mate, ruffled its feathers and poked its head under its wing when Isandor approached.

"Hey," Isandor said. He ran his fingers over the animal's side, feeling the warmth of the skin under the feathers. "Are you a bit jealous?"

The eagle lifted its head, and regarded him with an orange eye.

"Come on, let's go." Isandor untied the tether from the bar and led the animal to the open side of the stable. The bird was clearly less than impressed. Its snorting and squawking woke up a number of other birds, some of which hissed at him, and one gave the stuttering cry that males made when defending their territory. Isandor's eagle got skittish. He wrapped the tether around his wrist to hold the eagle's head close, and it made clear, through snorts and grunts, that it didn't approve of the situation.

Isandor stopped at the landing area. He loosened the tether and rubbed the feathery neck to calm the animal.

The top floor of the building looked out over roof of the city, the harbour and the bay and beyond that the ocean and the island of boulders before the coast where the Legless Lions frolicked.

The sun was at their back, casting long shadows over the bay.

"Going out, Your Majesty?" Rider Barton came up from behind.

"Yeah, nothing special, though," Isandor said. "Just a little trip to clear the mind. Too much to worry about lately."

Rider Barton nodded. Words about the lack of communication from the expedition hung unspoken between them. It had only been a few days, but they should have heard something. Except sometimes the telegraph didn't work.

A gull would always work.

Except they got thrown off course by too much icefire or bad weather.

"I can accompany you if you wish," Rider Barton said.

"All right." Isandor had intended to go alone, but Rider Barton was one of the most easy-going people to deal with. Besides, he could speak about the issue with Jevaithi in private.

Isandor waited with the eagle at the mouth of the stable while Rider Barton went to get his bird. It came without snipping or squawking, reminding Isandor that it might be a good idea to choose a dedicated bird for himself and that maybe he should go out a bit more often, because his skills were starting to go rusty.

Isandor climbed on the bird and the two let themselves fall into the air, spreading giant tan and white wings.

After flying over the city, the birds followed the coastline with its great many algae-covered boulders. The water was so clear that you could see the forests of giant kelp. Sea birds roosted on the rocks, taking flight at the sight of the two eagles.

The City of Glass lay in a bay to the north of a jagged tongue of land. A two-wheel track went over the ridge of the peninsula, zigzagging around boulders and rocky outcrops through the grass. A cart stood at the very end. The white speck in the grass would be the bear that belonged to the cart. Two fishermen walked over the shoreline boulders, collecting crab pots.

When he felt annoyed or disturbed, Isandor would normally land at the point and sit on the rocks to gaze over the ocean, but he knew that as soon as he landed those fishermen would come and start asking questions. He didn't want to talk to people, because he had no answers today, so he kept going along the western coast.

Rider Barton and his bird followed silently behind.

The western coast of Peria was rugged, uninhabited terrain with only the occasional farm. This land used to be covered in ice and the concept of farming was quite new. Many of the farmers were people from places like Bordertown or even Fairlight or other border districts in Chevakia. They had brought their crops and their animals when the snow had left fallow ground that could be farmed in summer.

A narrow, winding two-wheel track wound its way past all these farms. The farmhouses lay like little blocks in the landscape, each farmyard surrounded by fields of crops, usually grains. Most farmers also had sheep that roamed freely, kept out of the crop fields by walls made from loose stones.

Isandor and Rider Barton followed the track along the coastline. The sky was almost clear, the sea dark blue with occasional floating icebergs. The land was green, kept short by the sheep, with occasional rocky outcrops of grey rocks covered in orange and light green lichen. Golden sunlight gave the shore a warm tint.

Already, the sun barely cleared the horizon.

The road went up a rise where a land tongue jutted into the ocean. The other side of the ridge was in deep shade. Did Isandor see it correctly and was there a truck on the road?

Rider Barton whistled, pointing down. He sent his eagle into a downward dive. Isandor followed.

There were three people with the truck. Two of them had the third one holed up against the side of the vehicle. He held his arms over his head and crouched, bent over. Isandor noticed how one of the two others appeared to be *hitting* and kicking this person.

One of the assailants shouted and pointed at the sky and the two of them ran into the truck, leaving the abused man lying on the ground.

Rider Barton landed before Isandor did. He let himself slide to the ground as soon as the bird touched the ground. He ran for the truck, which was slowly moving away from the scene. The steam trucks were not fast, and Rider Barton easily caught up. Isandor ran after the truck, sliding his sword from its sheath. He'd debated not taking it, but now he wished he'd taken a crossbow.

Rider Barton yanked open the door of the truck. A flash tore from within the cabin, sending a wave of icefire outwards.

Isandor lifted the sword. It caught the golden strands and drew them into his hand. All that power sucking into him.

"Get out of the way!" he yelled at Rider Barton, who didn't need to be told twice.

A man jumped from the door of the moving vehicle. He carried a metal wand that sent out bolts of icefire, directing it at Rider Barton, but, being of the Pirosian clan, Rider Barton did not see or become affected by icefire. Isandor called the sizzling strands to him.

Who was this man?

The truck stopped. The driver came out as well, a mountain of a man in leather armour. He carried a sword so big as Isandor had never seen. He came for him at a run.

Isandor was about a third the size of this man and woefully out of fighting practice. He could do only one thing. He held the sword out before him and called the icefire he had just collected. It streamed in a golden, deadly bolt to the attacker. The man thrust up his sword, but the icefire hit him in the chest. It sprayed outwards, forming a giant web of threads that twisted around him. The second man hit at the threads with his wand. It sucked up icefire that engulfed the second attacker as well. His face froze in a horrified expression. The large man had toppled face forward into the grass, and the second one fell on top of him. The golden web went out, and there was silence.

Isandor lowered his sword. Rime ringed the edge of the blade and the adjacent part of the handle.

By the skylights, what was that? And what happened to the third person?

Rider Barton was already on his knees next to the victim.

Isandor strode over to the two attackers' bodies. Both men were much larger and broader than he.

Their armour was unfamiliar, dark leather, unmarked. Both lay with their faces down. The man on top had a blistering burn mark on the back of his neck, which Isandor could see because he wore his hair—sleek and black—in a ponytail. He also appeared to have tattoos on the side of his face around his ears. Most of the skin on his hands had burned away, leaving a weeping mass of flesh.

The leather armour of the second man had burnt crisp and black. Smoke still rose from it. In places it exposed the skin, red and raw.

Isandor felt sick.

These two men would not be going anywhere anymore, and wouldn't be answering questions.

He turned around to check the victim, and came across the wand that the second man had used—a simple rod of steel with, on top, an ornamental head of silver encasing a large stone. He didn't dare touch the stone. He had seen this type of thing before, and he pulled a cloth from his pocket to wrap around the wand. He'd have Brother Veshi look at this thing.

Rider Barton had the victim sitting up.

It was a young man, barely adult, his limbs still thin and gangly, his chin still free of growth. He was bleeding from a gash above his eye.

His clothing marked him as a citizen from the City of Glass. Isandor didn't know him, but he thought he had seen the young man's face before. Blood dripped from his nose and one of his eyes was gummed shut. He had a nasty gash over his forehead. Rider Barton pulled a cloth out of his pocket and handed it to the young man.

"Thanks." He wiped his face, smearing blood over his upper lip. Then he bowed his head while sniffing. "Your Majesty."

His voice was oddly light, and when Isandor met his eyes, he realised that this was not a young man at all, but a young woman and that she was, like Jeito, a man-girl. Isandor felt sick. Two big grown soldiers attacking a girl?

"Were those men known to you?" Isandor asked.

"No , they . . ." She looked around, her eyes wide. "My truck! Where is my truck?" She turned in a circle. "They took the truck! I have to have the truck back. My boss will be mad if I lose it."

"Calm down," Rider Barton said. "The truck is on the other side of the ridge. It's fine. I'd like to know a bit more about you and these men. What's your name?"

"I'm Jadan, Your Majesty. I did nothing wrong."

"I didn't say that you have done anything wrong. Please answer my questions. Who were these men? Do you know them?"

"Seen them maybe once. They're my boss' friends."

"And your boss is?" Rider Barton asked.

"The mechanic, Zaina. Do you know her? She's away on an expedition."

"We know," Isandor said. A seed of worry grew inside him. The men were *Aranian*. Zaina was Aranian. The expedition was probably close to Arania now. Aranians with icefire.

"I'm sure these men told you what they were after," Rider Barton said.

"They didn't, honest, sir. They wanted to know about my boss, and I don't know that much about her. She keeps to herself."

"What sort of things did they want to know?"

"A bit before she left to go on the expedition, my boss had an injury. They asked if she had seen anyone about it, and I said I didn't know. I said I didn't think so but that I had no idea what she might have done after work."

Isandor thought of how Zaina had come into the palace with the bruised face. "I saw her injury, but . . ." *She had been afraid to go out.* Afraid of these men? "Her eye was badly swollen. I'm not sure what a healer could have done."

"Oh no, it wasn't about that. It was about the wound on her side."

"I didn't see that."

"You couldn't because it was under her clothes, but she asked me to have a look at it, and it was awful."

"Like how?"

"Like . . . You know how the skin blisters for an icefire burn? It looked like that. But that's not really possible, isn't it?" Her eyes were wide. "Icefire is gone, isn't it?"

Like most of Isandor's generation, she must have been told to be afraid of it.

Isandor blew a breath out through his nose. He didn't answer the question because he didn't like to lie. So he asked a question of his own. "Do *you* believe that it's gone?"

She hesitated. "Well, I see these . . . flickers sometimes. I don't know what they are, but I've heard people say that those are flare-ups of icefire."

Yes, Isandor was right. The girl could see icefire. "You mean glimmers of golden light that creep over the boulders in the bay or the buildings in the city?"

Jadan nodded. "I just don't understand how they found out that she had this burn."

Because they might have caused it? Isandor asked, "So, did you tell anyone about her injury?"

"I went to see an apothecary, because there was only a little bit of the ointment left in our cupboard and it was all dried up and too old to be used. That is honestly the only person I told about it."

"Do you think these people were watching her?"

"Quite possibly. I may have seen them before, in the distance. There is one man who had red tattoos all over his skull. He shaves part of his hair. He even has paint in his eyeballs."

Rider Barton cast Isandor a disturbed look. "The red tattoos are worn by the high command in Arania," he said to Isandor in a low voice.

Isandor met Rider Barton's eyes. "What are they doing here?"

"Looking for this woman apparently."

Isandor thought of Zaina's fear. "Any idea who they are?"

"They speak with accents. I don't know what sort. Please, I want my truck back, and then I'm never again going to talk to anyone who comes into the workshop offering to take me to a vehicle for sale."

"Could I look through you boss' administration?" Isandor asked.

Jadan looked from Isandor to Rider Barton. "Can I refuse?"

"Yes, but it wouldn't look very good."

She opened her mouth and shut it again. "My boss would be upset with me."

"You think a lot of her, don't you?"

She nodded. "She is the best."

"Would you trust her?"

"Always, sir. She would not lie."

"She has dark secrets?"

"None that have anything to do with us, I don't think. Arania is not a very pleasant place to be as a woman, sir."

She had a point there.

Isandor had no more questions to ask her. He said he would visit or send someone to have a look at their books. Jadan declared that she was good enough to drive the truck, but Isandor and Rider Barton followed her into town anyway.

After having shadowed Jadan safely to the workshop, Isandor and Rider Barton returned to the eyrie.

"What an odd situation," Rider Barton said while they were both taking the harness and saddles off the birds. "Do you want me to investigate?"

"Please, do." Isandor hung his saddle on the hook on the wall next to the bird's cage. "Check the new register of Aranians in town to see if you can find out who these men might have been."

"It's not yet complete. Many Aranians in particular refuse to register. They are afraid that their authorities will find them."

"The authorities have no access to our administration."

"I wish I could unequivocally agree with you, but I would be the first to admit that we've been lax with our security in past years. We needed people to come here and help us build more than we needed to know exactly who these people were."

Isandor knew, oh, he knew. There had been a few cases of Chevakian criminals taking refuge in the seedy bars in the Harbour District. The place was heaven for young, angry political refugees. They found jobs in the warehouses and continued to plot their schemes at night.

The council had pushed the problem aside as being too hard, but it would come back to bite them.

"I'll get to work then." Rider Barton was quicker at packing away his riding gear than Isandor and was about to leave the stable.

"Just wait for a moment." Isandor quickly stepped out of his harness, hung it over his arm, left the bird cage and shut the door. He caught up with Rider Barton at the door.

"Anything else?" Rider Barton asked.

"Jevaithi did ask you to father her child."

"It is my royal duty." Rider Barton's face was blank.

"We both know that it will end in grief."

"Yes, but it is not my place to object."

He was right about that, it wasn't his task. It was Isandor's, and he had tried and failed to make Jevaithi see sense. "I'm sorry."

"Don't be." Rider Barton put a hand on his shoulder, like a favourite uncle. He was so much older than Isandor, had served under the dictatorship of Rider Cornatan and had seen so much hardship. "I can't claim to understand women—" He had a male lover. "But I did as she asked."

Isandor tried to imagine Rider Barton in bed with Jevaithi and could not. "I hope she was happy."

Rider Barton sighed. "I don't know that she will ever be happy unless she has that child."

"I'm worried about her," Isandor said.

"Yes." And then Rider Barton said nothing for a while. Having served in the Knighthood, Isandor knew all about their pledge to the queen. A Knight did *not* say anything bad about her.

But then Rider Barton said, "It seems to me she has stood still for twenty years while the world has changed around her."

"That's a good way of putting it. I wish I knew what we could do to help her."

"I guess if there was anything that would help her, someone would have done it already."

CHAPTER 19

Z AINA WAS WAKENED by a shout. She sat up, dazed, wondering where she was and why she was surrounded by feathers. A bird's head lifted from those feathers, white with a yellow hooked beak and an orange eye that cast her a baleful look.

"I'm sorry," she said, and scrambled to her feet. The eagle put its head back down on its wing, and Zaina scratched the top of its head, to which it responded by raising all its feathers.

"Yeah, I'm sorry. I'm going."

She collected her blanket and mat, wriggled between the two birds and jumped off the trailer.

Rider Tomason stood watching her. He would have been the one who had shouted.

His face remained impassive.

"I'm so sorry. I didn't mean to . . . I was so cold." Her mat slid from under her arm into the snow. She picked it up.

"I'm surprised the birds let you sleep there. They don't like strangers. You scratched that eagle's head. He's not the tamest of birds and would have bitten off anyone else's fingers. Have you handled a lot of animals?"

"No. I fix machines. Horses don't like me."

"Hmmm," he said and then he said nothing more, so she nodded awkwardly and dragged her mat and blanket off to the truck, where

Daro had just woken up. He looked scruffy, unshaven, huddled in layers of jackets and blankets.

"Can't wait until we go somewhere warmer." His breath steamed in the morning air. "I'm hungry."

Zaina was hungry, too. One of the Knights had started a fire, and whatever was in the pot that hung over it and produced clouds of steam smelled good. The sun wasn't up yet, but the sky glowed orange. Overnight, the camp had remained entirely peaceful.

Here they were, at the pass, and Nayek had *not* attacked.

Maybe his threats were all bluff. After all, how could you follow someone through this country and not be noticed? Here on the top of the world, you could see people coming long before they reached you, especially with the patrols on the eagles.

Zaina went to join the others at the fire.

The Knight in charge of cooking passed her a steaming mug of tea and a bowl of porridge. A couple of men had finished breakfast and were already starting up the boiler fires and repacking the trucks.

Zaina ate.

Rider Tomason joined the fire, accepting tea, and sitting down with his instruments. He was writing measurements in his book.

"Did you see the shimmering in the sky last night?" she asked him.

He looked up. "Shimmering?"

"Like blue and green and pink lights. Is that what you call skylights?"

"Yes, that's what we call skylights. I didn't see any."

"You were all asleep."

"Are you sure?" a Knight said. "The skylights vanished from the City of Glass when the Heart was destroyed."

"I'm describing what I saw."

The Knight gave her a what-does-an-Aranian-know-about-this look, but Rider Tomason flicked back through his book, running his finger over rows of numbers.

He said, "The truth is no one really knows what causes skylights. We tended to think that it was icefire, because the skylights only occurred near the City of Glass, but we really don't know."

"There are some rumours that icefire is coming back," someone else said.

"They're just rumours, aren't they?" Daro said. He spoke over the top of his hot tea, and his breath combined with the hot tea produced a cloud of steam.

"I received an official letter from the palace that there might be a flare-up," Zaina said.

Daro said, "Yeah, I heard about the panic that caused in the Harbour District. I still don't understand, because wouldn't that mean that the skylights would come to the City of Glass and not here?"

No one had an answer to that, and there was a lot of work still to do before they could continue, so the Knights handed in their mugs and bowls and went to work.

Zaina also had some tasks to do. Yesterday's towing had damaged the front of one of the vehicles, and she made some quick repairs. The result wasn't pretty, but at least if the vehicle needed towing again, the front panel would not fall off.

Rider Jeito, who had been missing from breakfast, came down on her eagle.

Zaina was close enough to the fire to hear the report she gave to Rider Tomason. The mist would lift soon from the valley ahead, she said, and there was no sign of any activity other than their own. Tomason asked if she'd seen any eagles, and she said she had not. He exchanged a dark glance with her. Zaina was sure that part of the reason they had come here was because the Knights had lost a team who had gone into the mountains.

Jeito reported on the status of the road, saying that a large section of paving had washed away. Tomason produced a map, and she pointed the way. She said, "There is a broken cart at the bottom of the land wash, all smashed up against the rocks. I presume someone didn't make it. The road is unusable there, but we can probably go down the glacier if we're careful. The road goes around and crosses the creek at the bottom of the glacier, but the bridge has washed away. The creek is quite small right now."

"We'll try the glacier," Tomason said.

"Get someone to walk in front with an ice pick to test the ground."

Tomason nodded, and then he said something to Rider Jeito that Zaina did not catch, spoken in a low voice close to her ear. Jeito looked past Tomason straight at Zaina. Tomason left, and Jeito beckoned Zaina to come over.

Zaina had just finished with the truck, but her hands were covered in grease.

Jeito held her eagle by the reins. She said nothing, but pulled the bird forward. It reacted by digging its claws in the snow and stretching its neck. The stroppy thing was not going to move just because a human said so.

"Come closer," Jeito said.

She was like an older version of Jadan, the tone of her voice similarly not very female and not entirely male either. Like Jadan, she was thin, flat-chested and hard-faced. Zaina cringed under her scrutinising expression, which made her painfully aware of every bit of her broad hips, big boobs and sensual lips. She *looked* the wrong type of woman for women like Jeito or Jadan to be interested in her.

"Come. Touch the bird."

The eagle wore a saddle that consisted of a leather seat with two pouches on the side for the rider's knees. It had a thick, fluffy bearskin cover that looked really comfortable. Zaina touched the feathered neck. The eagle did not react, so she dug her fingers between the feathers and rubbed the warm skin. Now the eagle turned its head, curving its neck so that she could more easily reach it.

"Yeah," Jeito said, glancing at Rider Tomason.

"I told you," Rider Tomason responded to her.

Jeito turned her attention to Zaina. "You're Aranian." It was not a question, but Zaina nodded anyway.

"Hmmm," Jeito said. And then she let go of the eagle's reins and went and got some porridge, leaving Zaina to stand there feeling awkward with this giant bird, watched by other Knights.

Well, what was that about? That was the strange thing with these Knights. They got into a conversation and then just broke off and started doing something else to leave the other person wondering what was going on.

"What am I supposed to do with this bird?" she called after Jeito.

"He's a bird. He can look after himself," Jeito said.

Zaina figured that the birds on the trailer hadn't been tied up overnight and that she hadn't, in fact seen any of the Knights tie up their birds during the trip, even though she had definitely seen them tied up in the City of Glass.

So she turned back to her toolbox, picked it up and carried it back to the truck.

Except the stupid bird followed her, stepping primly through the snow.

What the hell? She turned around and said, "Shoo!" for all the good that did. The eagle craned its neck and rubbed the top of its head against the back of her jacket.

Great. She had turned into a human scratching post.

Then Jeito whistled and the eagle turned and ran to her with big clumsy steps and its wings slightly spread.

WHEN THE COLUMN of vehicles finally started moving, it was almost midmorning.

The ground was treacherous. The slope of the glacier was quite steep and, even with the snow chains, the trucks needed to zigzag across. But because there might be deep crevasses in the ice, a Knight walked in front of the first vehicle, testing the ground with the handle of his ice pick. Their progress was very slow.

At midday, they had not covered a third of the way. They stopped briefly for a miserable meal of dry bread. There was no time for a fire, and most people wanted to keep going. A cold wind chased over the mountainside. Zaina had the feeling that they were being watched and hated the restricted view from the truck's cabin.

The glacier was not a quiet place either.

The ice popped and cracked, which was sometimes disturbingly loud. It was, Daro said, a river of ice flowing down a mountain.

The terrain got rougher in the afternoon as they approached the older sections of the glacier.

Not just that, the mist rolled in with squalls of rain and the ice became slippery where the water froze on the surface. Several times, the trucks lost their grip and slid aside, coming dangerously close to deep clefts.

Visibility was no more than a stone's throw and the Knight at the front of the column had to take extra care to check the ground before the trucks could proceed. The air team returned because the eagles did not fly in such poor visibility.

Then the Knight at the front halted. The first truck halted, too, and because Daro followed in their tracks, he stopped, too.

Rider Tomason got out, slipped and almost fell. He walked to where the Knight at the front was pointing down.

"What is he looking at?" Zaina asked.

"I don't know." Daro sat huddled in his jacket, his collar pulled up to his ears. He looked like she felt: miserable. "I don't care. I want to get out of here."

More people climbed out of their vehicles. Some of them walked past the truck and the truck in front, then stopped where Rider Tomason and the Knight still stood looking down and pointing.

Zaina sighed and opened the door. A gust of moist wind came in, biting into the exposed skin of her face and neck.

Ugh. She let herself drop to the ground—and almost fell. Whoa, it was slippery. She shut the door again and followed the tracks made by the others to where they all stood looking down into a forest of big jagged shards of ice, white tinged with clear blue, that lay between where they stood and the end of the glacier.

Down there, a clear mountain creek flowed from underneath the glacier across a riverbed made of loose stones.

"We can't get across from here," Rider Tomason said.

"Maybe if we back up, we can find a spot to get down off the side," someone said.

But behind them, the glacier went through a long canyon where sheer rock walls lined the sides. This was the first place where the terrain opened up.

"We'll have to go back," a Knight said, his voice morose.

Rider Jeito said, "No. I will fly over—"

A crack vibrated through the ice and echoed through the valley. Zaina could feel it through her feet.

People shouted.

One of the trucks back in the line listed, first a bit and then more. Ice cracked and collapsed in on itself. The truck tipped sideways and disappeared. It was a cargo vehicle and in getting out, the driver had left the door open. This door flapped wildly and was the last thing visible before the truck tipped off the edge.

"Everyone in the trucks!" Rider Tomason yelled.

Zaina ran to the truck and jumped into the cabin, where Daro still sat. She slammed the door shut. They waited.

And waited.

Each time the ice cracked and popped, Zaina froze, and Daro held onto the steering wheel with white-knuckled hands.

"We're going to die here," he said, staring ahead.

"Not if I can help it," Zaina said.

The ice cracked again. She winced. Because it had gotten so much warmer in the last years, these glaciers were retreating and not as strong as they used to be, especially at their edges. If she was alone, she would have reversed away from this dangerous edge, but the entire ground was treacherous.

"Did you see how far down the truck went?" Daro said.

"Not very far. We're at the end of the glacier. There is a creek bed below."

Supreme Rider Tomason had left his vehicle again. Zaina climbed down from the cabin, walked over the slippery ground to where he stood.

Rider Jeito had flown down to the fallen truck with her bird. The truck had tipped on its side. Most of the crates and boxes that had been on the back lay in a trail across the ice and river bed, some in the water. The roof of the cabin itself had caved in, and the door had bent at a strange angle.

"Lucky there wasn't anyone in the truck," Zaina said.

"Yeah." Rider Tomason shook his head.

Jeito walked around the vehicle, pulling items out of the water.

A second eagle landed on the stony ground. The Knight pointed downstream. Jeito spoke briefly with him, and then mounted her bird and came back up.

"He reports seeing some artificial structures in the valley," she said.

"What kind?" Rider Tomason asked. "Inhabited? Is anyone there?"

"He thought so. He said it could be a camp, but it's too misty to see and he couldn't come close enough."

"Chevakian? Aranian?"

She spread her hands. "Can't see in this weather."

"Damn, we're in a vulnerable position here. We need to get down from this ice, and soon."

Zaina said, "I'm sorry for interrupting, but I think we could use this break in the ice to make a ramp to bring all the trucks down. We need to start at the bottom. We can break off and crush the ice and pack it down and then pour water over it so the ice freezes together."

"That's a big job. How long will that take?"

"My guess is: shorter than going back around the pass and trying the old road that's washed away."

He nodded, slowly, while his gaze roamed the ice and the path of broken chunks of ice left by the falling truck.

"We need to get some people down there so that we can start from both ends," Zaina continued. She took their silence for agreement. She further explained the details: that the ramp needed to be at a certain angle, that they could use winches and use the weight of the engines to bring down the bigger engines, but that they would need to make the ramp so that the smaller trucks could come down unaided.

Rider Tomason simply listened, and when she had finished explaining, he said, "All right. Make sure that it is done."

Zaina asked Jeito to take a rope down and attach it to the fallen truck. This, they strung onto one of the trucks above. A few of the men pulled the rope to make it as taut as possible. Zaina fashioned a loop around the rope from a luggage belt and a leather sack, attached it to a thinner rope, and they used this contraption as a sling to lower some people down.

Zaina went down as well, swinging perilously close to jagged shards of ice with their eerie beauty of light blue. Daro was putting her toolbox in the sling when she walked around the fallen truck. The damage was quite a bit worse than apparent from the top. Besides the cabin, the boiler had dented. In a workshop where she had worked as apprentice in Arania, she had seen people die from an explosion of a damaged boiler. She didn't want this truck on the expedition until it could be properly fixed. She didn't think she could fix it properly here.

The men were already starting on making the ramp: hacking ice into bits, mixing it with stones and pouring the mixture in the gaps. This was going to be a long process. There was no way that they could finish this today.

Rider Jeito went out to investigate the camp that the other Knight had seen.

She came back in the dusk saying that there were lights in the mist. She told the others, "I can't get any closer. I was pushing the bird beyond its comfort as it was. I can only say that the mist protects us as well as it hides whoever is in there. We need to work fast to get on the move again, and hope they won't discover us before we're ready."

They also could not fire up the engines until they were ready to move, because the noise would give them away.

For the night, Rider Tomason deemed it safer for everyone to camp on the glacier with the trucks, so in the fast-falling murky darkness, Zaina helped haul everyone back up.

A circle of tired and miserable faces gathered around the fire in the dark. The Knights whose truck had fallen had nowhere to sleep. Zaina offered one of them a place in her truck because she could take the spot on the trailer with the eagles.

People left the fire to go to sleep early. Tomorrow, they would have to work their hardest to get the trucks down and past the camp that the Knights had seen.

Zaina was too tired to even worry about being cold. Her arms ached from hauling the rope, her back ached from carrying and smashing blocks of ice. It started snowing but, snuggled up between the birds, she kept dry and warm.

She didn't wake up until someone shouted harsh words in Aranian.

CHAPTER 20

WHENEVER SADY needed time to think and reflect, there was one place where he would go. He had found that people found it fair game to intrude on his life, even if he was at home with his ill wife, if he was in the bath, if he was having breakfast on a nice day in the garden or if he was at a private function.

But no one disturbed a person at a graveyard.

And sadly, an ever-increasing number of names on headstones were people he'd known in real life, like poor old Milleus, his brother fifteen years his senior, ex-general in the Chevakian army, ex-proctor and ex-goat farmer from the Ensar district, who had died a few years prior, aged eighty-one.

The family still owned the land, at the very point where Chevakia met Peria and Arania. It included a sprawling farmhouse where Milleus went to live after his marriage broke down and poor Suri killed herself, his sons walked out on him, he was voted out as proctor and when he could no longer make sense of the world. Fortunately, he had lived the last eleven years of his life in Tiverius, surrounded by his family. Suri's grave was next to her husband's, and Sady used to come here a bit because he felt responsible for her death, because he should have seen it coming, and he should have been brave enough to show his love for her so that she would have had something to live for.

There was also, in a different, old and leafy section of the graveyard, the grave of Lana, who had been Sady's housekeeper for many years, a woman he loved and should have married, and who had been killed by a magical beast at the time the sonorics cloud was threatening to invade Chevakia.

There were the graves of his parents, the headstones now both covered in lichen. For them, he had never been more than a second son, an inferior copy of the first, Milleus, their pride and joy. Sady had been a quiet, thin, non-athletic, studious kid. Instead of military training, he went to the Scriptorium. Meteorology was an upcoming discipline back then, but his father still didn't see the use in it and couldn't comprehend that the doga would pay someone simply to look at the weather. They never paid for a matchmaker and Sady had never married until he met Loriane in the squalid and desperate conditions in the camp for refugees from the City of Glass.

Sady would love to tell his father that he had now been in the job as proctor longer than Milleus, and that, despite his secret wishes, the doga showed no sign of becoming unhappy with him.

But he wasn't here in the graveyard for that. He needed to think of the next generation.

Faced with the issue of Lana wanting to go to Ysherra with Viki, what would Milleus do? He would say yes. But Milleus had two sons, and it was different for boys. His father would have said no, most definitely, but his father lived in a different time.

Suri and Lana, what would they have said?

He imagined Suri with her big brown eyes, terrified of Milleus, even though he never harmed her. She would have said little, but she would have cried inside, "Yes, let her go and please can I come?"

Lana would have been more practical. She would have said, "What does it cost?" And then she would have asked about how many clothes she would have to pack. Because Lana was used to having others make the decisions for her. She would have assumed that by the time she was notified of a plan, it had already been decided.

Well, that wasn't very helpful at all.

And the weather was not cooperating. It had been cloudy all day, but now the wind became squally and a few specks of rain hit his face. Not that this would be a major, drought-breaking rain, the meteorologist in him said, but it was enough to be annoying.

Sady had arrived at a different part of the graveyard. This section was much newer, and the graves were much smaller and less ornate. The people who had been buried here were of an unusual variety in age, but the dates on the headstones were close together, twenty years ago.

Whatever happened, and whatever he decided about Lana, he must avoid exposing Tiverius to another disaster like that one. When the machine in the City of Glass had blown up and the sonorics cloud had moved outwards, people had fled and had brought sonorics contamination into Tiverius. There had been that train of death from Fairlight that had brought most of the refugees from the south. Many of the bodies already dead on the train had never been claimed, and they lay buried at the far end of the graveyard, each under a stone tile with a number.

Most of the people here had been Chevakians who happened to be on railway duty that day, or who lived close to the camp, or had otherwise been contaminated.

Sady stopped in the middle of the path, looking out over the grey scene around him. Graves and more graves. He could still see the terrible sight of dead and already decomposing bodies piled in corners on the train while the living refugees, Loriane one of them, were covered in burns and filth. And no one in Tiverius had a clue of how to deal with these people and these types of injuries.

That was why he still performed his job every day: to honour the hundreds of thousands of Chevakians and southerners who had died in those days. He wouldn't be surprised if even Aranians had died.

In the light of this carnage, should he send his well-educated and smart daughter to the north to help find out what was going on there?

And, considering it in that light, was that even a question?

Sady returned to work a bit later, driven by his faithful guard Orsan in his familiar comfortable truck. Newer vehicles were smaller, faster and more efficient, but he liked the truck that had served him for so many years.

Orson accompanied him up the stairs, a good deal slower than he would have walked when he first started the job, and younger guards shepherded aside the line of petitioners who were waiting in front of his door in the hope to see him.

Sady had stopped seeing people two years ago. He was not proud of that choice—and occasions like this reminded him of that fact—but there was ever less time to accomplish the tasks that must be done. The majority of petitioners were sadly there out of self-interest. The really desperate people in the districts had discovered that he preferred to receive their pleas in writing and they no longer travelled to the capital to wait here. So he had to ignore the pleas for reductions in taxes so that the claimant could keep his shop open, or complaints about the study grades of a woman's son because the tutor was picking on the boy.

He feared he had become like Destran, whom he had replaced as proctor, who used to ignore submissions from the public all the time. For a while he'd thought that the claimants back then had brought more relevant complaints, but that was just his imagination speaking. There hadn't been enough time in the proctor's day to deal with public petitions for as long as there had been a proctor in office.

In his office, Sady found a multitude of reports on his desk that the secretary must have brought in while he was out.

Sady sat down, and Orsan went to get him some tea—he didn't even need to ask this.

Sady leafed through the reports. The status of the city's food stores was down again. Any time now the annual grain harvest should be hitting the depleted stocks, and he was keen to know what the damage was going to be. The harvest would be bad, that was all he knew, but he just hoped that, after he had given out farming licences to anyone who wanted one, there would be enough grain for the year.

Maybe.

Another document contained Viki's weather report and forecast, which had the current clouds vanish by tomorrow morning and had sunshine returning for another unseasonably warm day.

Then there was General Selidas' armed forces report. This document spanned several pages and detailed the activities, supplies and readiness of various sections of the armed forces.

Land troops had assisted in rebuilding several eastern coastal communities after a bad storm. The balloon division had completed a training exercise in the Ensar district. They had also sent out assistance to the northern town of Watya where a lot of refugees from the drought had gathered, most unable to pay for passage on the train further south.

This latter item worried Sady the most. The refugee crisis from Fairlight and Ensar had started with a trickle, after the sonorics machine had exploded but the cloud hadn't yet reached Chevakia. At that time, no one could have suspected how many people would come and the extent of the misery they would be bringing with them.

When Sady turned the last page, there was a handwritten comment from the general. *Contact me when you've seen this.*

He often did this, and Sady had expected it. The general had an office in the armed forces annex of the building. Sady asked his staff to check if he was there, and got the word that he was.

So he went out with Orsan, past the long line of petitioners who were probably about to go home for the day. They were arguing over their positions in the queue, which they would mark with chalk on the tiles. When they arrived at the top, one of Sady's staff would deal with them.

Now that Sady came out of the office, they assailed him with questions. Sady couldn't help hearing their pleas. All of them were about personal matters that would have been dealt with so much more efficiently if the claimants had gone to their local ward repre-sentative. But people tried anyway, just so that they could say they'd taken their complaints to the proctor's office.

General Selidas was one of those people relatively new to Sady's circle of influence, and who looked young enough to be Sady's son. He had managed to rise up quickly through the ranks of the armed forces through the balloon division and, as much as Sady remained a meteorologist, balloons were still his first love.

He greeted Sady with a stiff nod. "Good afternoon, Proctor."

Sady sat in the chair opposite the table. He came here often enough to be familiar with this room and its wall full of decorations and trophies, including prizes taken from Arania by Milleus.

The general was a man of few words. He often sent these strange types of summons to Sady or senators because he disliked both writing letters and long-winded explanations.

He simply extracted a roll of parchment from the desk's drawer, untied the ribbon and unrolled it on the table.

"These are the locations of our permanent units."

The map showed lots of dots at regular intervals from the Ensar district, where Milleus used to farm goats, in the south-western corner of Chevakia along the Aranian border all the way north to a small town to the west of Watya.

"We have travelling units," General Selidas said. He spread out a sheet of transparent film with positions written in black pen. The ink could be wiped off the film, and the sheet bore the hallmarks of having been wiped frequently. He lined the sheet up with the map underneath.

"And we have balloons stationed in these positions." He added another sheet with dots over the top. Two of the positions were marked in red.

"These are the stations I want to talk about. Those are the places where our patrols have spotted activity on the other side of the border."

"In Arania?" Sady gave him a sharp look.

The general nodded, a serious look on his face. "Arania is mobilising."

Sady heart's jumped. This talk was not at all going in a direction he liked. He should have known that the general wanting to see him was not a good thing.

"They've been quiet for . . . how long now? More than forty years." Was it that long ago already? He guessed they were all getting old. "Any idea what they're up to?"

"We're trying to determine that. We first noticed signs of activity across the border a month or two ago. It seemed they were building new towns and we thought they were relocating part of their population because of the drought that must affect them, too. But now we have other information that suggests they're garrison towns."

"This information comes from spies who have visited this area, right?"

"Yes. It's been harder to get spies into Arania recently." The general rose and went to the door. He opened it and spoke to someone outside.

A moment later, a young man came in, dressed in uniform. He bowed to Sady and saluted to the general.

The general said, "This is Yanes, one of our secret intelligence officers who completes missions across the border."

The young man was fresh-faced and clean-shaven. His expression was open and friendly. Pretty much everything Sady would expect a spy *not* to be.

His eyes were very light grey.

"Are you Aranian?" Sady asked him.

"Half-Aranian, sir. My mother is Aranian. I speak the language fluently."

Judging by his speech, the young man was far better educated than his rank suggested. Sady had heard about these "low-level spies" who were low level only in name and were embedded in the regular force to gather information not just on enemies but on potential discontent within the Chevakian troops.

"Tell the proctor what you have seen," the general said.

Yanes nodded to Sady. "As part of my act, I dress up as a peasant and go to the villages on market day. I listen in to the gossip that goes around these towns. Usually I pretend to be a farmer's son looking for carpentry work. The villagers will tell me about new buildings that are going up, whether or not the builders are looking for work. Then I go and have a look at the projects, but I don't usually talk to the owner or site manager. Often, it's just a house or a farm, or maybe a new bridge or town hall. But just recently, I was in a small town just here." He pointed at the map, northwest of Tiverius, the southern-most of the little red dots.

"The villagers sent me a long way out of town and I almost thought they'd finally figured me out and sent me into the woods to be killed, but then I came to a huge camp with a lot of building activity. They had set up rows and rows of tents, and carpenters were building a wall around this camp."

"For refugees?" Sady asked.

"That was my first thought, because I had heard people in other villages speak about drought and sand storms in the northern part of Arania. But then I realised the camp was in too much of a strategic position for refugees. The camp is set on a hilltop, with a ravine on the Chevakian side."

"Is this the river at the border?"

"No. The bottom of this ravine is dry. There are lots of spiky bushes in the gorge and it's not easy to traverse." He held up his arm, marked with lots of scabbed-over scratches.

"I hid in a copse of trees to check what was going on at the camp. The next day, while the carpenters were still working on the wall, a group of people arrived on foot. They were all dressed in black and carried similar packs on their backs. They took up residence in a couple of the tents. Later in the day and the next day, there were more of these groups. They all looked similar, they were all young men. The Aranian army does not have a strict uniform code, but I'm reasonably sure that they were soldiers, especially because they were all young men of similar age and build."

"Did they have any weapons?"

"Those first groups didn't, but then, later on, wagons arrived and those same men unloaded all kinds of strange equipment."

"What sort of equipment?"

"There were boxes that looked like the machines that meteorologists have in the weather stations, only bigger."

"Barygraphs? What would they do with those?" Especially *bigger* barygraphs.

He spread his hands. "I don't know enough about it. The next day, they started training with weapons that looked like wands, and they would put one of those machines in the middle of each fight. I tried to come closer to see what they were doing, but I got in trouble when the horses spooked when I came to the pen. I had to get away quickly, and I ended up climbing into the canyon. That's why my arms look like this."

The general thanked Yanes, and he bowed and left the room.

"That is the most current update," the general said. "We spotted something similar in another camp in the other spot. Only our agent couldn't come as close as this young man."

"Who is he, by the way? He's not as low-ranked as he looks."

"No, he's not. His mother is an actress, a princess of the Aranian court, one of King Orik's oldest daughters. She is very vocal in her protection of women from their barbaric motherhood culture. She rescues a lot of young girls who can make it over the border. He's grown up backstage and has absorbed the finesses of acting and applies it to his spying personas."

"I hope you pay him well."

"We do."

"What does the army make of his story?"

"I have a theory." The general hesitated. "I'm hesitant to mention it, because it encroaches on your discipline. But I think those machines the Aranians have created draw sonorics out of the air so that it can be used by their weapons. I've had extensive talks with the Perian Eagle Knights. Their problem is that most of their troops can't see sonorics. I am not aware that anyone in Chevakia or Arania can see it, but I suspect that to a southerner who *can* see it, that training scene in the camp would have looked very different."

Sady stared at him. Well, damn it. "So you're saying that the increases in sonorics we have seen, the unexplained spikes and the strange weather patterns might be because of meddling with sonorics by Arania?"

"It might be."

Double damn. Or, as Milleus would have said, *mercy*. "Does sonorics kill Aranians as much as it kills us?"

"If it does, I doubt King Orik cares. He uses the army to get rid of unwanted young men anyway."

Yes, there was that story going around about the odd Aranian culture. They valued mothers so much that they locked them away for the world as possession of the men, and their only task was to produce as many children as possible for their "owner". But worse than the lot of a young girl was that of a young nobleman of insufficient status to start his own harem. He was sent to a certain death in the army, carrying out futile missions designed for the sole purpose of killing soldiers. They lived for the promise of having their name engraved in the wall of heroes after their deaths. The camps across the borders were filled with angry young men who *wanted* to die for this cause, who did not care if sonorics killed them.

Sady breathed out a sigh. "So, I can only conclude that the Aranian army is amassing because they want to invade us."

"They probably want to pay us back for what your brother did to them."

Even if that was over forty years ago. "What can we do to prepare for the worst?"

"I have already ordered the distribution of sonorics suits to all units. I've increased the alertness level of the balloon units. Units are moving to these areas along the border as we speak." He indicated the two red dots.

"Are you familiar with any of their tactics?"

"Beyond what your brother has taught us about them, no. Virtually all the Aranians who come to us as refugees are women."

"And what Milleus wrote about Aranian warfare was based on very old information."

The general nodded, and they were silent for a while. Sady's head was spinning. As if having to deal with the drought wasn't bad enough.

Finally, he voiced his worst fear. "If they come across the borders, they will be headed for Tiverius, right?"

"That would be my estimate."

CHAPTER 21

JAVES STOOD in the middle of the tent, with all the windwalker people staring at the metal globe in his hand. They were mostly men, but some women, all of them with dark skin mottled with random matches of milk-pale.

"Where did you get that thing?" the elder Tiraa asked. His tone was serious.

"I came by it honestly," Javes said.

One of the men hissed.

"I swear. I was in the Field of Bones, and this windwalker came to me. He never said a word to me, but offered me this globe and then started raiding the body." He still shuddered at the memory of the snap of dead fingers being pulled off a hand. "I never knew his name, and he didn't ask me any money or tell me what to do with it. I don't even know what this thing is. That's why I came here: to find out. This is really, really old, right?"

One of the tribesmen said something. An old woman shuffled from the side of the tent. She took Javes' hand and held it, palm up, in front of her. She said a few words, and then a couple of others burst out with protests, judging by the tone of their voices.

Javes looked at Tiraa. "What is she saying?"

"She says you lie."

"I do not! I never even saw any windwalkers and didn't know any existed before I saw this man—if it was a man. I don't even know.

And if I stole this thing, would I come back here with it? Really? Would I come back here and show you that I have it?"

Tiraa spoke to the old woman. She again looked at Javes' palm, a frown coming over her face. An old man looked over her shoulder and made a comment. She snapped back at him, starting an argument.

"Will someone just tell me what's going on?" Javes called out.

"The windwalker who found this artefact has gone missing. He left the settlement over a month ago and has not come back. She says you have his soul."

"His soul? I have no such thing. I'm telling the truth. There was a dust devil and my tutor died. The people in the village didn't care much what happened to him, so I took his body to the Field of Bones. The man—is this a man or not?"

"It is Karlen, and we don't know. We think he's a man, but no one goes into Karlen's den so no one can be sure. It is said that his body is entirely white and that is why he never shows it. But we haven't seen him in over a month."

"I only saw him briefly. He had a camel with him, he gave me this as if I was the dead man's relative and took the valuables off the body in return. According to the villagers, this happens commonly. I didn't see where he went. I presumed he went to a town where he could buy or sell the gold. That's what someone in town told me windwalkers do."

Tiraa gave him an annoyed look. "People in the towns know nothing. Pah, they know less than you, because you had the smarts to take a camel. You were better prepared than anyone I've seen travel in the desert."

It was all knowledge he'd learned from Pashtan. Javes held the globe out. "I don't want to sell it, but I'd like to know what it is and where he gets these."

Tiraa said something to the people behind him. A man replied. The old woman argued, wagging her finger. Half of her hand was white, with blue blood veins shining through the translucent skin.

A couple of others chimed in. Their voices sounded angry.

Then Tiraa heaved himself to his feet. He jerked his head at Javes. "Come."

A boy scurried to him with a walking stick made out of a length of pipe with a red knob at the top.

Javes followed Tiraa to the front room where all the shoes stood. The boy knelt to put Tiraa's sandals on his feet. Javes stuffed his smelly feet back into his smelly boots.

The sun had sunk closer to the horizon and its golden light cast long shadows across the camp and surrounding hillsides. In the orange glow, the land didn't look quite so hostile. The camels stood peacefully, pulling hay from their feed troughs and chewing by moving their bottom jaw in a circle so that their soft lips wobbled and you could occasionally see their yellow teeth. They were silly animals, really.

Javes was surprised that he recognised his own camel amongst them. The windwalkers had taken the packs off—they stood in a neat pile against the side of a tent. The animal lifted his head and looked at him.

Tiraa noticed the exchange. "How did you get the camel?"

"I bought it with my own money, also because it was cheap because the merchant didn't get along with it."

"It is one of ours. It was stolen from one of our camps."

"I didn't know that."

"You damaged it."

"I made it calmer. I paid for the camel. I needed it to do work. I had no use for a breeding animal with a foul temper."

Tiraa nodded. Javes wondered if that was good or bad. If they insisted on keeping the camel, how was he going to get back to Ysherra?

They walked into the shadow of the giant bowl. The line of boys and girls had stopped moving up and down the ladder. They all sat on the edge of the pedestal, legs dangling down, talking and laughing. The children had black skin with white patches. Many of them had white strands in their hair.

"What is this big bowl for?" Javes asked.

"It is how we make our water. The ground is very salty and there is not much water. There is a well at the foot of the mountain but it is very muddy. The mud is too salty , so we carry it into the bowl and spread it out to dry. It gets very hot under the cover; the water steams and collects on the cover. We collect it as it runs down the sides."

"What was the bowl built for originally?"

"To collect rain water, when there was still rain in this area."

"Did the windwalkers build it?"

He laughed. "We're not that old."

"Then who did?"

"Old, old people. I don't know how long ago."

"The same who made the metal globe?"

"Maybe. Maybe. Many people used to live here. Many."

It was hard to imagine.

They left the tent camp behind and walked over the barren, rock-strewn ground. Their long shadows crept over the hillside. The orange hills were utterly desolate. There was not a tree, not an animal, not a sign of habitation.

"Does anyone go further north than this?" Javes asked, gazing at the hazy horizon.

"Some people do. There is treasure to be found. But it's risky."

"I can imagine that. How many days travel until you hit the cliffs?"

Tiraa gave him a sharp look. "Cliffs?"

"The place where the land ends and the ocean begins, but where the cliff faces are so tall that you can barely get to the water."

"There is no water out there."

"There is, if you go far enough. The land drops into the ocean."

Tiraa gave him a strange look. Clearly he had never seen a map of the world. Clearly, no one of the windwalkers had been far enough north to reach the cliffs that the captains who circumnavigated the continent had reported.

"We don't go far, because of dust devils, because there is no water and nothing for the animals to eat, and because the camels don't like going there. Too many dust devils. They get nervous."

They had reached an outcrop on a rocky and rubble-strewn hillside. Tiraa walked along a narrow passage between two large boulders to a space hidden in deep shadow. There was a *door* in the rock face.

Tiraa pushed it open, disappearing into the dark space beyond.

Javes followed him. He came out in a cramped room where Tiraa was rummaging around. A moment later, a light came on so bright that Javes had to shield his eyes. What sort of light was that?

The white glow reached into all corners of the room, revealing walls covered with shelves which contained boxes and boxes of strange items. There were bundles of coloured wire and large plates. Also panes of glass, few still intact. The room also contained a bed—hidden amongst the shelves—and a desk, on which stood strange contraptions.

"Wow," Javes said. "What is all this?" His voice sounded stuffy inside this dark dungeon.

"I said there was a lot of old stuff to be found around here. Karlen has a habit of collecting it. He told me once people pay good money for it."

"He didn't tell you what kind of people buy it?" It struck Javes that maybe even the Scriptorium might be involved with this, and if they weren't, they should.

"He does not tell me what and where the buyers are."

Javes looked at the rest of the mess on the desk. There were messy piles of calculations, descriptions and pages from a diary.

Javes picked up a couple of sheets of paper. One contained a rough map of the area. It included Ysherra and an area to the north where he'd marked a few spots without description. To the northeast of those spots, Karlen had marked an area as "foul".

He held the paper to Tiraa. "What does 'foul' mean?"

He shrugged. "Could mean anything. Foul hot and dusty, foul land—"

"What can be foul about the land?"

"No food, no water, the animals get nervous. You can't go across there when the camels don't want to go."

Javes put the map to the side. He was keeping that.

Then his eye fell on a piece of paper that protruded from the pile. It was different in quality from the thin rubbish paper that Pashtan also used to write his notes on. It was thicker, smooth, yellowish. The writing on it was in Aranian.

Javes didn't read Aranian. He recognised a few characters. They were all numbers. And then the row of characters, were they outlines of how much someone had spent on something, or how much Karlen owed this person?

That piece of paper was coming, too. And then the notebook, full of strange diagrams and graphs. What sort of man was this Karlen? Not one who had grown up with the windwalkers, Javes guessed.

He walked past the shelves, studying their content. He saw a couple more metal globes with wires. Each of them also had a hole in the side that was the same size as the hole in his globe. Clearly, it was for something to be inserted.

Javes scoured the desk for something of the right shape. He found a piece of wire with a small attachment at the end. With a bit of shoving, it fitted in the hole, but the other end of the wire still hung uselessly. You couldn't reconnect the other end of the wire so the it made a loop by which one could carry the globe, maybe around one's neck.

But it was too big to be a piece of jewellery.

The far end of the wire had a much smaller attachment that was too thin for the hole in one of the other globes. It clearly needed a different thing with a different sized hole.

It was all very strange. But he was keeping the cord.

By the time the oil lamp burned out, Javes had a small pile of odd objects. Darkness had fallen outside, and the sky was a tapestry of stars the likes of which Javes had never seen before. You could see the double stripes of the sky path, and the bright speck in the middle that was the Great Wanderer.

He understood why people came to Red Hill in order to watch the stars.

"You had better leave in the morning," Tiraa said while they picked their way across the hillside to the camp. The giant bowl stood like a black silhouette against the stars. A few pinpricks of golden light burned inside the tent camp. "If Karlen comes back, he won't be impressed that I've let you take things from him."

"I want to know where all this came from. Who made it? What could they do? What information did they have?"

"I'm concerned with Karlen. Where is he, why is he selling these artefacts to strangers. Those things are *our* history. I told him so. We had a huge argument before he left. I didn't want him to sell these things. He disagreed and ran out angry. I fear he's betraying us."

CHAPTER 22

*M*EN SHOUTED in the semidarkness.

Zaina sat up, shivering with the feel of the clammy air over her skin.

The air rang with the rough voices of Aranian men, and the pre-dawn light was tinged orange with the glow of fire. Something burned to her right, but the smoke and mist made it hard to see.

She scrambled for her boots and jacket and, those items located, made sure that her dagger was still inside her boot.

At least ten Aranian soldiers were attacking the camp, and fighting the Eagle Knights. The birds hissed and snapped. They were not tied up, yet didn't fly off. It was probably too dark and misty for them to see.

A man with a flaming torch walked past the trailer, and flung the torch in the back of the nearest truck. The contents caught fire almost immediately. Three Knights slept in there, and one of them jumped out brandishing a dagger, while the other two tried to extinguish the flames. More Aranians ran past, and a handful of Knights ran from their trucks to stop them.

The camp turned into a battlefield.

Zaina pulled her legs up against her chest and kept her head low between the eagles. Many of the Aranian soldiers considered a woman travelling alone fair game. She knew these type of men. Her mind told her to run, but up on the glacier, there was nowhere for her to hide and nowhere to go. They would find her and rape her and kill her. She was safer here, although she didn't think any of the Eagle Knights would stand up for her either.

She put her hand on top of the dagger in her boot, but had no illusion that she could fight and defeat this many trained soldiers. Who was she supposed to fight anyway? If she raised a weapon against the Aranians, they would declare her a traitor, and those were usually treated to the most painful and slow deaths possible. And her name, and worse, that of her mother, would be forever tainted. The memory of her mother didn't deserve that.

So she hid, pushing her head down between her knees, but it was hard to block out the cries of pain or death gurgles.

Both eagles on the trailer became agitated. One kept hissing, and rose to its feet. A rush of cold air wafted over Zaina, and she could see underneath the eagle's belly . . . straight to an Aranian soldier. His red-tatooed face split into a gap-toothed grin.

He yelled, "Oy, over here."

Zaina jumped up, but two men vaulted onto the trailer and dragged her down before she had a chance to pull the dagger. They were mountains of flesh and muscle in Aranian leather armour who laughed at her feeble efforts to kick them in places where it might hurt. They dragged her across the camp past a truck on fire. A man in Junior Knight uniform lay face down on the snow next to the truck, surrounded by spatters of blood. She couldn't see who he was.

A group of five Eagle Knights sat in the snow, their arms bound behind their backs. Rider Tomason and Rider Jeito were both in the group.

Where were the others?

All dead? Large blotches and sprays of blood tainted the snow all over the camp. Zaina spotted at least three more bodies. Her truck was on fire. And where was Daro?

Her captor pushed her down on the ground.

Another of the Aranians laughed. "What's that? They have *girls* fighting for them?"

"It looks like we got a little spy here," one of her captors said.

The tattooed man gave her a sharp look. "Dang it. She's one of us." He came to Zaina and drew her up by the front of her jacket. He was at least a head taller than she was, and the red tattoos on his face showed that he held a high rank, and was probably one of King Orik's second-favourite sons. One of his eyes was cloudy and a deep and ugly scar ran across the cheek underneath.

"Why didn't you contact your command?" His breath stank of chewing tobacco.

"I . . ." Zaina scoured her mind for ideas. Mentioning Nayek could be either dangerous or life-saving. She didn't know where this man stood with Nayek, and if he considered Nayek a competitor, he would take pleasure in defacing the woman that Nayek had picked. She'd heard the horrible stories of women who had been "cleansed" after having been freed from captivity of another man to make sure they didn't carry the child of a rival.

She straightened her back and said as loud and clear as she could make it, "What is your name?"

The Aranian words felt strange on her tongue.

He stared at her, his one light grey eye roaming her face.

One of the soldiers laughed, but the others gave her sideways glances. Zaina's heart thudded. Was she going to be convincing enough as a high-class woman?

She said in a low voice, "Never mind my southern clothing. I'm an agent for the king. Let us pass."

"Bullshit. You're a traitor."

"No, *you* will be considered a traitor if you harm us."

Zaina knew nothing about spying, and even less about the king, but hoped that by mentioning him, the men would be reluctant to lay their hands on her, lest they attract the king's anger. It was a gamble, but the only thing that came into her mind.

He harrumphed. "You better be right about this. I'll take you lot back to camp to ask my commander."

Yikes. Although that was better than being killed outright. But she absolutely had to maintain her haughty appearance, and sort out how to get out of this once they got to the camp.

"Do give me your name, because I don't like talking to nameless men."

The man hesitated. "Pritak."

"Well then, Pritak, let us continue on our way."

He snorted, but he set her down. "You better be speaking the truth, that's all I can say."

He turned around and made a hand signal to his men. One of the men came forward to tie Zaina's wrists behind her back. The others dragged all the other prisoners to their feet. Rider Tomason was injured. Rider Jeito looked furious.

"You let them know that we were here," she spat at Zaina. "I was suspicious of you from the moment I saw that letter soliciting jobs."

"I wrote it because I need work, genuinely."

"You lie. I never wanted you on the expedition, but you had the king around your little finger."

"That is not true. I've lived in the City of Glass for years and hardly even know anyone in Arania. Talk what you want. What you say is not true."

"Liar."

A soldier shouted in Aranian, "Shut up!"

Commander Pritak's eyes met Zaina's. His expression was suspicious. He might understand Perian. This might be a good thing or a bad thing, she didn't know.

She was precisely in the situation she had hoped to avoid. Her life in the City of Glass would be forfeit after this. No one would dispute Jeito's word, and she could not give any arguments against Jeito, because Jeito was right. She *had* betrayed the expedition. She should have told them that Nayek was following.

Then another thought: this commander he was talking about, that was Nayek, right?

Oh damn, oh damn, oh damn.

The soldiers dragged their prisoners down the icy ramp that they had almost completed the day before. One of the Knights, a man Zaina had heard the others refer to as Gilan, slipped and fell. A soldier kicked him in the side while he struggled back up.

At the bottom, next to the truck that still lay in the creek bed, stood a cart pulled by two strange animals with long pointy horns and a shaggy long-haired pelt. They had big wet noses like cows, but all the cows she knew had short hair. One of the animals was black and the other grey.

At the back of the cart sat a wooden cabin that looked like a box. A bunch of soldiers idled around the vehicle. One opened the back door. They lifted Jeito in. She kicked and bucked, but the men were too strong for her. A soldier climbed in and dragged Jeito into the darkness of the cabin by the back of her jacket. She yelled and swore at him.

Then Rider Tomason. His face looked pale and his side was wet from blood. He kept his chin high and said nothing while the soldiers lifted him into the cabin.

Two other Knights took his example.

Then Zaina. The soldier who held her lifted her up and set her on her backside on the cabin's floor. Before the soldier in the cabin could drag her in, the first one, a mountain of a man with a coarse face, shoved his hand under her jacket.

"Hey!" Zaina kicked him in the chest.

The soldier behind her dragged her up by the back of her jacket. "Keep you hands off this one. She's for the commander."

Zaina hissed, "I am for nobody. I work for the king."

"Whoa." He let go of her collar.

Zaina debated jumping off and running, but her hands were still tied, and there were too many soldiers to outrun.

The camp on the glacier was barely visible through the mist, except for the glow of burning trucks. A couple of soldiers had grabbed hold of the harness of one of the eagles and was dragging the bird down the slope. It resisted by putting out its claws in the ice. Another soldier was struggling with the second bird, which was hissing and screeching at him.

The soldier grabbed Zaina by the upper arm and dragged her into the cabin. The others already sat on the ground, each with their hands tied tightly to ropes that dangled from the ceiling.

It was dark inside the cabin, with the only light coming in through a little window at the front. He tied up Zaina as well, left the cabin, shut the door and bolted it shut.

"Fuck you," Jeito said in the dark.

"Shhh," said someone else.

Zaina's backside was getting very cold form the hard, dusty and gritty floor.

The cart wobbled from the men climbing into the front, while joking about what they were going to do to the prisoners. Zaina hated hearing their crude, Aranian voices. They brought up memories of hearing the soldiers march through the streets, of her mother hiding behind the door, hoping that they wouldn't come in.

Even in Arania, everyone she knew was afraid of these men.

The cart jolted into motion with the crack of a whip. The ground was uneven, and they moved slowly.

With every jolt, the rope cut into Zaina's wrists. She wriggled her legs under her, and that made it better. Out the window she could see a little glimpse of the sky and sometimes the mountains. Sometimes, too, there was the head of one of the men looking in.

After a while, the pace of the animals picked up. The men shouted to others. Maybe they were soldier on horses. Maybe there was a second cart.

No one in the cabin said anything. No one looked at Zaina.

She wanted to tell them she had no idea that the Aranian army had any presence in the mountains. She wanted to tell them about her situation, about Nayek, about the list and the lot of young women in the houses of princes. She wanted to tell them that she could never return to Arania and that for all she had done wrong, she was not a spy. But at least some of the men in the front cabin were likely to understand Perian. She could not risk it.

After a long time of bumping over the uneven road, the cart stopped. There were voices outside and the creaking of wood. Then the cart moved forward again for a short while before stopping again. Now the men on the front got off, and a moment later the back door opened.

Zaina blinked against the sudden light. Through the opening Zaina could see mud-trampled grass surrounded by tents. A group of soldiers marched past.

Two soldiers climbed in and started untying and dragging out the prisoners. Zaina was handed off to a tall man who grabbed her under the arms and dragged her across the mud.

The commander Pritak yelled, "Oy! The boss wants her clean."

The man set her to her feet and grabbed her upper arm while pushing her in front of him. It had started snowing, big fat white snowflakes that drifted from a leaden sky. Behind her, at the cart, Jeito's voice yelled obscenities. Zaina glanced over her shoulder. The other prisoners were being taken elsewhere.

The soldier took her into a large tent, where a couple of luxury couches stood on a soft carpet. A fire burned in an open heater in the middle.

A man sat in a chair facing the door.

It was Nayek.

"Here she is, Your Highness," the soldiers said.

"Good. You can go now."

The men bowed, leaving Zaina alone with Nayek.

He spent a long time just looking at her. His light grey eyes roamed over her body, coming to rest more than once on her chest.

Zaina's heart thudded in her throat. She did her best to stare ahead, and not let her gaze stray to his spade-sized hands or other parts of him, and imagine what he was going to do to her.

His mouth slowly curved into a smile, showing teeth browned through chewing tobacco. "I think I like your treacherous ways. You try to run away from me, but you are too stupid to escape me. You bring me the best prize of all: a high-ranking Knight and a female eagle rider. How delicious. I will enjoy myself today."

Zaina stuck her chin into the air. She wished she could say that if he intended to rape Jeito, she wished him good luck, but she could just see that happening. Because strong and quick as Jeito might be, Nayek would simply get two of his men to hold her down while he did his thing and then killed her. And it was her fault that Jeito would die.

Nayek pushed himself up from the chair. He took something out of his pocket and held it up to her. It was the counter. The little window in the front now said "three".

"Look at that. I have tried to warn you. I had hope that you would be useful to me in another way, but no, you were stubborn. You've tried to run from me and disobey me. An envoy of the king, how did that even enter your little head? As if the king would care about you. You're less than a dog to him, less than an ant, even. You're mine, because I took your name from the register. And sadly, I think you will just have to serve me in the usual way."

He reached out and trailed a hand, mock-tenderly over the line of her jaw. Zaina fought not to flinch. It was all part of his game. "I would think, from my experience, that you will put up quite a fight, and it will be one I enjoy winning."

He grabbed her shoulder and pulled her back into him. Through his clothes, through the leather, she could feel his hardness.

Zaina's heart was thudding. She recited to herself all the things her mother had told her: be quiet, be willing, don't fight, don't cry, don't scream, even if he hurts you.

And she knew she would not be able to do any of them. She would fight.

"I'm going to enjoy myself very much today." With one hand he held her upper arm and with the other he undid his belt. It fell to the floor with a tinkle of metal. The top of his leather pants fell open. He was wearing knitted woollen tights underneath. He pulled down the front of those.

There it was, in all its glory: hairy, red and engorged with thick veins running through the skin.

Zaina had to force herself to look away, overcome by revulsion.

He pulled at her jacket. "Take it off."

She did, slowly, her hands trembling. She hung the jacket neatly over the back of the couch. The knife was still in her boot. If she pulled it now, he'd simply take it off her. She had to wait until she could take him unawares.

Then he pulled her shirt. "Take that off, too."

"It's cold."

"Then come to the bed. I'll keep you warm."

"No."

He laughed. "You want it like this, huh? Standing up?" His dick poked her in the buttock. "That can be arranged." His hand came around her front, fumbling with the buckle on her belt. It came loose. He pulled her shirt up.

His rough, callused hand slid over her skin. Found her breast and squeezed.

"Ow!" Zaina whirled around, hitting him with her elbow.

He was taken aback, letting go of her arm. She ran.

He sprang forward like a hunting cat, much faster than she was. He grabbed her around the waist, lifted her in the air, swung her onto her back on the bed.

Zaina rolled aside, onto the floor, scrambled up—

And he grabbed her from behind again. Pushed her back onto the bed, leaned with his full weight onto her arms. In order to pull her pants down, he had to release one of her arms. Zaina rolled aside, unbalancing him. He kept hold of her arm, but they both fell on the ground. He tried to wrestle her onto her stomach, pulling at her pants.

She kicked and bucked.

He picked her up and slammed her over the back of the couch. Her pants hung halfway down her buttocks. He pulled them further down.

Zaina tried to push herself up, but there was nothing to push up against. The seat of the couch was too far down. She couldn't move. He held her by both thighs, and his hands were too strong. He pushed her pants down to her knees. Cold air reached in tender places and made her shiver.

This was really where her pride was going to end.

"Come on, scream."

"Never." She was not going to give him that pleasure.

He stroked her naked buttocks in mock tenderness, inserting his fingers between them, pushing into her and then spreading his fingers.

"Ow! Stop that!"

He pushed his fingers deeper. "Scream."

Zaina clamped her jaws.

He laughed, and pushed harder. "They all say they don't want it, but every bitch that's come to me is wet."

Zaina's eyes misted over with tears. It *hurt* and he hadn't even started. The slimy hardness of his dick slid over her buttock. There was that still to come, and he would fuck her in the arse as well, from what she'd heard. Then he'd cast her aside until she birthed his brat, and her life would be like her mother's.

She would rather die, be killed by him or his guards. But not without a fight.

With all her strength, she twisted her body sideways, reached with her hand over the top of the couch, and pulled up her knees at the same time. By sheer luck, her fingers found the hilt of the knife. She pulled it out of her boot, and thrust the knife backwards, blindly, because she couldn't see what she was doing.

There was a wet *squelch*. The warm presence of a body behind her vanished. No sound at all.

Zaina turned around. Nayek had fallen. The hilt of the dagger stuck out of his side. There was blood on his clothes, on his hands, on the carpet. His eyes rolled in the back of his head. His entire body shuddered with spasms and his breath came in short, wheezy gasps.

Zaina pulled up her trousers, did up her belt, tucked in her shirt and put on her jacket. She bent over him, grabbed the hilt of the dagger, closed her eyes and yanked it out.

Ugh. The wet *shhhhlp* when it came free made her sick. She needed to get out of here or she was going to spew.

She wiped the dagger on the bedspread, did up the buttons on her jacket, looked around for a useful weapon, but found none.

She was going to have to go like this, because the longer she waited, the more likely someone would come in. She guessed there were two guards and the tent's entrance. Likely, there were no guards at the back of the tent. His cloak might be useful. It was thick and heavy and made of fur.

She hefted the dagger. It sliced through the tent fabric until it got caught on a seam. The hole was big enough. Zaina climbed out. Damn, it was cold. Still snowing.

She threw the cloak over herself and pulled the hood over her head. The smell of oiled armour enveloped her.

All she could see was blood. All she could hear was the gasping shallow breaths. Damn, had she really killed someone? He deserved it, right? Her butt still throbbed from where he had attempted to stick his fist in it. Her crotch felt wet. She wouldn't be surprised if she was bleeding.

There was another tent a couple of paces away. She inched around the side, expecting to hear outraged cries any moment. But they didn't come.

She might have a chance to get out. But how?

A group of soldiers marches past. Zaina shrank between the tents.

They were talking about horses.

If she had a horse, she could get away. If she could find a civilian settlement, a village or even a farm, she could get a cart, or beg a lift. She could climb the pass and flee into Chevakia. It was dumb, it was the wrong season to be caught in the mountains, but she had to try.

She followed the group of soldiers at a distance. They were indeed going to the horse pens. Other pens contained the longhaired cows or whatever they were. Zaina had no idea how to handle those. She could kick a horse into a gallop and—damn, the camp was surrounded by a gate.

Maybe she could escape at night.

But by that time, the guards would definitely have discovered Nayek's body and would be scouring the site—

A shrill cry echoed over the camp.

Wait. That was an eagle up there.

The captors had brought and tied up two of the eagles. The expedition had three. Shouts rang out over the camp. A huge shape swooped down over the animal pens. Huge feathered wings flapped within the shelter. Men shouted, cracking whips. The free bird swooped again.

One man threw a lance, but it missed. The bird came back, grabbed the back of his jacket with its huge claws. It lifted the man straight into the air but his jacket ripped and he fell into the mud.

Several soldiers fired arrows at the eagle, but it wore a leather breastplate and they glanced off.

The bird landed in the animal pen. A man tried to hit it with a rake, but the handle broke. The eagle snipped with its beak through the leads that tied the other two birds. One rose in the air.

Zaina ran, and whistled.

The eagle arched its neck and regarded her with an orange eye. It was Jeito's bird, in full gear, including the soft saddle seat.

"Please, take me out of here," Zaina said.

She held out her hand. The eagle stretched its neck out to her. She scratched between the feathers. Then she grabbed the reins, put one foot in the stirrup that dangled over the wing, and swung herself into the saddle. A couple of men ran into the pen.

The bird, hissed, spreading its wings, and hopped aside. Whoa, she almost fell off. She grabbed the top of the saddle but there was nowhere to sit, and she couldn't figure out how to balance. The bird jumped into the air with whooshing and flapping of wings. Zaina held on for dear life. She managed to get one knee into one of the side pouches and then the other one. The camp was already gone in the mist, but she could still hear men shouting, but their voices faded fast, to be replaced with the whooshing of the huge and powerful wings.

Zaina settled into the rhythm of the eagle's wingbeats, even if the biting wind made her fingers numb.

The eagle rose and rose. The mist became thinner. Bits of blue sky peeped through. And then the eagle broke out of the clouds into bright sunshine. The sun hung low and held little warmth, but the view was incredible.

The eagle soared between the snow-covered mountains, into the sunlight. Zaina didn't know how to steer it and hoped that it knew the way home.

CHAPTER 23

$\mathcal{A}$FTER LEAVING General Selidas' office, Sady went back to his own. He bypassed the long line of claimants on the stairs deep in thought.

After the door closed, he took a couple of dusty books from his bookshelf. They had sat there, pretty much untouched, since Lana was born. He opened the top book and leafed through the pages.

Memories of disturbing times came back to him. Times when he'd worried about distributing sonorics suits to the people of the border regions, times when he'd had to sound the sonorics alarm, when people had to stay indoors and board up the windows.

What should he do now? If the Aranian army used sonorics, Chevakia was pretty much defenceless. Distribute suits? The stocks of suits had been decommissioned. As far as he knew, a huge pile of them sat in a warehouse in the army barracks. Would there be enough for everyone? Probably not.

Would they still retain their protective value? Not as much as they used to, as the outer coating tended to deteriorate with age.

How could they get new and better suits?

Did anyone at the Scriptorium still work on sonorics? That was all done and dealt with. At least that's what he and everyone else had thought. Not so, apparently.

He also remembered the Most Learned Alius of the Scriptorium, and how he had promised protective pills against sonorics; and only days before the cloud reached Tiverius, he had admitted that the promise of these pills was a lie. He had killed himself, leaving Sady and the others to fight sonorics without any help.

Tiverius had suffered many, many deaths of soldiers and civilians. Many more had died within the years following the cloud, because low-level sonorics exposure acted as a slow killer.

Sady made several attempts to work on the jobs that needed attention, but he couldn't concentrate. If things were as General Selidas said, Chevakia faced a deep threat, and he was very sorry to the doga, but that warranted more of his time than the agenda for tomorrow's sitting.

He grabbed his cloak and went into the foyer. Orson rose as soon as he entered.

"I want to go to the Scriptorium," Sady said.

They went down the stairs, where the petitioners were getting ready to go home. Several were unaware of the protocol that they could not heckle him when he was on his way home, but none of it mattered anyway. He rarely saw people anymore and didn't understand why they still queued up. Yet the queues grew longer, not shorter.

They went down the stairs and out the main foyer, across the forecourt and out the gates.

The Scriptorium was in the northeastern corner of the main square, its round tower bathing in low sunlight. The main hall was an oasis of calm after the noisy and sometimes crassly political corridors of the doga assembly building.

Sady climbed the stairs that wound their way along the many bookcases in the tower.

The Scriptorium's position of Most Learned had gone through a quick succession of academics recently. There had been sex scandals involving students that forced holders of the position to resign, the untimely—and natural—death of one candidate, and one of the academics retiring to the country in order to help the home district that had helped fund his studies.

At the moment, the position was in the hands of a young man called Sameron—a native of Fairlight—who was in his late thirties and one of the youngest ever to hold the position. He had made his academic fame, required for the position, with his advances in medicine.

Sady knocked on the door of the office at the top of the tower and was told to come in.

The Most Learned Sameron sat at his desk, and jumped up like a spring when Sady entered.

"Oh, Proctor. I wasn't expecting you at all!" He pulled a chair back for Sady. "Can I offer you something to drink?"

"No, I'm fine, thanks."

"How can I help you?"

"I would like to say that I won't be long, but I'm afraid I can't guarantee that. If you need to go home or have something else to attend to, let me know."

"No. I don't," Sameron said. He had an unusually severe face, with a large nose. His hair was very dark, almost southern in its sleekness.

Sady started by explaining the situation with Arania and the unexplained bursts of sonorics. The latter Sameron should know about, but the expression on that severe face became more severe when Sady spoke of the machines in the Aranian army camps that might be some kind of sonorics device. "My most important question, I guess, is this: has there been any progress made in the past twenty years about the effect of sonorics on Chevakians and how to prevent it?"

"Well. No. Not really. We all thought that we would no longer need that research, so no one has continued that line of work. Alius tried to produce pills, but since he couldn't get his method to work—and it was clear why it was flawed and could never work—we considered the work irrelevant."

"What about protection?"

"You mean suits?"

"Yes. Has anyone developed better protective gear, or even any gear at all?"

"I'm afraid not. We dealt with the threat. Protective gear was not deemed necessary anymore."

Damn, it really was as bad as Sady had feared.

"Do you have any people who could start working on something soon?"

"I don't have any people who are free. I could allocate people, but it depends on which project I can take them from. The doga should decide about that. Then I'll have to check which people would be in the best positions to change. There would be some retraining involved. Very few of the young academics know much about sonorics and its effect on human bodies."

"Could you start this training soon?"

"How soon?"

"Well, these Aranian troops could be in Tiverius within a week. We'll try to stop them of course, but if they have effective sonorics weapons, there may not be a great deal we can do to prevent them charging to Tiverius."

"A WEEK?" Sameron's eyes were wide.

"That *may* be all the notice we can get."

"What does the doga expect me to do within a week? This kind of project you're talking about takes months, years even."

"Start that type of project as well, but give me the best advice and the best protection you can find for the frontline troops within a week."

Sameron stared. "Really, is it that bad?"

"It might be." It was hard to believe that after having kept quiet for so long, King Orik would do this. Where Peria and Chevakia had grown closer, Arania had remained detached. "I hope we're wrong about this, but the amassing of troops along the border doesn't look good at all."

"The doga should send an official letter to King Orik."

"Oh, we will be doing that as well, but the king is not known for responding kindly to our messages." Chevakia had tried to reach out a few times, most recently after Milleus had died, since he had been the most influential figure in Arania's defeat in the war. Sady had written that the death of his brother meant the end of an era and that he hoped another era would begin. The Aranians had sent a package in return, a neatly wrapped handmade box containing a human turd.

The object in question, now dried out and odourless, stood inside a cabinet of curiosa in the upstairs hall of the doga building.

The Most Learned Sameron promised that he would do what he could, even if he conceded that it might not be much.

Sady went back to General Selidas where he discussed what he had heard from the Most Learned Sameron, including protection for the troops. The general would make sure that if Sady could unearth the sonorics protection suits, they would be sent to the troops on the border.

Then Sady remembered having heard about a sonorics sink that the Eagle Knights used, so he went back to his office again to write to Supreme Rider Barton in the City of Glass. Poor Orsan was then tasked with the job of folding the message and putting it in a little cylinder around the neck of a messenger gull. The doga always kept one or two of those birds. When released, they would always fly straight home to the City of Glass.

When finally all that was done, Sady could go home.

It was late in the evening and the streets were dark. A fine haze hung over the city, visible in the light of the street lamps. It probably came from wildfires in the hills on the outskirts of town.

The lamps on the veranda cast a golden glow through the front yard. Warm light also showed in the little window next to the front door. Orsan sped up the path and opened the front door. Sady went into the empty hall. He found Myra and Loriane in the kitchen.

"You're late," Loriane said.

He kissed her on the top of her forehead. Her skin was warm against the freshness of the night that still cooled his skin.

Sady sat down and accepted soup and bread from Myra. He ate quietly, blowing the steam off the soup. Myra said she was going to fold the washing and left.

"Busy?" Loriane said.

"Yeah." He hated keeping information back, but he didn't like to worry her. It might be bad for her health. Likely nothing would happen for a while, and Loriane didn't *need* to know about his worries. He would probably tell her soon, but . . . it just hurt him to look at her. She was so incredibly thin, her cheeks sunken, her hair more grey than black. The lustre had gone out of her eyes.

"Has the healer been here today?"

"Yesterday." She stared at the table. "I'm tired, Sady."

"I'll take you to bed. You could have gone there already. You know sometimes work gets late, and I don't mind if you go to bed before I get home."

"No, I'm tired of being sick."

Oh. He nodded. He could imagine.

"I'm tired of the pain and the weakness. I'm tired of seeing your faces, trying to hide your pain because you know what will come, and you don't know how long it will be, and you're afraid of that day."

He reached out and took her hand, warm and dry-skinned in his. "Yes, I'm tired of that, too, but life is as it is, and I will do everything for you for as long as possible."

She whispered, "I'm sorry about being a burden."

They sat silently. A tear tracked over Loriane's cheek. "I will go on for as long as I can. I haven't yet found out where they all are."

"Who?"

"All my children."

A light went on inside Sady's head. The books she'd been studying, the long list of names, the monument. "You've been looking for the nine children you sold to nobles?"

"I want them to know that their mother was not some breeder whore, and that I would have cared for them, if I'd been allowed to do so." Another tear ran over her cheek. She looked up at him, her mouth trembling. Her eyes filled with tears.

"Oh, Loriane. You could have told me. I can help you. I will let you meet them if we can find them."

He hugged her and so they sat for a while. Her shoulders shook with quiet sobs.

Sady's eyes misted over, too. He couldn't stand the thought of losing her.

He released her when Myra came back into the kitchen. She offered to take Loriane to the bedroom and get her ready for bed. She wheeled the chair out of the kitchen.

Yes, Sady should go to bed, too. He sat for a quiet moment at the table, leaning his head in his hands. He feared the future. He was too old to be dealing with hostile actions from Arania. He was no army strategist. On top of that, if he had to choose between spending long days in the doga and spending the last days with Loriane, he preferred to be with her.

Maybe rather than waiting until someone unseated him, he should just step down. Yes. He should call a doga meeting and resign. Let someone young and fresh use new ways to tackle the problems. He'd be happy to mentor and consult, but, as Loriane had said, he was *tired*.

Sady was about to get up when fast footsteps sounded in the hallway.

The door opened and Myra's husband Farius burst in, his face red. "Sady, come."

Sady followed Farius out of the kitchen, into the hallway where the front door was open. The groundsman stood staring into the front yard, one hand holding onto the door, his other hand covering his mouth.

Farius opened the door further.

On the path from the gate to the door, a man lay face down on the ground, his arm outstretched towards the veranda steps.

Sady crouched. "Is he—?"

"Don't touch him," Farius said. He showed Sady his pocket barymeter. The needle sat at seventy motes per cube.

Damn it. Sady retreated and they all stood staring, not sure what to do.

The man didn't move. His clothes were so filthy that he hadn't immediately been recognisable as a soldier of the Chevakian army, but Sady now noticed the uniform under the grime.

If he was alive—and that was a big if—the level of contamination required to make him radiate this much sonorics would certainly kill him. There hadn't been a cure for sonorics illness back then, and there wasn't any now. No one had done any sonorics research. They hadn't thought it was necessary. Everyone had been terribly, fatally *wrong*.

"He had this in his hand." Farius held a piece of paper under Sady's nose. It was not the usual type of paper, but a thick, yellowish, card-like paper. In large, ugly letters, it said, *The time has come for you to bow to us.* "What in all of the seven heavens is that supposed to mean?"

Orsan came up the path. He walked around the man in a big circle, stepping off the path and through the garden bed. "This man was deployed to a unit in western Ensar."

"And how did he get here?"

"His truck is outside."

Yes, Sady could see it, parked awkwardly in the street. "Why? I don't understand."

"He won't answer us anymore. He used his last strength to drag himself up here. The truck is a mess."

Yes, Sady could imagine that. He held up the piece of parchment. "Any idea who wrote this?"

"I have no idea. I'm sorry, Proctor. There was no envelope that I could see."

But, Sady realised, the writer had used an Aranian style of handwriting, and he had seen that yellowish paper in Milleus' library: the peace agreement that the Aranian royal family had been forced to sign after the Chevakian army had pushed all the way into Kadrish, and had caused the heaviest defeat suffered by any army in living memory.

Combined with the observations made by the spies, this note was not a random threat. It was a declaration of war, sent in the vilest, most insulting way Arania could muster. They'd sent a message, and contaminated him enough for him to die a horrible death on his leader's doorstep, an image that would shock the genteel citizens of Tiverius, and that would forever be remembered.

Sady said, "Orsan, call up the emergency council."

Orsan nodded, and then left to do as ordered.

Sady went back inside and washed his hands in the bathroom. He dried them and then washed them again, even though he had not touched the body. The lamp side-lit his face, showing the deep crags and folds that had come with age. He was too old to deal with a war. Far too old.

Back in the hallway, he hesitated outside the bedroom, but went in anyway because he knew Loriane would hate it if she didn't know where he was. The oil lamp sputtered on the bedside table. Loriane's eyes were closed. Her hands lay relaxed on the bedspread, one of them still on the book.

Sady blew out the light and left.

Was it too much to hope that she would peacefully go to sleep before war blew up?

Myra stood by the front door. A couple of guards had arrived in sonorics suits, and they were in the front yard removing the body.

Sady put his hand on Myra's shoulder. "Go to bed. Everything is under control."

Myra looked up at him. "Has the young mistress come back, then?"

Lana? Sady met her eyes. Myra was right. Lana had gone to a

student meeting. She would normally come back pretty late, and he guessed it was pretty late, but she hadn't come back yet, he didn't think. . . .

Orsan called from the street, "The truck is ready. The emergency council is about to assemble."

The suited guards lifted up a stretcher with the body. Sady followed them to the gate. He glanced down the street, where a street lamp cast a pool of yellow light. Where *was* Lana? And, more worrying, how could he keep her safe?

"Orsan, I've changed my mind. I'd like to make a quick visit to the Scriptorium first."

CHAPTER 24

*L*ANA WAITED at the front of the room, nervously looking over the audience.

The Scriptorium's student astronomy meeting was still a bit light on attendance, because of the absence of all the fourth year meteorology students, but the news from last month's controversial meeting had spread and everyone else was there.

At the last meeting, Lana had presented the theory posed by Tamerane in the City of Glass, that the world was round and that the City of Glass was at the pole and Tiverius close to the middle.

It challenged the prevailing view that the world was an island set in a large sea where the water fell off the edges into an abyss. There had been a lot of talk in the corridors in the days following that meeting. And, apparently, some of the third year students had been ridiculed in class.

"Everyone here?" Lana said, looking around the room.

She felt uneasy. The student who normally led the meeting was in Fairlight, and he might be less than impressed that she had brought controversy to the gathering.

She missed the familiar faces of her fellow students. Everyone in the room was younger than her, except for the two junior academics at the back whom she suspected to be informants for the established academics of the Scriptorium. They did not normally come to meetings. Of course the Most Learned Sameron could not lower himself to attending a student meeting, but it was a measure of how much talk their little, insignificant astronomy group had generated.

She hoped this meeting would not be as controversial. Lana disliked being controversial as much as she disliked information based on dogma.

She picked up the series of plates that she had brought for tonight's meeting on the table and leaned them against the wall. The students in the room fell quiet and squinted at the projections she had made on the roof of her house at night.

They were poor in quality, because of the lamp in the street below, and because she hadn't wanted to leave the plates out too long because she didn't want stripes this time. Also because she had used the looking glass to project an image onto the plate, and the edges of the image were blurry.

"I looked at the Great Wanderer and its children this week," she began.

The Great Wanderer took up a prominent position in the sky in this time of the year, but it wasn't until the recent introduction of spyglasses into astronomy that people had noticed the children. They were a line of four dots, sometimes three, that followed the wandering star.

Her projections showed how much the position of the children changed over a couple of days. One image showed three children on the left and one on the right, then the next, taken later the same night, showed two on the left and one on the right. The next showed two on the left and two on the right, but it was the fourth image that was the most interesting, because it showed one child on the left, two on the right, but the Great Wanderer itself seemed somewhat elongated.

"Whatever is that?" asked Pavin, a fourth year student in war tactics, in his usual brash manner.

Lana brushed off his tone that always suggested that she'd done something wrong. "These images show us that the children move from one side of the Great Wanderer to the other. I think this image caught one of them as it was going in front of the Great Wanderer."

"Or behind," Pavin said.

"Yes, or behind."

He frowned at the rest of the images in the series. "Do you have any more? Is this all there is?"

"I've brought all the plates I made." Some people already said that she was only here so that she could show off how much money she had to spend on these trivial projects. Light plates were not cheap and this set represented what would be a fortune for some students. Lana was well aware that the money she spent on plates could feed a poor family, but Pavin had no such objections. His family was a lot richer than hers.

He wrinkled his nose. Not good enough, clearly. "It's a pity there aren't any more, because this way, I can't tell for sure if what I think is true. You should take more images, a few hours apart, every night."

"Maybe it would help if you told me what you think first." At times she came close to snipping at him and wishing him gone; but he was too smart to ignore, even if he was also an arrogant prick.

He pushed himself up with a sigh, came to the front of the room, picked up a piece of chalk from the table at the front and drew a small dot on the blackboard. "This is the Great Wanderer." He made the dot a bit bigger and then drew four smaller dots, three on one side, one on the other. "We see the children in many different positions. Sometimes we see only three, because one of them is in front or behind the Wanderer. The only way I can see this working is if the children all describe paths around the Wanderer, and they all do so at different speeds and at different circles, so that they don't hit each other. But to prove that, we need more images."

Lana nodded. She had suspected something like it, when first developing the images and seeing the changes in the line of dots.

"What does this mean?" another student asked. "What do you think the Great Wanderer actually is?"

"It is a star that has worlds going around it. This . . ." He pointed at the biggest dot, the Wanderer itself. ". . . is the star, a sun. We are like one of those little dots. This is one of the best arguments I've yet seen for the case that our world is not flat or fixed in place, but floats in the air, like the Great Wanderer's children. We move around our sun, and our moon is another one of those children and that's why it gets bigger and smaller and sometimes it disappears, because it's on the other side of the Sun. We're like this." He drew a large dot and wrote "Sun" underneath it, and then another, smaller, dot and called it "Earth" and a second one called "Moon".

A couple of first year students argued about how the world could be round, and why people didn't fall off. Others said that you could see the curve of the horizon and it wasn't the illusion of distance, as was the prevailed wisdom. Then someone wanted to know about the edges of the world.

Pavin rolled his eyes and glared at Lana, hoping, maybe, that she would cut this discussion short. They'd had it during the last meeting.

But the two junior academics in the back of the room were talking to each other. According to the Scriptorium's teaching, the world was an island, and she didn't want to argue against their teachings. Much as she believed that those teachings were not based on the type of evidence that they could now collect with spyglasses and by talking to people in other parts of the world, she also believed that those old academics had done a lot of good, and didn't want to upset them.

"What do the Aranians say about the edges of the world?" someone wanted to know.

"Sizek says that the water from the ocean cascades off the side into a cloudy abyss." This was a female second year student. She was normally very quiet at these meetings, but very useful because she was half-Aranian and spoke the language well. Aranian was the language of astrologers.

"What happens to that water?" another student asked.

"He says it turns into clouds that rain the water back onto the land."

"Has anyone ever seen this abyss?"

"There are a lot of stories about it."

"*Stories,*" Pavin said loudly, rolling his eyes, and the girl cringed. "There are plenty of myths, but are there any eyewitness reports about this edge of the world that are recent and credible? Most of these stories are hundreds of years old. They are about the myths of the Mother and the Child. They are Aranian fairy tales."

"Why are you attacking her?" Lana asked. Just because he was older and was training for a high position in the army didn't mean that he could yell her into silence.

He scoffed. "I'm not attacking her. I'm just pointing out that myths exist for reasons other than recording the truth. Because the aviators are saying the ocean curves, so how can the water fall off? Where is it going to fall?"

She agreed, but why did he need to be so terrible about it? The two men in the back were busily writing.

Another student said, "But if the world was round, you could travel around it."

"You probably could."

"What is on the other side?"

No one knew the answer to that. Pavin spread his hands and sighed, annoyed, as if this was all perfectly clear to him and he didn't want to have to stoop to the depths of having to explain it.

Seriously, these army people could be so annoying.

The Aranian student said, "There is one quite old Aranian text that says that if you go far enough out to sea, you will meet the Mother."

"Myths," Pavin said and snorted.

"There could be truth in it," Lana said.

"*Meeting the Mother* is probably some weird Aranian euphemism for dying."

"Will you just stop being such a boor?"

He had the audacity to look surprised. "What? I'm telling the truth."

"No one knows what the truth is."

"Well then." He spread his hands. "Explain to me what this 'Mother' thing is then, if not some sort of goddess of fertility."

"That is exactly what I mean! The Mother is part of Aranian culture and beliefs. You may not believe in it, and I don't believe in it either, but that doesn't give you the right to mock it in front of someone who may believe in it."

He met her eyes, and crossed his arms over his chest. "I thought this was an astronomy group, not some sort of cultural discussion circle."

"Culture and truth often mix."

He sniffed.

"The Mother is real," the Aranian girl said.

"So, you believe in the Mother?" Pavin made it sound like an insult.

To her credit, the girl didn't flinch. "There is no 'believe'. The Mother is real. All the fishermen say so. She is fat and round and you can see her rising out of the ocean when you go far enough from the land. She was chased from the land and fled to the sea."

"Well, that's no surprise, that," Pavin said. "Seeing as how Aranians treat their women. You seriously believe a goddess lives in the sea?"

Lana glared at him. She resisted asking him whether this was how he talked to his mother. Likely it was, and likely, he wouldn't even get the irony. If only he wasn't so genuinely smart, then she'd have kicked him out of the group long ago.

Lana apologised to the girl after the meeting ended.

"It's all right," she said. "I get this all the time. People see that I'm half-Aranian and they want to make me look ridiculous or try to get me to make a fool of myself."

"I'm still sorry. I sometimes want to kick him out, but he makes a lot of very good points. I just wish he wasn't so arrogant about it. *I* enjoy your cultural comments, if that's worth anything."

"Thanks." She smiled.

Lana stacked her light plates between her books, inserted the whole pile into her bag and grabbed her coat. Then she turned down the wick in the lamps so that they went out, and left the room—and almost ran into someone.

"Whoa—what. . . ?"

"Calm down. It's me."

Her father. What in all the heavens was he doing here? Worse, how long had he been here and how much had he heard?

He jerked his head. "Come."

They walked silently for a while. The meeting had lasted so long that the library was deserted. Most of the other students had gone home, librarians had turned off the lights and were preparing to go home themselves.

Then he said, "I didn't know you were with the astronomy crowd."

Lana cringed. No, she had never told him specifically about these meetings, because meteorologists couldn't be seen to be studying the sky beyond weather and clouds; because, if he'd known, he'd probably tell her not to waste her time.

So what was this going to be? A lecture about how she needed to be more serious about her studies? "We talk about all kinds of things."

"Mainly stars and skies? I noticed young Pavinius there. He's a very smart and assertive young man. He'll go far."

He's an arsehole. "I think the study of stars and the sky compliments meteorology."

"They're unrelated. Meteorology is an essential science, the study of the sky is a bit of frivolous fun."

"It's not frivolous."

"Aranian astrology? You could not call that serious with all the will in the world."

Lana clamped her jaws. It always came down to this and she was sick of this discussion. Would he still talk like this when they proved that the world was round and that you could sail around it, and that on the far side there was another land with untold riches?

"Anyway, I haven't come here to argue with you. From rumours that are circulating around the halls, I'm guessing you're getting enough arguments already."

"No, you've come to drag me home again. I'm no longer a child." Although his tone disturbed her. She wasn't sure anyone in the group fully comprehended what would happen if the academics got wind of this. For one, all of them were students, and the academics controlled their grades.

Maybe she should stop while she still could.

"I have actually come to tell you something I will surely regret, because I really don't think you're mature enough for it. I'm going to let you go to Ysherra with Viki."

What? She stared at him. She'd put her admittedly outrageous request aside. "Really?"

"Yes, really. Mind you, I still don't think you are mature enough to handle it, but your mother says we will never know if we don't try."

This had to be a joke, certainly. She had never even left Tiverius alone. He would never let her go, no matter what her mother said about it. Come to think of it, he had been out of sorts the last couple of days, and why was he still here at this time of the day? He would normally be drinking tea with her mother, in his dressing gown, and the only work he'd still do would be leafing through some papers for the next day.

"Wait—Dad, why are doing this? What is going on?"

He looked away, pressing his lips together. He blew out a breath.

"Is there something to do with Mother?"

"No, not that." He stopped walking. The light from a lamp lit his face side-on, showing the deep crevices in his face. "I was underway to the emergency council meeting."

Her heart jumped. "What happened?"

He told her about movement of troops in Arania, and how a soldier stationed in the Ensar district had come to the house with a note from the Aranian royal family, and how this man had been affected with sonorics and had died on the path to the front door.

"We thought we'd finished with sonorics. No one has any protective suits left. We're having to find them from the old stores. No one has done any research on it in the last twenty years. The Aranians are coming for us with sonorics weapons."

Lana felt sick. She had grown up hearing stories of the fear and terrible burns that sonorics left on their victims. "What can you do to defend us against it?"

"That's what we were going to have a meeting about. It's why I want you to leave. If the Aranians come, they will be coming for Tiverius. I want you to be safe, out of here."

Her heart jumped. "But what about you?"

"Sonorics don't harm your mother. I can't possibly leave."

Lana looked into his light brown eyes, the eyes that had always been ringed by wrinkles since she remembered. She understood why he had looked so worried and been so irritable. And she had acted like an entitled brat.

"I'm sorry, Dad." She had to do her best to stop her voice from cracking.

"Sorry for what?"

"For thinking only of myself. Astronomy is not as important as everything else. It's an indulgence. I love you. I don't want you to be killed either. I want to stay here and help."

"For once, I want you to do as I say. Please go with Viki and be safe."

He hugged her.

CHAPTER 25

*D*URING THE NEXT few days, the daily reports delivered to Isandor by the Knights contained a lot more violence than usual. A man was murdered in an inn room, and three shops suffered arson attacks. The Knights had to diffuse a street brawl, and two men were put into the dungeons for thuggery, but two more escaped by ship.

The perpetrators and victims had one thing in common: the were all Aranian.

The news chilled Isandor, because the register of foreigners was still incomplete and Rider Barton had not identified the main troublemakers.

He called for the council's Aranian advisor, Rider Farey, who was half-Aranian and who had served in the Knights for a long time.

"The rumours are that Prince Nayek was killed," said Farey. "No one can definitely confirm it, but the powerful men are so keen to win the favour of the king that they jostle for the best positions anyway."

In Arania, jostling involved dead bodies.

"Does any of this jostling involve people in the City of Glass?"

"Rumours also say that Prince Nayek was operating out of a room in the Silver Gull in the Harbour District. I have not been able to verify that. I've been to the room, and the people who have seen the man in question certainly describe a man of high ranking, but if it was the prince, he was not using his own name."

"What would he be doing here?"

Farey spread his hands. "It could be something as harmless as business interests."

"But because he was here under a false name, it is probably not as harmless as that?"

"Aranian princes often travel under false names. They have rivals everywhere. The truth is that he was well disguised, and I wasn't aware of his presence until I heard rumours that he might have been killed, this morning."

"Where did this happen?"

"Again, I'm not clear on details. I don't think it was in the city because we would have heard more, but many of the Aranians are nervous for what's going to happen next. Prince Nayek is considered a forward-looking moderate. He's too interested in money to want to go to war. He'd rather trade with us than fight a costly war. Some of his rivals, in particular his older brother, are a lot more traditional. Those rivals have had pledges and promises from friends and backers that they will be pulling in now that they have a chance of getting selected as the king's heir. That is probably why we are seeing these small disagreements between Aranians. The pledges to the rival princes may have been small: a certain amount of money, two sons to go into the army, a daughter for the harems."

Isandor closed his eyes and blew out a breath. This was what he had feared: foreign events influencing a significant part of his city. "The heir doesn't *just* get selected based on how many children he has? That is a myth, isn't it?"

"It's not the only issue that determines selection, but it's an important one. The heir gets selected because of how useful he is to the king. Having lots of sons on whose loyalty one can count is important, as well as having lots of daughters to trade with men whose favours you need."

ZAINA'S WORKSHOP was in the Harbour District, in one of the streets that led up the hill away from the waterfront, a place where a lot of businesses were located. It was a solid stone building with large rolling doors through which people could bring vehicles and machinery. Two of those doors were closed; the third was open.

"This is the place," Isandor said to his guards. They'd come up the hill with him, having left the coach at the waterfront. Isandor hadn't wanted to advertise his presence here, especially while the wave of unrest among Aranians continued.

Zaina was Aranian, and while the use of icefire weapons on her and her workers was probably unrelated, he didn't want to cast more suspicion on the workshop than necessary. Jadan was Perian, and so were all of Zaina's mechanics.

He told the guards to wait outside. They, too, wore regular uniforms and not royal livery as they did in the palace.

On the workshop floor, he found some of Zaina's workers: three young men, all of them not twenty years of age, surrounded by machines, trolleys with tools and bottles with oil and other things the purpose of which Isandor could only guess. When he travelled in Chevakia, he'd learned a bit about engines, but he counted himself far from an expert.

There were two engines in the workshop; one was a truck, the other some sort of grinding machine. The young workers downed their tools at the sight of the visitor, scrambled to their feet and bowed.

"Your Majesty." Jadan came outside the little office at the back of the workshop. She eyed the two guards who remained inside the door. Since the attack, her face had gone an interesting shade of blue and yellow.

"Have you had any more trouble?" Isandor asked.

"Not since the guards keep an eye on the shop, thank you very much. That's just as well, because there has been so much trouble in the district in the last day or two."

"Yes, I heard about that. It didn't affect you?"

"No, not at all. Thank you."

Isandor gestured at the door to Zaina's office. "Can I go in?"

"Sure. I've pulled out all the books and correspondence from just before she left."

The office was very small indeed, with barely enough space for a desk. The bookshelf overflowed with folders and account books.

"How long has the shop been in operation?" Isandor asked.

"It's been seven years now. First the shop was owned by a Chevakian, but he wasn't very good, or didn't care much. This was before I came here. Zaina bought the shop five years ago. She sacked all the staff and trained her own."

"Have you been here since that time?"

"No. I only started three years ago."

Isandor sat down at the desk. A neat pile of books and folders lay there. He opened the first one.

"I'll go to work then," Jadan said. "I'll be in the workshop. Call me if you need me."

Isandor said that he would, and leafed through the book.

Zaina kept a neat administration, much better than any he had ever seen. The account books were neat, with total income and expenditure listed at the bottom of every page, with orders, payments and salaries listed on separate lines.

Another folder listed her customers. Isandor leafed through. The list was a who's who of the upper class of the City of Glass. Zaina serviced their trucks, their heaters, their shop machines, their ships.

He idly turned pages until he happened across the name used by one of the companies owned by House Mara. It was to fix a truck. Across bottom there were several notations. *Reminder sent* with a date and then *Second reminder sent*. And then in big letters, *PAID!!!*

The next page was similar and the third page said, *Quote only. Ask for upfront payment before commencing any work.*

Well, that was interesting, if not what he'd come here to find out. He *had* often wondered where the nobility found the endless supply of money that seemed to sustain them. Maybe that supply wasn't so endless after all. That would also explain Tamerane's father not letting her keep any of the money she earned.

Isandor set the folder back on the shelf, not sure if it was his business to know this about Tamerane's family. Maybe it wasn't, but he cared about the way it affected Tamerane. The thought of a man selling his daughter's body to rescue his business made him feel ill.

Another folder on Zaina's shelf included information about shop supplies, which she got mainly from Arania. The folder with recent orders for new machines was fascinating. He was, of course, familiar with the trucks, but there were also ships, and sawmills, and machines for cutting stone and things that he didn't even realise you could use machines for. Most of them, apparently, were shipped in parts and assembled locally

Maybe he should look into getting a truck. It was not cheap, but not as expensive as he had thought either.

By the time he'd gone through all the material Jadan had put out, not only had he found nothing about Arania, he found nothing out of line in the books that justified thuggery. Nothing to question at all.

He wandered into the workshop and questioned the mechanics. They said that Aranians sometimes came into the workshop, but that Zaina never treated them differently from her other customers. They were locals.

The mechanics did not remember any violent or threatening customers. They didn't know of disputes over payments or any other issues. And to the question of Zaina ever going back to Arania, Jadan laughed out loud.

"Why would she, the way they treat their women? The rich men own their women, and they are considered more powerful the more children they have."

"Did she escape a deal like that? Did she ever mention anything of the sort?"

"No, she wouldn't talk about Arania at all."

"Most Aranians don't," one of the young mechanics said. "They're all petrified. I don't know what they think the Aranians can do on foreign soil, but they're petrified anyway."

When Isandor went back into the office to collect his cloak from the back of the chair, his eye fell on a red book in the bookshelf. Unlike all the other books, it did not have anything written on the spine. He pulled it out.

The book was a type of diary, but not the kind that chronicles daily events. Rather, it chronicled a process of learning. The first half contained details about the working parts of machines and how to maintain them, how to avoid wear on certain parts, how to fix breakages and possible ways for improving parts of engines.

The later part of the book went into future developments. It contained letters from people Zaina had corresponded with—mostly in Chevakia—and drawings of concepts and possible new techniques. Often she would have noted things like "this method needs better control of pressure to be safe enough for public use." Some of the discussions would venture into the realm of using icefire, with the notes that it was certainly not safe.

Isandor felt slightly uneasy reading this. This woman was not a simple mechanic. She was highly literate and studied machines.

Isandor leafed through the loose letters inserted in the back of the notebook.

One letter of several pages in Chevakian described a machine in great detail. At the bottom it said, "Mind you, I'm not sure that this was how it worked. Unfortunately, the thing is broken, and has been for a long time."

The writer of the letter had made a sketch of a square-looking contraption that looked like a bundle of pipes folded like a sheet. The notes included no reference to the size of this machine, but it had to be quite big. The design reminded him of drawings he had seen in the very old books, which described even older technology.

Was this the second Heart they were looking for?

No. The writer said that the machine was dead.

But where did he find this?

On the back of the last page, where the outside of the letter had formed the envelope so as to save weight, the name of the sender was listed as Shen Mani, and it was stamped at the telegraph office in a place called Ysherra. Where was that?

Isandor closed the book, put the other items he had collected on top of it and draped his cloak over his arm.

Jadan had taken a part of the truck's engine apart: metal rods, gears and cylinders lined up on a wooden table.

"I've finished," Isandor said.

Jadan straightened, wiping her hands on a cloth blackened with grease. "Did you find anything?"

"Yes and no. Your boss runs a very efficient business and I can't find any evidence for extortion or foul play. But I'm taking this note-book." He held it up. "I'll bring it back soon."

"Oh. I'm not familiar with that one. I guess we could miss it for a few days."

Isandor left the workshop.

❄

OVER THE NEXT FEW DAYS, Isandor copied the drawings.

He wrote to Tamerane asking if she knew about it. He asked if she would like to come to see him in his office.

He waited one day, and then two and three.

There was no news from the expedition.

There was no reply from Tamerane. With every heartbeat, he ached for her. At night he went to sleep hugging himself.

Once, he spotted Jevaithi and Rider Barton walking through the garden. By the way she smiled at him, Isandor guessed that Jevaithi would soon announce yet another pregnancy that would end in yet another disaster.

He wished he could stop it, but there were no rules regarding the legal status of the "brother of the queen". The long negotiations for a proper constitution that properly recognised all the non-Knight members of the council were almost completed, but they couldn't vote on the final agreement until the expedition returned, because Jeito needed to vote in it.

All those thoughts made him angry and frustrated and after yet another day without reply from Tamerane, he pulled out official paper and the royal seal. He sat at his big desk, spread the paper out with his hands and wrote,

Forget the breeding arrangement. I want to see you every day and every night. I want to marry you and I'll pay for all your work and all the children we may have. I'll pay your father, too, if that is what he wants.

But that was too informal, because her father would read it and know that he had found out about the family's financial troubles. Part of him didn't care, but the sensible part knew that it was not the way a king, not even a lame, powerless one, proposed marriage. He scrunched the paper up and put it aside.

Then he wrote, *Hereby I, Isandor, heir of the Thillei Clan, officially propose marriage to Tamerane of House Mara.*

There.

It looked stupidly official, but anything less would not do. He folded it up, sealed it, and went to collect his cloak.

The guards in the entrance hall asked him if he needed transport. When he said that he could walk, two guards offered to go with him. He almost preferred not to have them, but there was no avoiding it.

The walk to Tamerane's house was short.

He caught her shutting the door behind her and coming down the front steps.

He ran to her. "Tamerane."

She turned around. The sight of her full lips and clear eyes cast light into his gloomy mood. He was certain: he wanted her and no one else.

"Oh! You didn't say that you were coming." Her cheeks went red.

"I was just about to give you a letter."

"Oh." She seemed out of sorts. Had he done anything that unsettled her?

"Can we have a talk?" he asked.

"Yes, sure. Come with me."

He expected her to go back inside the house, but she strode through the front yard to the gate. Isandor had to walk fast to keep up with her. What was going on?

"If you don't want to talk at your house, we can go to the palace or the eyrie."

"I don't know . . ." She glanced over her shoulder. Anyone watching her? Isandor's two guards followed at a distance.

"Is anything wrong?" That was a silly question, because clearly there was something wrong.

All of a sudden she pulled him into a doorway of what turned out to be a teahouse. "I'll buy you some tea."

All right. Isandor made a gesture to the two guards to wait outside.

The tea house was one of those dainty places with ornate tables, flowered table cloths, pretty cups and plates and little sweet cakes displayed on a set of shelves.

Tamerane went to the counter, where an attendant bowed to her. "My lady, you want the usual?"

"No, bring a pot of tea to one of the rooms upstairs for myself and my guest."

The man met Isandor's eyes and bowed even deeper. He gestured at the staircase behind him, with red-carpeted steps that led to a gallery that ran along the perimeter of the tearoom.

"I come here a lot," Tamerane said when they were climbing the stairs. Their footfalls were soft on the carpet of the upstairs gallery.

Through the bars of the ornate railing, Isandor could see snatches of the pretty room below.

So many old paintings hung on the walls that the doors opening onto the gallery hardly stood out. They were closed, painted different colours, and a little table stood next to each door, sometimes with a tray containing empty cups.

Tamerane opened one such door. It led to a neat but small room with couches and a table. A fire blazed in the hearth.

The teahouse attendant followed them into the room, carrying a tray with a teapot, cups and a plate with little cakes. The man set this on the table and poured tea before leaving the room.

After the door had shut behind him, Tamerane extracted an envelope from her pocket and put it on the table. Isandor's full name was written on the front.

"Read it," she said.

Isandor knew what it would say, but he unfolded it anyway, his hands sweaty.

Sure enough, the first line said, *I'm expecting your child.*

Isandor's face glowed. "That's . . . that's wonderful."

"Read on."

The rest of the letter dealt with details about payment and transfer of the child to him. It was a very dry text.

He looked up. "Your father told you to put all of that in?"

She closed her eyes. "My father told me to put *all* of it in the letter."

He realised what she meant. "You're not really expecting my child?"

"I could be, but it's too early to tell, and even if I am, with a contract like the one we signed, I wouldn't be hasty to claim success."

Every word she said hummed with implications. "Why? Does your father want money that badly? Didn't we agree that I would buy you an apartment?" But wait, he had his own letter that would solve everything for her. He took it out of his pocket and gave it to her.

She inserted her finger under the flap and ripped the seal. She unfolded the paper.

Isandor's heart was thudding like crazy.

She read. Her mouth fell open.

And then she said nothing for an agonisingly long time, just stared at the paper.

"Tamerane?" He reached out for her.

She raised her head. Her eyes brimmed with tears. "You're serious?"

"I have never been more serious in my life."

She whispered, "I want to marry you. I want it so much."

All the tension of the last few days fell off him. He shifted to the couch next to her and closed her in his arms. She buried her face into his shirt, sobbing.

"Calm down. It's all right now. I'll look after everything." Including Jevaithi. She would just have to get used to the fact that she didn't own him.

Tamerane pushed herself away. Her face was red and blotchy. "No, it's not all right at all. I really want to marry you." Her voice choked with tears. "But I can't."

What? "You're serious?"

"You think I'd say something like that just to tease you?" Tamerane wiped her eyes with the back of her hand. "I'm not the teasing kind. I love you. For the past weeks, I've lain awake at night wishing, hoping that you'd come back. No one has ever taken my interests seriously. No one has ever taken *me* seriously—"

"Then marry me."

"I can't. It's the ugly truth."

"But by the skylights, why?"

"I can't talk about it." Her shoulders shook. "My father . . ."

"Stop worrying about your father! You're old enough to decide for yourself. I will tell him to leave you alone. I'm the king." Without any form of legal authority. Ledor would know that.

Tamerane hid her face in her hands, shaking with sobs.

"Let me talk to him."

"There . . . is no . . . point."

"Of course there is a point. I'll pay him if money if that's what he wants. I don't care how much. I don't care about money. I just want you." Hell, he was close to losing it himself. Why was this man so terrible to his daughter?

"Please, stop it or I'll kill myself." She rose from the table. "I shouldn't be here." She threw her cloak over her shoulders and went to the door.

He cut her off. "Just tell me why you think you can't marry me. Whatever problem, I'll solve it. I'll pay, I'll order things done, I'll fight. We have a contract."

She faced him, her cheeks wet with tears. He felt like someone had stabbed a hot knife into his heart and was twisting it with both hands.

She said, in a low voice, "Something has happened. Please, don't get involved, because they will kill and crush you and the queen and the Knights and everyone and everything in this beautiful little, vulnerable country. Keep safe."

She went to the door, opened it and then she was gone.

A Word of Thanks

THANK YOU very much for reading *Sand & Storm*.

As author of this book, I would appreciate it very much if you could return to the place where you purchased this book and leave a review. Reviews are important to me, because they help readers decide if the book is for them.

In book 2 of the Moonfire Trilogy, *Sea & Sky*, Aranian fighters move across the border. Javes faces a long journey back to Tiverius in the company of a whiny little girl. Both Sady and Isandor are caught on the back foot by Arania. And one person finally breaks through Jevaithi's shell.

Also be sure to put your name on my mailing list, which I use to notify subscribers of news and new fiction. For everything else, please visit my website at *pattyjansen.com*.

ABOUT THE AUTHOR

Patty Jansen lives in Sydney, Australia, where she spends most of her time writing Science Fiction and Fantasy.

Her story *This Peaceful State of War* placed first in the second quarter of the Writers of the Future contest and was published in their 27th anthology. She has also sold fiction to genre magazines such as Analog Science Fiction and Fact, Redstone SF and Aurealis.

Patty has written over twenty novels in both Science Fiction and Fantasy, including the *Icefire Trilogy* and the *Ambassador* series.

pattyjansen.com

BOOKS BY PATTY JANSEN

More information:

PATTYJANSEN.COM

ABOUT THE AUTHOR

PATTY JANSEN lives in Sydney, Australia, where she spends most of her time writing Science Fiction and Fantasy. Her story *This Peaceful State of War* placed first in the second quarter of the Writers of the Future contest and was published in their 27th anthology. She has also sold fiction to genre magazines such as *Analog Science Fiction and Fact, Redstone SF* and *Aurealis*.

Her novels (available at ebook venues) include *Shifting Reality* (hard SF), *The Far Horizon* (middle grade SF), *Charlotte's Army* (military SF) and The Icefire Trilogy consisting of *Fire & Ice, Dust & Rain* and *Blood & Tears* (dark fantasy).

Patty is on Twitter (@pattyjansen), Facebook, LinkedIn, goodreads, LibraryThing, google+ and blogs at: http://pattyjansen.com/.

In the Earth-Gamra space-opera universe
The Shattered World Within (novella)
RETURN OF THE AGHYRIANS
Watcher's Web
Trader's Honour
Soldier's Duty
Heir's Revenge
The Return of the Aghyrians *Omnibus*
The Far Horizon (For younger readers)
AMBASSADOR
Seeing Red
The Sahara Conspiracy
Raising Hell
Changing Fate
Coming Home
Blue Diamond Sky
In the For Queen and Country universe
Whispering Willows (short story)
FOR QUEEN AND COUNTRY
Innocence Lost
Willow Witch
The Idiot King
The For Queen and Country *Omnibus* (Books 1-3)

Fire Wizard
The Dragon Prince
The Necromancer's Daughter
In the ISF-Allion universe
His Name in Lights (novella)
Charlotte's Army (novella)
Luminescence (short story)
The Rebelliousness of Trassi Udang (short story)
Shifting Reality (novel)
Shifting Infinity (novel)
Epic, Post-apocalyptic Fantasy
ICEFIRE TRILOGY
Fire & Ice
Dust & Rain
Blood & Tears
The Icefire Trilogy *Omnibus*
MOONFIRE TRILOGY
Sand & Storm
Short story collections
Out Of Here
New Horizons
Shorter works
Looking For Daddy (absurd horror novella)
This Peaceful State of War (Writers of the Future winning novella)
Visit the author's website at *http://pattyjansen.com* and register for a newsletter to keep up-to-date with new releases.